FISH ANTHOLOGY

2020

25:13

& Other Stories, Memoirs & Poems

love you pidget x

www.fishpublishing.com

Some people feel the rain.
Others just get wet.

Bob Dylan

Published in Ireland by
Fish Publishing, 2020
Durrus, Bantry, Co. Cork

The *Fish Anthology 2020* receives financial assistance from the Arts Council of Ireland.

the arts council an chomhairle ealaíon | funding literature | artscouncil.ie

ISBN 978-0-9956200-3-2
A catalogue record of this book is available from the British Library.

Cover Image – *desk* by Liam Rowe

For details on Fish Publishing's annual competitions write to:
Fish Publishing, Durrus, Bantry, Co. Cork, Ireland
email: info@fishpublishing.com
or see: www.fishpublishing.com

FISH ANTHOLOGY
2020

Winners of the 2019/20

Fish Publishing

Short Story Prize

Flash Fiction Prize

Lockdown Prize

Short Memoir Prize

Poetry Prize

Edited by Clem Cairns

Fish Publishing
Durrus, Bantry, Co. Cork, Ireland
www.fishpublishing.com

Contents

LOCKDOWN

SHORT MEMOIRS

POETRY

Acknowledgements

COMPETITION JUDGES

Short Story ~ Colum McCann

Flash Fiction ~ Tania Hershman

Short Memoir ~ David Shields

Poetry ~ Billy Collins

Lockdown ~ Clem Cairns, Adam Wyeth, Mary-Jane Holmes.

SPONSORS

Anam Cara Writers' & Artists' Retreat
(Ireland) anamcararetreat.com

Casa Ana Writers' Retreat
(Spain) casa-ana.com

COPY EDITOR & DESIGN

Jula Walton

E-CONSULTANT

Phoebe Bright
(Vivid Logic)

ADMINISTRATION

Sally Elsbury

WEB DESIGN

Tom Walton & Justin Bowley
(Emblime)

EDITORS/READERS

Mary-Jane Holmes

Simon Humphreys

Tina Pisco

Laura Harris

Judith Hinman

Tessa Gibson

Adam Wyeth

Paul McMahon

Guy Simpson

Zara Baker

Pierre Antoine Zahnd

Cressida Peever

Sally St Clair

READERS

Kevin Jackson

Ray Travis

Zoe Walton-Cairns

Nicholas McLachlan

COVER IMAGE

Liam Rowe

Introductory Note

In the time that it took to compile this Anthology, the world has seen for the first time a landing on the dark side of the moon, female imams lead Muslim prayer, an image of a black hole, a global lockdown, an albino panda in the wild. There were fires the size of small countries, the Greenwich compass points true north after 360 years of deviance, Black Lives Matter has become a household name, a global pandemic has manifested. Wokeness exploded and Cancel Culture emerged as a serious threat to freedom of expression. And that's not the half of it.

And there are still the perennial matters of love and life, loss and hope that writers weave into their stories, memoirs and poems. Thank you to those whose work is published here, for making this a vibrant, varied and eminently readable collection. And thank you to all the writers who entered the Fish competitions, many of whom were a hair's breadth away from making it. It is all of you who make this publication possible. *If I could carve the prize into twenty-five pieces, or thousands of pieces, and give them each the top award, I would.* – Colum McCann.

A big thank you to Colum McCann, Tania Hershman, David Shields and Billy Collins for selecting the work that is in this Anthology.

An extra category is included this year – *Lockdown* – in order to preserve the personal perspective of COVID-19 – the fear, the isolation, the bewilderment, the bonding, the sense of peace even, that many felt as the world slowed to a stop. As a result of the *Lockdown Prize*, 13 micro pieces are published in this Anthology and over €4,000 has been donated to Oxfam's fight against COVID-19.

Clem Cairns, Jula Walton: July 2020

Notes from Colum McCann

Every February, in my job as a creative writing teacher, I read literally hundreds of short stories from people all over the world. I know that at some stage I'm going to make a mistake. It's natural. Maybe I just can't see the one line or one paragraph embedded in the story which suggests that a promising writer is embedded in there. Maybe I bring my own preconceptions to the text. Maybe I don't have the range to hear the music of the text. But undoubtedly I will get it wrong somewhere along the line. That's one of the reasons why I am a little reluctant to judge literary competitions: they are a wonderful forum for a new writer, but they have limitations. And so I'm always torn when I get asked to judge. The most promising voices to me might have already been sidelined. Or I might overlook something myself. I might not be able to see through my own preconceptions.

I have been the beneficiary of awards in the past and I know how they can kickstart a career. In particular, in judging this prize, I was looking for talent that would possibly last. Voice was very important to me. Style. And then story.

I feel a certain guilt about aiding and abetting a Literature Olympics because in truth there is no gold, silver or bronze. There were many fabulous stories in the final batch that came my way. I could see great stretches of imagination. I saw experimentation. I saw novelty with voice and style. I saw sentences that embraced both meaning and music. And in the end that was why 25:13 came in what we call first place: it has the music and it has the intention. It has all the landmarks of a true writer. I expect we will hear great things from the author. So too with Oh Bend Your Backs! and I think a little time in the editing room could really sharpen this voice into a Kevin Barry-like maestro. And there was something very genuine and earnest and well crafted about Fearfully and Wonderfully. And yet all the stories had something wonderful in them ...

Keep writing, keep reading, keep creating. And rage on ...

Short Stories

25:13

Tracey Slaughter

It is raining out on the field today when I get back from the hospital, and I find myself smiling, as if I called it up. I stand at the ranchslider that squares my lounge off with the turf and watch the downpour chasing off the onlookers. There are mothers out there who've thought to bring shelters, staked out a shanty claim of plastic on the sideline, parka'd up the younger kids. They've squatted in spiny pop-up deckchairs pre-game to guarantee their view is prime. Those mothers fight the longest. They're still in place when a rush of umbrellas heads off, the deluge whirling from their red and white panels. Everything club-coloured, chillybins and snap-backs, pvc ponchos and first-aid kits, bumping in retreat along the flooded green sod. In the end it's just me and those mothers, huddled in resistance beneath their branded tarps. Watching the team still stumbling the muck, as the sky proves no one can hope to stop it.

When Ryan was a child we had to rush him to hospital. I remember, the walls were lemon then too, and the frieze was a march of ducklings, grins of goofy fuzz with blue gumboots on their webs and sky-blue plastic hats. It was raining on them, but that only made them cuter. I hated the things, galoshing around in the splash, their peach beaks smirky and dimpling. I think Ryan hated them too. He hated the whole room, and everyone in teal that entered into it, carrying wires to the bed, and liquids, and trays, and needles, and lastly, straps. They'd plug and stick him, maintaining near-smiles, and gag his howl with clear-gloved fingers. We never had to guess his hatred. He screamed at them all, loud belts of terror, pitched from the struggle of his trunk, his blond-white hair spiked with fever, his milk teeth in fits. And it was my job to hold him down, to pin the tiny hammer of his heartbeat to the trolley, to lock down his clattering flannelette pj's with their pattern of choo-choos all jumping the track. To use my whole body if I had to, like a vice, bear down on my baby, his flailing heels and wrists. Mutter everything I could find of comfort, while his head swung side to side and bludgeoned up at me. Keep on with a babble of falsetto sweetness, crossing my heart with fake promises. Hating the ducks the whole time, their chubby parade around the walls where the squeaky-clean blobs of entertaining rain would never drop down hard enough to drown them.

Let the rain come. Last weekend, when there was another minor incident, I stood at the window and watched while the ambulance coasted, low-profile, through coloured margin flags. While the stretcher was manoeuvred off, swift, unobtrusive. While the game played on. And those mothers never moved. Except one. But she wasn't from the home team.

I've taken to wandering over to the back of the clubrooms, on some nights that I can't sleep. Maggie sees me coming, where the spotlights smudge the mist above the field, and taps out a couple of smokes. We sit on a pair of overturned white buckets she's scrubbed out by the bar door. With the heel of my runners I fiddle with the handle, so it keeps hitting the concrete with a thin silver click. I don't know why I do these things, but I find myself falling a lot into rote motions like this, waking up with my unthinking body caught in little drones and tics. I tap and rock. It might be my own therapy, I don't know – my body trying to jerk out a new mode for itself – but if it is, it's a poor joke on the exercises I watch them putting Ryan through each morning, his big frame stranded on the bed. He blinks at them when they call it training, when they cast the tiny twitches of muscle as heroic, when they chant in big explosive hoots for the vacant limb they haul through its range of movement. It's my job to make the same noise. And I do. I'm relentless, an overage bogus cheerleader, flapping my nonstop applause. There are pinboard panels on the ceiling of the therapy room and he blinks up into them. I want to give up and stare with him, count the black array of dots, an unmoving hole-punched universe. But I don't. I'm still full of promises, I brim with them. I swear, I vow, I pledge. I set targets, forge pacts. I'll get him up on his feet again. If it's the last thing I ever ...

I don't have to press my body over his, to block his protest. He never makes a sound.

We're still in the children's wing, which would have once humiliated him. But now he doesn't care. The frieze this time is of giraffes, the long freckled glide of their spines around lanky trees, the doped friendly glaze of their eyelashes. A patch of them skipping, dorky and cloven, that's meant to be adorable. I just stare through their hides to their happy bones towering, the way I watch the vertebrae of figures who gleam at home from our late night TV, picking up nothing of the plot, tuning out the buzz of dialogue, so my husband will sigh beside me, hard, on the couch, scoffs of reproach he doesn't aim straight at me but over at the brown scrawl of curtains or down into his can of DB. But I go on staring at the bodies on the screen, the seamless way their hidden bones arrange their easy movements, their sliding thoughtless links beneath the well-lit skin. Waiting for the sudden crack.

Maggie has known me since secondary school. She used to be a bitch to me back then – but I had it coming, a stuffy little priss, part barbie doll, part religion. I'd put on lipstick, quote scripture, and girls like Maggie, with spiky fringes and home-made tats of maryjane and khaki army-surplus satchels, would have to hold themselves back from lobbing a fist at my sanctimonious pink mouth. She makes me laugh about it now, as we sit on our tubs, and inhale and huff, and sometimes munch on the odd leftover courtesy meat pie. She still has the bad ring-a-rosie of metal stuck along her left ear's cartilage, a silver pick-and-mix – I remember when she lanced the first one, in a bathroom off C Block, where I hid in a stall, and tried not to sick up, as I watched her school shirt spat with safety-pinned blood. I love the toughness of those studs now, the saggy ammunition of them trailing their curve, the grey roots tracking out her way-too-red-dyed hair, the lined mocha slur of her smile. She sneers at everything. She's worked the club since she was in her twenties. A couple of weeks back when her cellphone got pinched out her ute, the boys hunted the culprit and pounded him, a lesson delivered bigtime. She's an institution now. Revered. So fucking watch it right?

Her son too has something wrong with him – though it wasn't the game, he was just born with this. Sometimes she has to bring him in, and sets him up at a station in the kitchen. He likes to butter the big yellow sleeves of bread, flicking marge out the tall white boxes and striping it with a wide grin onto the slices his Mum has chequer-boarded around the stainless bench. He has to study hard to close up each sticky pair, a drool of twenty-something concentration. I don't know if she just dumps the bread. No one's ever had the guts to ask. And she doesn't ask about my son either, doesn't offer me any cheap proverbs, or trite old tags. When people do, I'm tempted to follow her example and aim for the fat goal of their smiles, take some platitudinous teeth out. We just sit and lick pixels of piecrust out our gumline, and blow the air with tired fuckyous of smoke. And Maggie takes the piss about how uppity I used to be, 'tight-arse little princess, but me too, eh, I could be a bit of a dick. Hangi-pants too. Check us out now. Haha. Ah well. Is what it is.' And we'll watch the last of the tanked-up kids still lacing through the carpark, the topple of trios of high-heeled girls, their tube-frocks moist with oblivious sick, and we'll wish the dumb young fuckers well in their stagger home to normality and think of our sons.

Inside the club, there's still a picture of me, marrying my husband. There's a whole wall of club weddings spanned across the decades, but girls that win the captains, like I did, still rate at the top. And she's right, I am a tight-arse princess, iced into white satin, strapped into a shiny cylinder of it, so I wince each show-offy breath through the dress's boned column. I'm so goddamn delighted with myself. I've struck a trophy pose, and my husband has the logo on his blazer and stamped on his diagonal tie. He's a thickset honey, his tousle of hair greased back, with a beautifully munted smile. He's a team player, and I'm marrying the whole team – and I don't mind, I feel like a matchfit goddess. We've even bought a section that fronts onto the club grounds, and he's going to knock us up a house right there, like we're in permanent reserve, with his own rugged number-eight hands. And I'm going to get myself knocked up, and feel my babies ruck inside me, and let my captain stroke the globe of my stomach and crack lame jokes about them kicking, coach them through my waters with his gruff game-play commands. 'Be dominant,' that's his favourite one, the one he'd roar from the sidelines while our son blitzed by, a hulk of strain and froth, thudding through the cross-grain of bodies, braced around the ball, gouging forward, 'Ryyyyyyy-an,' the syllable stretched like a curse on his opponents, 'be dominant.'

Be dominant.

Plummeting the turf to a soundless stop. While the crowd kept bawling my baby's glory.

And later, while he lay in the rattle of the hospital, his body in the throb of the tubes and the tests and the strobes, more than one person posted the outcome to his Facebook page, *mate, we wasted 'em*. Even a mother, oblivious. *Letting you know the score! We took it out 25:13!*

They're decent, the boys. It could be the same bunch that worked over Maggie's thief, that are head down over a stack of lumber in the back yard when I get home from the hospital today. They've volunteered to help with the ramp. There's a row of them, good value kids, and a couple of dads, and the skeleton's going up quick, piles thumped in, a good frame righted in struts. The lads are trying to out-hammer each other, and one or two are going at warp speed, jerking in guffaws off the end of a nail gun, until they get yelled at, *don't arse about or I'll knock your bloody heads together*. For the most part, they've stripped off their t-shirts and wear them stuffed above their bums, so when they swag around the lawn their sweaty flags flail around. One has his tee collared back over his scalp so it girlifies him with a long blue veil. There's not a drop of sunscreen on any of them, and the ozone glints on their torsos already, a promise of third degree.

When I pass them, their antics go quiet. The hassle, and clatter, and joshing stop. They half-drop tools, stare at their gawky hands. They don't exactly grin, but their mouths do something sweet and bungled. There's a muttering that sounds respectful. But it could just be fear.

I'm an institution too. But no one knows what to say to me.

I watch for a while out the kitchen window, their klutzy progress, their loose aim, their uncouth trunks. They swing boards round, only half hoping to miss, a mongrel ballet, slapstick, amateur. They don't skip a chance to roughhouse each other, tousles of sudden punch, and passing scrags, topped off with hefty laughs. I think of my boy, their captain – of course he was their captain – who should be out there calling the shots, pulling a blokey pose overseeing the work, mock bawling-out their foul-ups, clocking the back of their scalps if they clash too much. Then I think of him, three, in the clobber of his dad's tool belt, taking goofy outsize stomps to keep up its leather anchor. I think of him, six, lying head to head with me on the cooled trampoline to stare up at the milky chinks of star: I think of the smell of his wonder, the black mat buzzing as he waves up the disbelieving wriggle of his hand. I think of his fontanel, the soft pulsing gap of it fronded by his cottony hair, a thrum of feathery bone I could touch my mouth too, cradling, as he fed. I take out supplies to the boys. I take out a tray of tomato sandwiches, Mountain Dew and Coppertone. I take out a handful of my son's old caps, the scent of his skull still moulded in their stiff domes. There's half a handprint of red paint daubed onto one, a mucky blotted lifeline. There's the coast of his temples, sweated in a fine grey tremor that leaks along the white of the peak. Today in the hospital he hadn't wanted anyone near him, so I'd had to wait till he slept, to edge closer on his pillow, to creep to his crewcut hair, where the stubble sticks out like his last crop of nerve endings. But here in the back yard I hold out the stains of him, all the rip-shit dents and scuffs – he was always going for broke at whatever activity he was attacking, full tilt, brute force, a mighty irrepressible blur. He was a feat of nature, my boy. A reckoning in teen male skin.

The boys don't talk to me. Bar one. Daniel's the one who's turned up most to the hospital, although my son still refuses any visits. I see him down by the letterbox, faking a standoff with a hi-top, like it's packed with stones he can't bash out. I know it's an update he wants. So I wander over, chuck him a tube of sunblock, pretend a half-hearted telling off. But he's too tender, this boy, for the sheer hulk of him, the stout block of muscle which is his jaw. The stocky throat wobbles, his eyes glaze too quick above his heavyset smile. I think of the nurse I liked best at the hospital, an elegant singsongy male, who trilled at us coyly as he swished through his work, and blabbed bits of high-pitch nightshift gossip, but touched us, firm, a genuine no-bullshit touch, and sometimes even a hug, his grip a sincere grab right to his ribcage, matter of fact with suffering, and crooning some comfort. When Ryan wouldn't see the kid, he'd steered him away by the shoulderblades, propped him on a park bench outside and nodded as he snivelled, lit him a relay of smokes. But my husband has clout in this small town – they don't forget you here once you're captain – and behind the scenes he made sure no more male nurses were rostered onto Ryan's case. He told me of his victory – it was the least they could do for him, things were going to be hard enough, without the extra humiliation of … he couldn't bring himself to describe the scene, the handling of our boy's body, its longterm needs. He didn't see my rage. And I make sure now I don't show it to the boy by the letterbox with the too-soft eyes.

Instead I tell him of the day I first brought Ryan back from hospital, a tiny warm survivor, squashed into a car seat, sleeping off the unexplained battle of the last few days. The scrape of the instruments, the evil figures in teal, the march of the ducks. And I'd parked and lifted him out of his seat, a wobble of wool and limbs and shuteye, and my husband had come to the car door to help and I handed him over, a see-sawed transfer of weight. But when his body left me it was sudden. I found myself on the gravel, crumpled, relief gulping my ribs. Wracked with deliverance, giving great gasps of spluttered prayer.

I won't know that feeling again.

There are things the boy could say to me. He could come out with some banality, the slogans they drill them in over at the club. I hear them nearly every night, shouts that echo from the field, their barks of courage, stale and trite. But he doesn't. He takes the cap I offer out to him, and he slides it on, so his face darkens, thickened with shade. He farts his palm with sunscreen, fumbles it over his face. That's what makes his eyes red. He's a tough boy. And he is learning. I don't know if he'll be visiting Ryan again.

The rest of the boys don't say his name to me. My husband assures me though, our son's a legend to them. Nothing will ever change that. He tells me later there's plans, for the boys to line up along the drive on the day we bring him home, guard of honour. They'll do the haka for him. Kia kaha. They'll be spruced up, their thick bodies jammed in their formals, sternums huffing under blazers, throats tweaking yanked ties, awkward with clean-shaved ahems. Then the shout will fire up, and their hands will rout and clap, they'll outface, their shins will thud. It will be bloodthirsty and beautiful, a boom on the earth as their big limbs thunder out a warrior's welcome.

And I'll wheel my son past them, where we've tucked him in his contraption. Where he doesn't want to live.

There are traditions I can't stop. I know that tonight, when I hear the haka pounding the dancefloor over at the club. It's been a big game, a decider, and there's a band in: I watched them unloading the van from my ranchslider earlier, a clapped-out troop of musos dragging in amps and light bars, stopping mid-pack-down for a fag, a trio on the sunset blockwall in matching black tees. I know it's a zero-sleep night: if I bother to lay in my bed the bass will only detonate my chest wall, a deep controlled bruising. And I've lived alongside club nights long enough. I can pick out every item in the soundtrack: the shrill as the hatchbacks of girls arrive, their preloaded silvery high-heeled squealing. The hoots as the old blokes, sinking their brews since mid-avo, start pulling their stumbled boogie, weaving the girls in harmless nostalgic jolts, getting freaky with their senior hips. The line-up for the feed, the clack of plastic, shovel of chips round the steel bins, squeak of the arse-end sauce, the wrangled chops. I even know the tone of funerals, or weddings, or birthdays, the shift in decibels, the dead or alive playlists. And this: the tribute of half-cut boots thundering the wood floor. A spasm of remembrance, before the band cranks up its millionth Sweet Home or Simple Man, and they're all too plastered to stagger any further. The frieze around the walls is of themselves, as gods. There isn't a stretch where they're not mighty, ranged in their divisions, lined up in their frames, fists held hard on their wide-planted knees or squared across their chests, no mistaking the set of their jaws. Here to dominate. Season after mud-gold season. The frames rattle as their stance hounds the floor. There are traditions that aren't up to me. If they have to thump their grief against their sternum, if they have to stomp and bellow it, then so be it. Grief is not a language I understand any better.

I think what I want to sign mine is a whistle.

I think I should be allowed one. It's a whistle I want when the doctors half-explain to me, when the dash starts shrieking on his ray of machines, and they sprint into the room, and the sound of their efficiency, played against the vinyl and sterility and metal, terrifies me, their mouths moving in fast-paced clips of jargon that make every blip feel terminal. There needs to be half-time, they need to let me call it, take a breather. And it's a whistle I want when the journalist, who's been told no, hung up on, many times now, tries to sneak in and steal a bedside soundbite to headline their hard-hitting expose. When the same reporter stakes out the dayroom and catches my son's girlfriend, ringed with her besties, who try to tone their giggles down to ICU levels, but who still spill details, of the backless ball dress his girlfriend wouldn't be wearing, can't resist all its chic sequinned specs, and the night they won't be spending at the Sun Kist Inn where he'd booked *like the actual honeymoon suite, OMG, supersweet*, for their first time, clumsy and gentle, a room with a waterbed in padded crimson velour and a dozen red roses he'd pre-ordered, and how sad, but they'd heard it could *still be, you know, um, managed*, in the longterm, *you know*, there were ways it could be sorted, all blushing in simpers, making tragic corny bats with their lashes, little measured blinks of semi-wet tint, because it was all so (dainty sob) *like ultra saaaaaad*, while the journalist sketches down their soft-core handicapped dreams.

And it's a whistle I want, tonight, when I'm walking to the clubrooms now for my out-back toke with Maggie but she heads me off, jumpy under the spotlight, clearly aiming to stop my gaze falling on the girl who's groaning up against the wall, and it's not like it's a shock to see a girl corralled there, staggering the brickwork with a boy in control, so her head is bobbing on the end of his thrusts, and she's maybe even tipping out a little pre-mix puke mid-groping, then tripping off after, a high-rise tip of a walk, like her shoelaces are tied, and her torso a-trickle, oblivious to what's been pumped into it, except she's been anointed by one of the boys, so she can afford to zigzag back to the hall and gabble her baptism to pals on the dancefloor, and drunkenly point to the boy who's left his mark, imprimatur on her greasy thighs, and dream maybe he'll hit her up for more, maybe even let her wear the hallowed branding of his first fifteen jersey to school on Monday, *way romantic*, it's hardly a shock she's there, but I want a whistle when I know that it's her, it's my son's girl, straddling a hard-at-it boy, not a gentle replacement, but a rough-as-guts fuck, though the boy's grunting dopey endearments while he's blocking, and she's rambling something too, some drivel about broke hearts, cold facts, lost love, but she's already forgetting what she's lost, except all the remains that will drain from her later and the brickwork remembered on her spine in lagered bruises.

And if the boy turns I know he'll have too-soft eyes.

'It is what it is,' says Maggie beside me. And somehow that works as well as a whistle.

And what is there to do then but let Maggie lead me round to the rear mess door, and prop me against the barred screen while she fetches us a couple of quiet ones. And then let her lead me, white tubs in hand, to the mini crane-lift that they service the floodlights with. She's an institution in this place, and she's got the keys – *too right*, she eyebrows me, as if there was any fucking doubt. She bangs the yellow crate, *up ya get*, and fiddles with some mechanism over on the frog-green cab. Then she hoists her arse over the rails herself, and upends the tub with a hollow pop. 'There you go. Throne, ya uptight princess.' Her ragged teeth are grinning at me, pushy and gapped.

I do as she says, and climb on. Maggie's tough thumb joints jog at controls and we're aloft, a slow grinding rise above the field. It smells like rust and ascension and turf. The mist is coming out, a float of it over the green, and we drift over its illumination. The floodlights are like some sleek artillery from heaven.

'I used to do this with my boy sometimes. He was into it. There've been some choice moments.' She nods at me. 'Not much eh. But something.' She answers herself, 'Well I reckon anyway.'

The altitude is radiant, a good place to get pissed. So we do, careful to do it mostly silent. Although I tell Maggie once, or maybe more, that the lift-tray makes me think of when Ryan was little, how he used to love to huddle in the plastic laundry basket, and beg me to launch him overhead. And how somewhere, over my baby, locked in his terrible isolation, there's a line of giraffes extending their lonely wet eyes to out-of-reach trees. And once, in the clubrooms, I remember him nicking off with someone's Nana's wheelchair, and hooning it, on long giggling burnouts round the hall. And Maggie blows listening grooves of smoke and says nothing. I look out over the lines of the field and think of the old man who comes to mark them, who's done it for years now, a patient ploughing of the paint roller, jittery and silver on the grass, along the string lines he's measured, meticulous, pegged out, recalibrated, offside. He's religious about it, kneels on the turf, doublechecks, genuflects, before he stamps it white. When Ryan was little he'd sneak out our fenceline and follow him, poor man, stuck with a toddler, rowdy and fidgeting and nonstop nattering beside him as he yanked round his trail of paint. And everything would grow through it, burst, bloom, smudge, break, the bodies just scrape away its borders, so he'd have to come back and do it all again before the next game.

Oh Bend Your Backs!

John Mulkeen

You'd think of a whale as being a simple fucker, but the truth is more like, nuanced. A blue whale, for instance, has a brain the same shape and size as a Volkswagen Beetle. Whales have a language with over two thousand words. They have distinct personalities and insecurities and they form complex, flawed relationships. There's been documented cases, within whale pods, of altruism, platonic bonding, infidelity, body dysmorphia and transphobia. In the waters off Nova Scotia, scientists have catalogued killer whales with distended pectoral fins, which they get by using kelp as a form of resistance training. In Japan, fishing boats have reported that when a processed unit is returned to the water, grey whales behave in a manner that closely resembles a Catholic wake. Whales are as diverse as they are plentiful. But when the whale came back to Derry in the spring of '17, that thing was compelled by the one impulse shared by every whale in every ocean on the planet. It wanted blood sacrifice, and nothing else would do for it.

I was the first one to see it.

It was a May morning; the air was like fresh bedsheets and I was looking down from the New Bridge. The New Bridge is the largest bridge in Ireland, three thousand feet long and five hundred feet high and straddles the Foyle, the fastest, deepest tidal river in Europe. The river where the Nazi U-boats surrendered and where ten thousand coffin ships set sail for the New World. Once a day, when the river empties, herring gulls frolic among the bones that stick out of the mudflats like rotten teeth. The riverbanks are lined with supermarkets and the rest. When we got peace, this place could have been fancy like Amsterdam or Belfast. Instead we got great brick toads that lap up people like fleas and waggle their holes at the heart of my town. After the next war I swear we'll build beer gardens in the rubble. We'll dig out the banks and let fish chew fungus from our feet as we sup on fermented conifer sap.

I sank my Orchard Thieves and squashed the can in my hand. I've had big hands ever since I was wee and though the backs of them are covered in scars like thran mouths, the palms are soft as fanny lips. I pinged my empty and watched it fall to see how far the ripple would travel. But there was no splash and I saw there was a hole in the river, and I was not surprised.

Then the water began boiling and frothing and the dark heart of the Foyle rose up. A gnarled giant, encrusted in barnacles, shimmering black and blue, swelling like a tar pit bubble with two crucified wings on either side, and just when it loomed impossible, the water stopped bubbling.

A whale. A whale! A whale-fish I cried but the words failed in my throat.

It had only one eye, a glistening black orb full of narcolcptic rage like my Da would get before he went into one. The other side of its head was a wreck of vicious scar tissue. It blinked once. Then every air particle exploded, and long-dead hatchet men screamed, and I fell on my hole.

A jet of spume as high as the bridge.

Everybody knows that when the river takes you, she only gives you back after nine hours, nine days or nine weeks but I swear to God, when my empty clattered on the road behind me, it was but nine seconds from it hit the Foyle.

I bolted from that bridge, screeching warnings that the town might wake up and before I knew it, I was in the alley by my old house. I pressed the back of my head so hard against the rough brick wall, it drew blood. Then that painted maze, the glass fangs, the 'Kill Touts', it all went away, and I was grabbing me ma and hiding my face in her nightie and whispering "Not me Mammy. Not me." And she was gorgeous. Eventually I wiped the spray off my face and left.

In fairness, that first day was class. The council announced a Whale Festival and the whole city turned out for a jook. Anybody working dobbed, people milled about, tapping their thighs to gentle techno playing from the back of a Tesco lorry. There were food trucks and face painting, and the smell of churros and weed made your cheeks tingle. The ziplines from the Cancer Festival were still up, so ones could fly across the river holding selfie sticks for a fiver a pop. Under the bridge, there was a cracker mural done on top of all the names, of a whale saying “Yes” out its blowhole.

Swarms of drones followed it as it swam in slow circles. They landed on its back like flies on a rhino and each time it spumed, they took off in a pulsing black cloud. The whale sang as it swam. Eerie, jarring songs like a keening Shee. Songs about genetic purity and folklore, cringeworthy in all honesty and though people were low-level affronted, nobody said nothing.

People watching online started wondering about the holes in the fins and what did that to its bake? The ould ones knew of course. They knew its name too.

Omar Gillespie used to post videos of himself doing his sword, and though everyone knew Omar was a skank and a hood, his videos always got likes and shares. Omar loved being a hood more than anybody I know loves doing anything, and that sort of passion is infectious. The CCTV shows Omar roaring as he walks out along the bridge that first night. At the bottom of the screen something glints in the dark. Omar stands on the railings and steadies himself. When he jumps, his face pixelates and as he falls, a gargantuan mouth opens. Omar lets go the sword and his arms start windmilling. He lands in the mouth and disappears. A second later he leaps out again and grabs the sword mid-air. The mouth closes and waits. Omar hangs for a second and then falls again straight into the ravenous jaws, again shooting out just in time and so on.

Whoever Boomeranged the video did a good job. In the Boomerang Omar escapes for a bit at least. When that video blew up, things changed. Everybody knows Omar was mental, but his brand was consistent, and people appreciate that in a world that wipes its hole on expectations.

By morning the city was out for blood. FTF began appearing on walls. The whale mural, still fresh, got two big cocks drawn on it and its eye crossed out. Young ones started pegging bricks and fireworks at the river, screaming obscenities. Anybody sticking up for the whale torn apart online. FTF. Fuck the Fish. And a whale is a fish and if you don’t know that, then I can’t help you.

There´s ones who say that it was only doing what came natural. There´s people who’ll contort themselves like they’re the midnight show in

Phuket, to forgive anybody except their own. They're the ones who'd have been happy with an apology video, whale sincerity, heavy on passive aggression. Sad.

The next evening Pajo Hegarty necked fifty Sunrises hoping to poison the thing. Pajo was doing his masters in maths but if his sums that night represented his best work, he'd have been better fucking it off and doing english. Fifty pills to a thing that size is like you or me double dropping. A moot point, for as he fell from the bridge, belly-full of Sunrises, the whale timed it and thwacked him with his tail, clean out of the park. They found most of Pajo in the grounds of Boom Hall, his toes still twitching. Them Sunrises are lethal lad.

Now there were crowds camped out the banks twenty-four seven, with oil drum fires piercing the nights, barrow lights flitting mute across the dark water and ones on the shore feeding names into the blackness.

I fled to the Park Bar and bought the ould boys Harps, and they told me about the first time the whale came to Derry.

They said they were glad to see it, true as God. A big fish swimming around the Foyle was a bit of craic between abominations. They called it Dopey Dick and everybody was delighted. The whole town lined out, and the Brits barricaded themselves in Fort George peering out through infrared binoculars. The demonic images relayed to London convinced top brass they'd finally caught the heathen paddies worshipping their ould pagan gods and they planned accordingly.

And after Neil Burgess and Sam Tracey, two dock workers out at DuPont factory went missing, most people didn't want to point fingers at Dick, despite the fact the whale had begun singing songs that were considered racist, even by the standards of the day.

It was the incident with the Prehen Rowing Club which changed everything. The chairman John Collins should have known better, but he was posh and wouldn't be told. He led the club out on the water, Andy Porter, Francis Hamill, Pete McDevitt, Harry Davidson, Cormac O'Neill and Juliette Devine and they looked like Rhubarb and Custards in their wee red and yellow canoes with matching life jackets. Out they went towards Dopey Dick and on the banks, people stopped talking. The sounds of Collins calling instructions and the gentle lapping of the oars carried across the water. They got close enough that they could have stroked the glistening, barnacled skin. Collins beamed and gave a thumbs-up. On land people began to whoop. Then Dopey Dick lifted the great tail in the air and smashed them all.

After that it went mental. An IRA sniper shot Dick in both fins from the top of the Guildhall. The UVF tried to make a bouncing bomb and when they couldn't, they blew up the Fergal Sharkey statue instead. The INLA, fearing exclusion, launched a petrol bomb attack from Top of the Hill. Most of the bombs didn't reach the water and, due to the strikes, didn't contain petrol. Nevertheless they rained down on Spencer Road causing minor traffic delays.

The lads told me of the peace treaty organised by the one from the bog, and how a huge parchment was fashioned at the Limavady printers, and how the big pen was commandeered from the city's Ulster Giants Festival. They said that on the day of the signing the air crackled with the sound of Phil Coulter singing a specially commissioned song over and over again from the back of a Woolworths lorry.

When the bell rang noon, the Rosemount Hells Angels led a procession to the water and the Apprentice Boys followed with the parchment, rolling the pen on a wheeled platform. And when Dopey Dick hoisted himself onto the banks beside the Guildhall, he squashed a bin and nobody said nothing. They told me how one of the Apprentice Boys shouted and how they all scattered and how the cannon fired. For it was no giant pen at all but Roaring Meg, the city's last working cannon. They told me how Dopey Dick paused, a cavity in his face, how meat rained down on the road and how he slipped back into the river. Those who grumbled about the skank soon quietened when the celebrations began, and the Roaring Meg Festival was born.

It was a quare tale but it reeked of the desperate exaggeration that occurs when you feed lonely ould boys pints of Harp.

Una Doherty knew all too well about the power of spectacle. As she walked stiffly through the crowd on the bridge on the third night, she was wrapped in duct tape and clattered with razors head to toe. As she struggled to climb the railings, two legends from the crowd grabbed her legs and helped her over, getting sliced up nicely for their troubles. Una probably got the closest out of everybody, her razor armour splitting Dick´s leathery lip. And even though they reckon the water shattered her spine, Dick was seen holding her underwater and thrashing her about for hours afterwards.

The city was a no-go area. The tourists cancelled, and our fresh paintings of old wars went unlooked upon. The council declared a state of emergency which achieved exactly nothing. Sure the Brits are no more, and Dublin wouldn't touch a whale with yours after their own shanty town unpleasantness.

The Bogside Young Satanists held nightly black masses. The Park Bar Sociologists developed theories of immigration and populism. The council took leave and so a better one was created. Thirteen members, the leader of every gang plus me, the town crier, messaged late into the nights.

Deccy Donnelly, slabber extraordinaire, should have stuck to smuggling fags but he took notions. He led his squad down from Top of the Hill, body-popping along Spencer Road followed by a silver Mitsubishi, blasting Tupac and pulling donuts. Cheering crowds lined the pavements, live streaming the procession. Deccy's crew hopped the fence and climbed the ladders to the ziplines. James Doherty, Blink McMonagle, Doots and Fly Sweeny, Cormac O'Neil Og, Doc Callan and Deccy himself. They attached themselves to the zipwires and shimmied out above the water. When the rolling waters and drone clouds were spotted, the screams from the crowds on the banks levelled up in pitch and intensity. Deccy was still trying to get his first petrol bomb lit when, through sheer tyranny of will, Dopey Dick breached, thrusting his whole body from the water and hovering dreadfully, blacking the sun, before crashing down through the zipwires and sending a corrupted wave over Spencer Road to scatter the crowd.

The solution came from the philosopher Petang. In Top of the Hill, Petang is like a saint, having drove the cats from the estate around the turn of the century. Word reached the New Council that Petang sought confab. He held court in the smoking section of Anne's Leaping Hole and it was clear that he was bitter about not being part of the New Council. His scarred lips sneered and spat insults until we agreed to announce a

Philosophy Festival in return for his help. He hoked around in the entrails of a pigeon. He told us all about the cats as he tells everybody about the cats. Like you do one great thing with your life and then ruin it by spoofing about it for ever. He told us how he used lasers as a distraction before dropping paving slabs on them which caused a shouting match from the New Council. It had taken Derry twenty years to get the money to fix the pipes at Stinkers Creek, a laser was unthinkable but still Petang talked and when we left Anne's, our trousers were tucked into our socks on account of the place being swarming with rats.

Still, we had a plan. Emerging from the chaos was hope, barely there, like a web glistening in tear gas. We knew rightly how things like this end where we come from, but still.

No sooner had D-Day arrived than half the city lost the bap and the thing was postponed. A day later D/LD-Day arrived leaving everybody scunnered.

Everybody knows how it turned out. But they didn't see the organising, the messaging, the lorries full of dyes and fabrics brought down from the Sperrin Mountains. They didn't see the dawn congregation in Brooke Park. They didn't hear the poet Olivera make her speech. They didn't see me standing on the plinth where the statue of Padre Pio once stood, looking out over the sea of sesh heads and stews and scumbags, my hands shaking and my mouth a fur boot. The New Council all speaking finely and me only whispering "keep her lit lads".

People know about the gathering by the water, but they haven't heard the sound of ten thousand pairs of Vans tramping the empty streets. The clanging as Olivera rapped her hurl on the railings. Dopey Dick approaching the banks. Olivera roaring. They've heard about the incandescent glow of the dresses. The parade along the banks, the last great parade, with a thousand Irish dancers hammering out a grade four two-step while D-Ream blasts from a sound system on the back of a Sainsbury´s lorry. Dopey Dick hypnotised, swimming on his back, rubbing his belly with his fins.

Brendan Kehoe wasn't mad or loud or anything really growing up, except for stubborn. He was that alright. Ran with the gang, owned a great Mitre Delta, fancied the one with the curls, everybody did but

Brendan *really* did.

The parade arriving at the bridge; Dopey Dick insensible below.

Everybody got booted out of the gang at some point. You had to wait it out, that was all. Easier for some. Some could go back to their own houses. And when it was time, you came back and never spoke of it again. Everyone knew the score. Brendan knew it. And he still fucked it.

People know about the statue of Padre Pio dropping from the bridge, Pio's sword aimed directly at Dopey Dick's exposed heart.

Brendan went but he didn't come back. When it was time, he just mooched around by himself. And when we realised that he wasn't coming back, we turned on him. We spat at him and called him a pansy. We egged his house and slagged him about his da. We battered him on the green after school.

The chains wrapped around the base of the statue.

Then Brendan turned to stone, which threw everyone for a loop. They took him out of school, and everyone felt lousy. It was decided that Brendan was forgiven, and Brendan's ma cried so hard when we called in for him again, us beaming around a shiny new Dunnes trolley. From then on, we wheeled him everywhere with us. We decorated him for the bonfires and pushed him down Lawrence Hill and surfed on top of him. We wrapped him in scarves for the football and tied fireworks to him at Halloween. He was integral to the gang, more so than anyone else. And even though no one had seen Brendan in years, when it came to D/LD-Day, it was only right that he was sent for and wheeled up to the bridge in a shiny new Sainsbury´s trolley, his hair gelled down by his ma the same way he wore it all those years ago when he was last real.

Ones talk about the sound of the chains tearing the side of the bridge. Nobody mentions Brendan's eyes popping out of his head.

For reasons including ballast, aesthetics but mostly prophecy, Petang told us that a sacrifice was required. Had he been able, no man would have put his hand up quicker than Brendan. For he'd have known that his mural would be four storeys high and that his page would be filled with all the hearts and likes. And up in Heaven, there would be forty pawpaw hallions waiting to ride him in his silver trolley until the one with the curls got ould and died and then she too would give him the touch for eternity.

The Galliagh hoods brought the statue of Padre Pio on the back of a Maine lorry and balanced it on the railings. Brendan made an epic hero, his chains attached to Padre Pio's legs. We turned his trolley to meet the rising sun and his wet eyes sparkled. Even the City football top he wore worked perfectly as an ironic gesture to parochialism and corporate sponsorship. This monster slaying is brought to you by the Derry Disaffected, and Donegal Creameries.

Ones have seen the blur of Brendan being flung from his trolley. They've heard the one with the curls calling out, "They'll mind how you went Brendan! Not how you were!" a second before he was ripped from the bridge.

Ones have seen the statue hurtling, the chains unravelling, the trolley and Brendan, Dopey Dick oblivious, the sword holding the distilled rage of a whole city bear down upon the creature.

They've seen it miss.

Missed by a fair bit in fact. It's a tough thing to judge, the height plays tricks on your eyes. The statue hit the water and poor Brendan shattered, shinbones splintering through his legs. Dick rolled nonchalantly over.

The bridge was silent apart from D-Ream singing about woods and trees.

Without another word people began climbing the railings. They bared switchblades, high heels, machetes, mobile phones, compasses, teeth, fingernails. I looked around me at strangers, weans with life carved into their painted faces.

I pressed my face through the cold railings like a man can nearly taste freedom, and though every tendon in my neck strained to look away I peered into the heart of the river. I've been beat like a man, by a man since before I could walk and it made me who I am, but when I finally beheld, all I wanted was my mammy and to gouge the eyes out of my head.

As the weans of the city fell, Dopey Dick mashed them. He chewed them and gargled them. He swallowed them whole, thrust them underwater and churned them, each one a blush in the froth. I'll paint your names, every one of them, high on the walls and under the bridge and keep them fresh. Forgive me for I am truly rotten, a grateful coward clinging to the bars of his cell. I cried out, but bubbles flooded my mouth.

Every hour, a whale's heart pumps eighteen tonnes of black blood along nearly a thousand miles of veins, each one as thick as a cage fighter´s forearm.

A week after D/LD-Day Ruairi Lynch walked from the Park Bar to the New Bridge, pausing only to stop in the Culmore Road Texaco to pick up a can of petrol. Once there, he doused himself and placed the can carefully on the path. He sat on the railings and after twelve attempts he got himself lit and dropped like a stone. No last words, no bother to him, classic Ruairi. He didn't get near Dick, but I wonder if the last thing his brain registered was the river going up in flames. I wonder if he thought he landed in Hell.

Whilst the weans had been hurling themselves at the fish, the council and the owners at DuPont had agreed to open the pipes and were pumping the Foyle full of foulness, that it be desecrated for man and beast. When Ruairi Lynch hit the water the whole thing went up. The heart of my city.

When they named the whale they didn't ask its permission, for a christening requires no consent. They called it Dopey because they thought it was lost, that it didn't belong. The ones who slag us say that by baptising it we gave it a home, but you know, and I know, whales are cuter than that. That hungry mouth in the Foyle is older than the names we give it.

Sometimes a skeleton gets pinged from the river, usually landing on Spencer Road, causing minor traffic delays. I drink here, in the Park Bar, and it is warm and full of shadows, and I close my eyes and am swallowed and with me in that scarred place are the voices of senile old gods, sparking flints and endlessly misquoting each other. Sometimes in the morning, there are fresh mouths on my hands.

I watch for my phone going dark so that I'll know it has begun. I wait to be asked something, and for a few Harps I'll tell you anything about anything, except for my name. I'll not tell you that. Not yet anyway.

Fearfully and Wonderfully

C S Mee

We had sent in our samples and opened an account months before we felt ready. I received the odd email reminder and would log in to browse the familiar options, fiddling with combinations, lining them up, pairing them off and then deleting the selection to start again. The possibilities seemed infinite and I had no idea what I was doing.

Then one day we made the decision. The reality of it was so cold and functional it shocked me. As simple as ordering a mattress or a hob. We sat together in front of the computer, clicked the website we'd tagged and logged in to our account. We made our selection. Just one item in the basket, no more shopping for now. That made us laugh.

My husband admitted later on, that he hadn't been convinced to begin with, while I was certain it was his idea in the first place.

I read out my credit card details and my husband typed them in. We'd stopped laughing and were focusing then. He still typed the wrong numbers three times and I snapped at him and took over. We were that tense.

Then one click and it was done. Ping of a confirmation email in my inbox. Next day delivery. We dared a glass of prosecco in celebration, in relief.

I took the day off work to be home. The kit was bigger than I'd expected; five large boxes, filling the hallway. The delivery man was not as careful as I would have liked. I signed with a hysterical squiggle, eager to be rid of him.

I wanted to tear the boxes open, but we'd agreed to wait. One of the top flaps was loose and I slid a finger beneath it to peek inside. Small packages nestled in layers of polystyrene. I picked one out at random and opened it carefully. Inside, embedded in protective foam, were two sets of miniature finger bones. I shut the box and my eyes tight.

My husband came home early, keen to begin. We cleared the kitchen table and wiped it with a cloth. That didn't seem enough. We sprayed it with disinfectant and scrubbed our hands. For the first time in our married lives, I saw my husband clean under his fingernails.

'Shouldn't it be in the fridge?'

We had our first argument.

'How would we fit all this in the fridge?' I started to panic.

'Maybe we should have bought a special fridge.'

'Did it say anything about keeping it in the fridge?'

'It must say in the instructions.'

'Where are the instructions?'

The instruction manual was as thick as a Bible. There were fifty pages of hazard warnings at the beginning; toxic substances and choking hazards to avoid. I sat down to read them. My husband wanted to skip the warnings and start straightaway.

'I'm looking to see if it says anything about storing it in the fridge.'

He opened a beer.

'You're drinking?'

'One beer.' He started picking at the flaps of a box.

'Don't open that until we know what we're doing.'

He waved his beer at me. 'Do you want one?'

'Of course not.'

I turned back to the instruction manual and heard the television come on in the living room. I sat up for hours reading the hazard warnings. There was no mention of storing the kit in the fridge.

By the time I'd finished, the television was silent. My husband was sitting on the sofa with the remote in one hand and the empty bottle in the other, staring at a blank screen.

'It doesn't say anything about keeping it in the fridge, but we mustn't immerse any parts in water, unless instructed, or set fire to it, or stick it in a plug socket. And they're very down on domestic pets, but I think your tropical fish will be okay.'

'So long as we don't immerse it in the fish tank.' He smiled.

'Unless instructed.'

He got up and put his arms around me. We stood long and close.

'This is more stressful than I thought.' He sighed. 'I mean, I knew it would be stressful, but …'

'Let's go to bed.'

'Let's start tomorrow.'

We began with the spinal cord. Our hands trembled as we removed the vertebrae from their foam shells and laid them out following the numbered sequence in the instruction manual. The bones were tiny and awkward. I hardly dared to handle them, afraid of snapping a spinous process. We started with the atlas and the axis then lined up the vertebrae in a long tail, ending with the sacrum and coccyx.

As my husband reached to set the box aside, he knocked the coccyx to the floor. It skittered under the table and hit the skirting board. I dived to retrieve it, banging my head as I came back up with the comma of bone. My husband washed it and disinfected it and rinsed it and dried it before placing it back in line.

The intervertebral discs were harder than I'd imagined. We set them in place then began the long slow work of stitching the bones together with the ligaments provided. We'd barely begun on the thoracic vertebrae when my husband put a hand on my arm.

'Let's stop here for tonight.'

'Shouldn't we finish?'

He nodded at the kitchen clock. The night would be short before the alarm.

We left the unfinished spine curled on the table like a dormant snake. It was untouched and unmoved when we returned, stretching and unrested for our morning coffee. We drank standing against the counter, afraid of spillages, afraid of knocking those precious bones.

Over the following evenings we sewed ligaments until every vertebra was attached. Triumphantly, we threaded the spinal cord through the channel of bone, surprised by how easily it slipped through and found its place. The finished spine was tight and flexible. It curved into a C and we began to imagine her back curving in our arms.

The instruction manual provided a schedule, mapping out the weeks and months ahead of us. We consulted our calendars and divided the labour between us, planning days of leave at crucial stages.

'Shall we tell our managers?' I thought we should make it official.

'Not yet.' My husband wanted to wait. 'Let's make sure we're off to the right start.'

I worried that he wasn't sure we'd made the right decision. We couldn't go back now.

We shared the secret with no one, not even our families. My husband needed time to adjust to our new reality, time to make it real for himself. If I'm honest, so did I. She was so small, so fragile, so incomplete. I was afraid of making a mistake, misreading instructions, misconnecting vessels. I was afraid of losing her before she was half formed.

We stitched her with anxious fingers, pulling bones together with ligaments, laying tendons and muscle, threading veins and arteries. We constructed organs using parts from the kit, gluing and stuffing, pressing and occasionally stapling. We created parts for her that we didn't know she needed; the glands of Zeis, the sinoatrial node, the locus coeruleus and other features that we'd never heard of before. We thought back to anatomy classes at school and realised how little preparation we'd been given. The importance of every task overwhelmed us. We felt inadequate and unqualified.

In those early days it was hard to think of her as a person becoming. When I glued together the cavities of the heart, I knew I was doing something important, something vital, but I couldn't relate to that jellied organ, lying cold and still in my palm. I struggled to picture it racing with excitement, skipping with surprise or slowing in sleep.

In those early days I struggled to picture her racing or skipping or sleeping at all.

It took weeks to assemble the lungs. The bronchioles were fiddly and never ending, overflowing from a stack of boxes onto the kitchen table and scattering the work surface in half-formed tangles. Each morning we greeted the sight of them and the previous day's small progress with dread. I read somewhere that this is the stage at which most couples give up and I began to understand them.

That was the time of our most bitter arguments. We were wired with tension and the importance of our task. The instructions weren't always clear, comprising intricate diagrams and few words. We interpreted them differently and we argued.

'It's all common sense.' My husband liked to say.

When we were sitting there with bronchioles strewn around us, examining the assembly diagram with a magnifying glass, I begged to disagree. We wrangled over the instruction manual, each passionately defending our own opinion on the best way to construct her.

'Don't attach it there. That's the wrong way round,' I shrieked.

'If we don't do this right, she won't be able to breathe,' my husband snapped, seizing a half-formed lung.

Then he suddenly stopped and carefully laid it down.

'Let's call the helpline,' he said quietly.

It was at that point that I realised how much we both cared for her already.

We spoke to a young man with a Scottish accent who was casual and jokey. He directed us to an online tutorial. 'You wouldn't believe how many couples struggle with the lungs. It's a miracle any of us can breathe!'

I laughed and felt the air fill and empty reassuringly through my own manmade respiratory tract.

We studied the tutorial and completed the lungs exactly as shown, but we were never certain that we'd done everything right. Even years later, whenever she panted or seemed out of breath, we exchanged worried looks.

For all those months, making her gripped our own bodies, reshaping us around her, around the kitchen table where her parts lay scattered and forming. For all those nights we sat curved over her, until our backs burned and our eyes blurred. Our day jobs shrank in importance, compared with our evening task.

There came a time when we began to look forward, thinking beyond the kitchen table, making space for her in the rest of the house. We talked of cots and changing stations. We read catalogues and took measurements. We chose colours.

We began to imagine the person forming, how she might be, how she might grow. We pictured her animate and breathing, lifting the arms we'd built for her, wriggling the toes we'd glued together. I imagined her eyes looking into mine and I wondered what words would move her tongue.

Our secret left the bedroom, moved beyond the kitchen and escaped out into the world. We tested it on close family and friends. Their excitement was contagious. We told managers and colleagues, those who hadn't guessed from our distraction and days of leave. Some were kind, made allowances, muttered supportive comments; others were impatient with our new slowness, disapproved, issued unwanted advice. It was always clear who'd been there before us. There was light and sympathy in their eyes. We were so grateful for their kindness as we stumbled through the days.

The midwife visited for regular updates and pep talks. She glanced over our progress and checked our blood pressures to ensure that the stress wasn't too great.

'We've never done this before,' said my husband.

'We don't know what we're doing,' I added. 'What happens if we make a mistake?'

'Don't worry,' the midwife reassured us. 'Just follow the instructions and you can't go wrong. Nature is well made.'

She fobbed us off.

The inspections were more thorough and serious. There were only two, at 12 weeks and at 20. Only two chances to check our work, make sure we were on the right track, that we hadn't left anything out.

The inspector arrived at our house carrying a heavy bag of instruments and a folder spilling notes. She cast an expert eye over the kitchen table, and I worried that she wasn't impressed with our progress. Having politely rebuffed my husband's offer of tea, she unpacked her bag and sat down with concentration. We watched as she examined our work in ominous silence, scribbling in her notes. My husband and I exchanged anxious glances.

'Is everything okay?' I couldn't contain myself.

The inspector looked up with an unexpected smile. 'All in perfect order.'

Then she gave us a tour of that tiny body that we already knew so well. She named its parts as though we were seeing them for the first time. The spine, the stomach, the two halves of the brain, the chambers of the heart. An anatomy that we knew more intricately and intimately even than our own, or each other's.

I felt possessive then, defensive. She was ours, wasn't she? I didn't like this official person who might judge her inadequate, who might judge us inadequate.

After the second inspection we began to feel more confident. Gone were the early days when we were silent and focused over her bones, not daring to distract ourselves or each other. Now we were used to the daily ritual, accustomed to the rhythm of our evenings and weekends. Bending over her body, our heads almost touching as we glued and stitched, we grew to know a new intimacy. We did argue, but we also helped each other, debated problems and solutions, collaborated.

In the past we might have coexisted in the living room, each absorbed in his or her own phone, or sharing a takeaway and a box set from opposite ends of the sofa. Now we worked together, discussing everything, sharing every stage and triumph. For the first time since I'd met my husband, we were working on something that was entirely and uniquely ours.

I came to see a new side to him, a patience that I hadn't appreciated before. As I watched him delicately carve her outer ear, curling the ridge of the antihelix with total concentration, I loved him more than I'd ever loved him before. He told me several times that I'd changed, that he was impressed by my determination, my ability to focus through the small hours. If I'm honest, I impressed myself.

As we shaped her, she shaped us.

I was tired when I assembled her hands. There were so many tiny bones. I had a headache and my eyes itched. My husband was working late, putting in extra hours to finish projects before she was complete. I was alone in the kitchen and irritated by his absence. My fingers were clumsy and brusque.

As I pressed her left index finger to fix muscle to bone, the intermediate phalange snapped in two.

I dropped the finger with a gasp. She could feel no pain. I hadn't hurt her, but I was devastated. How could I be so clumsy?

My husband returned home to find me sobbing on the kitchen floor.

'What happened?'

I showed him the broken bone. He was calmer than I expected. He called the helpline and they arranged for a replacement phalange to be sent out by express delivery. It arrived the following day and we completed her hands together.

The guilt never left me.

By that time, we were both tired, worn down by the long months of work. My husband painted her left iris beautifully, blending colours in a regular pattern that was lovely to behold. But when he coloured her right iris, he splodged the paint, leaving a mark that's still visible today. He was disappointed and wanted to order a replacement, to try again. I reassured him that her right eye was no less beautiful than the left, that the unusual imperfection would be her own unique mark.

Towards the end we could think and talk of nothing else. The body on the kitchen table was the centre of our lives and the heart of our home.

We'd constructed her organs with diligence, but it was only when we began to work on her skin that she became real for us. As I shaped the buds of her milk teeth and embedded them in her gums, I began to see her as a baby, as our baby. We plumped her lips, glued her nails to their tiny nail beds, sanded her skin to the smoothest polish and stitched her scalp with a fine down of dark hair.

We chose a home animation. It was more intimate, more personal and the risks were low.

Everything was ready. We'd painted the nursery, set up the cot, bought nappies and baby grows. We followed the instructions to the last, laying her on a soft cloth on the kitchen table, where she rested, naked and still. We fussed over her. Right until the doorbell rang, I was touching up the birthmark on her left calf.

The midwife carried out a final inspection. I didn't like to see the way she handled her, moving her quickly and confidently, even if she was an expert. I wanted to say that she was fragile. I thought of the parcels of kit when they arrived. Handle with care.

After the inspection came the preliminary tests.

'You might want to sit out for this part,' the midwife suggested. 'Most parents prefer to wait for the final animation.'

We brewed calming tea and sat nervously in the living room, alert to every sound, as the midwife tested her circulation and nerve connections, respiratory tract and brain function.

It was late into the evening when she called us back into the kitchen. I glanced over the body on the table, reassuring myself that she was just as we'd left her. There was more paperwork. The midwife certified our work with an official signature and stamp of approval. My husband filed away our certificate.

'Now,' said the midwife. 'Are you ready?'

It happened so quickly. There was a jolt and a cry as her heart started and her lungs filled with their first breath. She didn't open her eyes at first, but lay panting, her skin growing warm and pink. We watched breathless. The miracle of life as her temperature rose, and she moved her muscles for the very first time.

Over the months we'd become so accustomed to her stillness that it was uncanny to see the body we'd built move of its own accord, animated by its own spirit.

'May I pick her up?' I asked, shy of this unfamiliar creature.

'Of course,' said the midwife. 'Please do. She's your responsibility now.'

Seeing us hesitate, she leaned over and gathered our little girl into her arms, then passed her into mine.

I gazed down at my daughter and she gazed back.

She was ours, but she was perfect, fearfully and wonderfully made.

The midwife packed up discreetly and left us alone with our baby. It was only hours later, as we examined her in the morning light, curling and uncurling her fists, that we noticed we'd attached her thumbs back-to-front.

A Letter from the North

Donna Brown

Just north of Manchester, in a small terrace house, lives a man who is a wood carver. His name is Arthur. On sunny days Arthur can often be seen sitting on a wooden dining chair outside his house, penknife in hand, poised over a piece of wood, watching the people come and go.

Sometimes he carves little figures of the children on the street. Usually, he gives the figure to the child and tells them to paint it if they want. More often than not the figure falls from a bedside table into a toy box, which then finds its way under a bed and is forgotten, at least for a little while. Occasionally, though, the child does paint the figure carefully with their best set of paints. If these are watercolours, then the paint job doesn't last long and they are back to a plain wooden figure quite soon, but that doesn't matter so much; it can always be painted again, although it seldom is.

One day a photographer is wandering about in Arthur's town, looking to capture working-class scenes: scenes of human interest. *Round here it's mainly red brick terraces and red brick mills, so I suppose there's historical interest, don't know about human …*

When the photographer gets to Arthur's street, he sees Arthur sitting in his chair and Jacob and Oliver Nesbit playing on the pavement nearby. It's the middle of the day so there are less parked cars than usual, what with nearly everyone being at work, otherwise he'd probably never have spotted Arthur at all. Well, this is exactly the sort of human interest he wants – the type of scene he has come all the way from London for – so he asks Arthur if he can take a picture.

"Hi mate, mind if a take a picture of yer?"

"Ay?" Arthur looks him up and down, trying to place the accent.

"Can a take a photograph? It's for a magazine. Human int'rest. Working-class scenes. Y'know? Name's Paul Miller, see." Paul hands Arthur a business card.

"Human interest?" Arthur sucks his teeth at this and the children snigger.

"Everyday scenes. Y'know."

Arthur shrugs. "Maybe I'll be famous yet: a workin'-class hero," he says to Jacob. Then, turning back to Paul, "Yer'll have to ask their mum if yer want them in it."

A head appears at the window opposite. "What d'yer want? What does 'e want Arthur?"

"A picture, Sal. For *human* interest."

"Human what!" Sally Nesbit laughs out loud. "Ten quid, then," she thinks for a moment then adds, "each." She slams the window shut and appears a moment later at the door, "including Arthur."

Paul mutters something unintelligible under his breath and hands Sally thirty pounds. She retreats to her step and watches. Paul sets up his scene.

"What's so interestin' about them, then?" Sally asks.

"We're a workin'-class scene, love," Arthur answers.

Sally laughs. Paul mutters again.

"Well, work's a relative term, isn't it? This your work, then?"

Paul takes a deep breath. "Yeah, this is my work. Freelance. For magazines."

"And they pay yer?"

"Yeah."

"How much? What d'yer get for one photo?"

"Depends. Might not sell at all."

"Aw, well, it might." With that Sally shrugs and goes back inside, slamming the door behind her.

Paul breathes a sigh of relief. *Now to work.* He lifts up his tripod and moves away down the street to a point where he can get a portion of the mill in the background. Shame there's no chimney anymore, he thinks. Just then the sun comes out, and he gets the red brick mill against a blue sky. *Sweet.* The little figures of Arthur, Jacob and Oliver dance in the foreground.

"Carry on playin'," he shouts to the children. Jacob pulls a face and puts his hands in his pockets. He is seven. You can't play to order when you're seven, so he struts up and down, wanting only to go and watch Arthur, who carries on with his carving, his head down.

"Show me how yer cartwheels are coming on, Jacob," says Arthur, glad to have the sun warming his back.

Jacob braces his legs, his arms raised, ready to attempt the spin. The cartwheels, however, need work. Oliver laughs and tries to copy.

Arthur keeps his head down as he smiles. "Keep practisin'. It takes time."

Jacob's brow furrows as he tries again. This goes on for a while, and eventually even Arthur half forgets about the photographer.

Paul finishes taking his pictures, thanks Arthur, then disappears. Two weeks later Arthur gets a letter. He opens it, and inside the envelope are a clutch of photos. A4. Black and white. Arthur chuckles to himself, thinking what an old bugger he looks in his flat cap. Then he wonders for a moment how the photographer knew his address. When he realises, he chuckles again and goes across the road to show Sally.

* * *

A few days later, Arthur is whittling again. This time the children are out with Sally, and he is alone, making a little model of the photographer from memory. Arthur has a good memory, and that comes in handy when you want to visualise something and carve it from wood. When he finishes, he wraps it up carefully in tissue paper and puts it in a padded envelope on which he has already written the photographer's address. He writes a short note that says, 'From one working-class hero to another,' then he seals the envelope, tapes it up with parcel tape for good measure, and ambles off to the post office to send it.

* * *

When Paul Miller gets the parcel, he is suspicious and prods at it for a little while. *He isn't expecting anything. What could it be?* Eventually, curiosity gets the better of him and he opens it. Now it's his turn to smile. He studies the figure for a time, then checks in the mirror to see whether he really is that bald, whether he really has a stoop and a paunch; he can't see either when he stands up straight. When he reads the note, he laughs out loud, but he still doesn't see himself as a working-class man. *You don't get your hands dirty taking photos, after all.*

* * *

Secretly, Sally Nesbit is pleased with the photo. Andy Nesbit, however, is not pleased and makes no secret of it.

"Creepy, that is. Coming 'ere, takin' pictures. Did 'e say what magazine?"

Sally shrugs, realising she probably should have asked. She hasn't told Andy about the thirty quid either. That's between her and Arthur, and neither Jacob nor Oliver have mentioned it, so she's assuming they didn't notice.

Andy doesn't know what else to say, so instead he picks up the photo and toys with the idea of tearing it up. Just then, Jacob comes in.

"No, Dad, please, I want to draw it."

"He's been drawin' pictures all day," Sally tells Andy.

"Let's see 'em then." Andy puts the photo down and his face lightens. He used to draw a bit when he was a kid. He was quite good too, but that was a long time ago now. Now his fingers are always sore and dirty from working outside all day.

Jacob appears with his sketches and Andy nods, suddenly happy again, forgetting his irritation over the photo.

"Might 'ave done 'im good, seein' that photographer," he comments to Sally later, over a mug of tea. "The drawin's were good. Good likenesses. Did yer see the one 'e did of Arthur?"

Sally shakes her head. "He was quiet all afternoon. Never been big on drawing before, has 'e?"

"No," Andy answers, "but then, I was always drawin' when I was a boy."

"Yeah, I know," Sally nods and passes Andy a chocolate biscuit then gets up to put her mug in the kitchen. As she does so, she slides the photo off the side table and hides it in the paper rack for safekeeping.

* * *

The next day, Jacob and Oliver are playing out again. Jacob sidles over to Arthur, who is on his chair as usual, and sets a piece of paper under his nose. Arthur puts down his penknife.

"What's this, then?" he asks Jacob.

"Who d'yer think it is, Arthur?"

Arthur nudges the boy and chuckles to let him know he's only joking.

"Can y'er tell who it is, Arthur?" chimes in Oliver, looking up proudly at Jacob.

"Looks like some old feller t'er me," Arthur says, and winks.

"Not very old," says Jacob, suddenly serious again.

* * *

Down in London, Paul Miller has bought himself a gym membership. He works out three times a week and still worries about whether or not he's middle class. *The seed of doubt has been sown.* The little figure that Arthur made sits on the mantelpiece in his tiny flat and he too is secretly proud of it. It never occurs to him to paint it. Anyway, he likes it just the way it is – *full of sunshine.*

The picture he took of Arthur, Jacob and Oliver hasn't sold yet. He's tried it in both colour and black and white. He still likes the black and white one best.

One day another envelope arrives. This one is flat, and it's addressed to 'Paul Miller, Working-Class Hero'. Paul smiles and concedes the point. When he opens the envelope, he finds Jacob's drawing inside, and he knows this because Jacob has signed it in red crayon. The picture is a perspective drawing in red, grey, brown, black and white. It shows Paul with his tripod, three small figures, one seated, and in the background the mill, which seems to have regained its chimney. This gives Paul pause for thought. Jacob, it seems, has added the dimension of time. Paul puts the drawing on his mantelpiece next to the figure, then tentatively adds his own photo – the black and white one. Somehow, it all works. The pieces fit together: artist and subjects, past and present colliding. The artist in him nods. Sale or no sale, the project is complete. *Or is it?*

* * *

Back in Manchester, Andy has scrubbed the dirt off his hands and set about some model making. He started with a kit comprising a series of machined balsa wood discs and built a swan, but now he's got more ambitious and is making a model of the mill, complete with its missing chimney. For this he is machining his own pieces, each correct to the millimetre, each brick identical. *The engineer has turned master craftsman, with an eye for detail that astounds even his wife.* Like Arthur,

Andy is using wood. He'd forgotten how good he used to be at woodwork too.

Andy is working from a photograph that Arthur gave him, showing how the street looked in 1955. Arthur is helping him. Now they have a crowd of wooden mill workers too, none bigger than three inches high. The whole thing started on Sally's kitchen table, but now it's getting too big, so it has moved across the street to Arthur's house. Arthur lives alone, so there is much more room. Jacob and Oliver are helping. There are lots of bricks to paint. It feels a bit like Lego, but you have to glue the blocks of bricks together.

It takes Andy and Arthur six months to finish their project. It's a scale model, pristine and unsullied by smoke. The bricks shine red, the chimney rises like a spire and the little Perspex windows gleam. Andy has an idea. He sends a photo of his model to the Museum of Science and Industry in Manchester and asks them if they'd like to display it. It should fit in well. There's a huge array of working looms in the museum that have been preserved so that visitors can learn about the Industrial Revolution. Jacob went on a school trip there; he said they were very noisy, and the cotton bobbins spun very fast.

The museum agrees to display the model.

Andy is over the moon. *He is a 3D artist. His work is on display in the city.* Sally and the boys are very proud of him. Arthur raises a glass to him in *The Friendship*. No one thinks to tell Paul Miller, who, you might argue, set the whole thing in motion. Such is life, however, and Paul is doing well at the gym.

When Andy mentions his next project idea to Arthur, the old man laughs and tells him he should partner up with Jacob this time.

"Me," he says, "I like bein' a workin'-class hero best."

Statue of the Future Martyr

Stephen Flanagan

Annette Moore first learned about the statue on a rainy Saturday afternoon at the library with her father when she was seven years old, and from that moment on she was captivated. They looked it up together in the *Encyclopedia Britannica* under the approving eye of the librarian. It was, as the book put it, an artwork whose fate was sealed. Or at least, *should* be sealed, if its creator got his way. Esteban Tennyson Clarke finished the statue on December 16, 1920, and specified in his 'terms of ownership' that it should be destroyed by gunshot a century to the day later – December 16, 2020. He called it the Statue of the Future Martyr, and offered it for sale at the substantial price of $1,000.

But sadly for him, no-one paid much attention. The shadow of the First World War hung over the world, and there was limited appetite for futurism. By the time Annette became fascinated with the story, in the mid 1970s, the statue was an obscure part of the collection of the National Gallery in Washington DC, and was rarely on show. The curator thought it vulgar. Then in 1984, it turned out that the gallery didn't actually own it, and the statue was just on long-term loan from the Clarke family, who were now asking for it back. It was duly returned to them, and then, as far as anyone knew, the Martyr disappeared.

For Annette though, it remained an obsession. She learned everything she could about it and its creator. She thought of studying sculpture, but found her interest didn't extend far beyond this particular statue. There was something about its story that gripped her, fascinated her – a destiny playing out over a century, completely dependent on the actions of others. She often told people about the statue and could never understand their looks of mild interest. How were they not as consumed by the story as she was?

It turned out she was just early. In 2015 the statue began its world tour under the masterful guidance of Pendula Clarke, Esteban's daughter.

Pendula's life to that point had followed a fairly standard path of declining generational wealth, but now in the evening of her days she discovered a new talent: creating online controversy. In eighteen months the statue went from obscure to well regarded to well known to famous to global icon. Pendula asked a simple question: What would you do? Would you destroy this beautiful object because of a request written in the shadow of war? Or would you save it, redefining it as a symbol of hope? Everyone had an opinion, and thanks to the internet everyone had a way to share it.

In Annette's life, meanwhile, she studied economics and took a junior role in her father's company. Then she met William Moore. He was not the type of man you'd expect to have gotten a PhD or travelled the world or started his own business, but in fact he had done all of those things. He was a long-term thinker, and the materials science he studied in the late 1980s didn't become relevant until the early 2000s. By which point Annette, who managed the finances of their shared company, saw a precipitous and scarcely-believable rise in their net worth. William celebrated by assembling a garage of rare Corvettes, but remained otherwise unchanged.

Annette, on the other hand, began a new phase of her dreams of the Statue of the Future Martyr.

Ownership.

* * *

Donna Jameson lived in a small out-building which could generously be called a 'shed' or more meanly a 'shack'. Yet for Donna the shed was perfect: it was cheap, and she didn't have to worry about noise. She had a long workbench along one side and it was crowded with the tools of her trade – files, hacksaws, grinders, reciprocating saws, blowtorches, welding machines, vices, clamps, all scattered around chaotically but exactly mapped in her mind. In her twenty-two years of life there was nowhere she had been happier than in that space working on her sculptures.

But for the last several weeks, she had a problem. She had been aware of the Statue of the Future Martyr for years, of course, a curiosity in the world of sculpture. She was surprised by its re-emergence, and more surprised still by how the story had taken off, sweeping around the world.

'You're a sculptor, Donna,' her friend Rebecca had asked her when the story caught fire. 'What do you think should happen?'

But Donna didn't particularly care what happened to the statue. It wasn't an important work in the history of sculpture. And the amounts of money people were talking about were obscene – if it went to auction, one prominent cultural critic said, it could be the first billion dollar artwork. To Donna, that was so crazy it was offensive. A Giacometti or a Modigliani cost a tenth of that. A billion dollars for a curiosity created by a relative nobody? It was nuts.

And yet. Somehow the damn thing had gotten into her head, and she was finding it hard to focus on her own work. The Clarke family, to nobody's surprise, announced that they were going to auction the Martyr off a month before what Pendula called the 'destruction deadline'. The story reached a new level of intensity. Donna found herself thinking about it more and more. She read up on Clarke, and it seemed to her that what he most liked were controversy and money. The sculpture was already sullied, in a sense. Better to save it as a symbol of enlightenment than to crassly destroy it, she thought.

She resolved to put the whole story out of her mind and focus on her work. But the state of peace and flow she usually reached so easily was suddenly unstable and elusive. Her current work was a set of gentle geometric waves pierced by harsh industrial rods, all the metal reclaimed from a skip near the shed. It was a horrible piece, violent, rapacious, and when she had started it the very thought of it made her heart beat faster. But now she had to force herself to work on it.

In her workshop a week before the auction she picked up a grinder and let it spring to life at her touch on the trigger, the familiar high-pitched whine. She brought the cutting disc to the metal, a spreading arc of golden sparks flowing from the cut. But her movements were uncertain, uncommitted. When she looked at the cut she could not decide if it was progress or a mistake.

She put the tool down, closed her eyes, rolled her neck.

She would give in, and engage until the story was over.

* * *

William Moore knew that Annette wanted to continue their talk about the statue, but he also knew that the process could not be rushed. Decisions for her were multi-phase affairs. He was in the garage of their Washington State farmhouse, tinkering with the carburettor for a 1967 split-window Corvette, when she came to find him. She was still dressed for horse-riding.

He put down his wrench.

'You know I want the statue,' she said.

'You have made that clear.'

She sat down in an old much-patched leather chair. 'How far would you go?'

'I told you. All the way.'

'All? It's just crazy. That you would even consider it. That I would even consider it.'

'Ten left is plenty. And it leaves us one nice, round, bid.'

'It would be so crazy, though!' She jumped to her feet, walked around the workshop. 'I think it could be my destiny,' she said finally.

'It could be.'

She bit her lip unconsciously in a way that made him think the decision was already made.

* * *

The Burroughs auction house was packed with the wealthiest and most powerful people in the world. Billionaires, oligarchs, actors, heads of state, CEOs, sports stars, influencers, people famous enough to have one name or rich enough to have none – they all trickled in to take their seats. Journalists were penned in at the back of the hall, security staff discreetly monitoring them. Near the front were a scattering of sports stars, looking strangely naked because they were not permitted to show even a hint of their usual logos. In the front row were the artist's descendants, trying and mostly failing to look at home and not overly avaricious. Pendula Clarke sat in stoic silence, working on the safe assumption that there would be a camera on her for every single moment of the proceedings.

At the centre of the stage, a set of heavy red curtains formed a velvet cylinder around what was presumably the statue. The attendees found it hard to take their gaze from it. The *Financial Times* said that about a trillion dollars of spending power was in the room, depending on how you counted the net worth of the shadier of the attendees. Perhaps in reality it was much higher.

Every seat was full. People who never waited for anything were waiting intently, expectantly. The hall was at maximum capacity. The atmosphere built from electric to hypercharged.

Finally, when it seemed the anticipation was becoming intolerable, Edgar Burroughs walked tall and straight to the lectern.

'Ladies and gentlemen,' he said, and total stillness fell. 'Welcome to the Burroughs auction house for a very special event.'

Only silence greeted his words, but if the silence had a voice it would have said: *Get on with it get on with it get on with it.*

'In 1920, Esteban Tennyson Clarke created a most remarkable thing,' he continued. 'Yes, he created a statue. But he also created a moment. A single, remarkable moment. One of decision. Of truth. Of resilience. For him, the moment was in the distant future. And now, here in our time, the moment is upon us.'

Total silence.

'Today, ladies and gentlemen,' Burroughs said, 'one of you will inherit Esteban's moment. You will be bridged through space and time to the artist himself. And what to do with his moment will become your burden to decide. The fate of the Martyr will be in your hands. Ladies and gentlemen, it is the greatest honour in the history of this house to give you: the Statue of the Future Martyr!'

The red velvet dropped in one flowing motion, like released water. The statue stood in perfect light. It was slightly smaller than life size, of white unadorned marble. The subject was a strikingly beautiful young woman, her hair gathered over one shoulder, wearing a long flowing dress. She had distinctively-shaped eyes and cheekbones and a delicate jaw, as if she was modelled on a specific woman, and yet there was something of the everyperson about her. According to surveys the word people most often thought of when they first saw her face was 'pure'. Had there been no further distinguishing attributes, and if the statue was standing in a long line of similar statues in a museum, you may or may not have stopped for a second look. But what made the Martyr stand out in a most unmissable way, leaving aside the story that whirled around her, was the large red 'X' gouged into her chest as if with a blunt knife. The lines intersected right over her heart, and the ripped flesh of her body and the ripped material of her dress were both represented in stone with a skill bordering on the satanic. Doctors had studied it and pronounced the fidelity to be extraordinary.

'I hate these stupid rich bastards,' William whispered to Annette, looking around the room. They were sitting near the middle, befitting their status as mid-tier billionaires. Annette was staring at the statue as if trying to impress every detail of it upon her mind. 'It's beautiful,' she murmured.

'I wonder would you really destroy it, if you had it.'

'That's the only completion of the arc,' she answered.

'Different, though, if it was yours,' William whispered back. 'Right in front of you. At the end of the barrel of a gun. After you've dreamed of it all your life.'

'Maybe,' she said. 'I suppose that's really the question.'

On stage Burroughs announced: 'Ladies and gentlemen, the hour is upon us. Who will give me one hundred million dollars?'

Hands went up all over the room, joyously. Finally. *Finally.*

'Two hundred million?' Lots of hands.

'Three hundred?' Lots of hands.

'Four hundred?' Fewer hands.

'Five hundred million dollars?'

The battle lines were drawn now. The bidders-for-fun were gone. This was the price of the previous record artwork. But dozens of hands remained.

'Six hundred million? Thank you sir, in the front corner. Seven hundred? Several hands I see, but the lady to my left was first. Eight hundred? Thank you sir. Nine hundred? *Nine hundred million dollars?*'

It stalled. The room felt breathless, as if something extraordinary was happening.

'Nine hundred million dollars,' said Burroughs slowly, carefully, as though each syllable of each word was a little rolling celebration. 'Ladies and gentlemen, can I get nine hundred million dollars for the Statue of the Future Martyr?'

Nothing. Nobody moved.

Then: A hand went up. A ripple ran around the room. Who was it? Gates? Musk? It was someone in the tech corner.

'We have nine hundred, thank you sir! Ladies and gentlemen – nine hundred million dollars!' Burroughs was an expert and he kept the moment alive, blowing into it like the first spark of a fire. 'And now – who will give me *one billion dollars*?' Each of the last three words was like a sentence in itself.

The centi-billionaires in the room all knew one another and they made glancing eye contact over the heads of the deca-billionaires and billionaires. Who would place the first billion-dollar bid in history?

Silence hung and hung.

Maybe nine hundred was the number.

'Going once at nine hundred million dollars,' Burroughs said. If there was a trace of disappointment in his voice or bearing, it was undetectable. 'Going twice, ladies and gentlemen. Going three times ...'

William Moore put his hand in the air.

'Ladies and gentlemen, we have *one billion dollars!*'

Gasps, shrieks, spontaneous applause, centi-billionaires and deca-billionaires on their feet trying to see who was the bidder.

One of them said to his companion in a shocked whisper: 'Whoever it is must be spending basically everything he has on it.' His friend could only nod back, equally perturbed.

'Ladies and gentlemen, a new bidder in the centre of the room!' Burroughs almost shouted. 'One *billion dollars*!' He just loved saying the number.

'You did it,' Annette said to William. She kept her voice calm but her hand gripped William's with the full extent of her surprising strength.

'Is this not our plan?' he answered.

'It's exactly our plan.'

'You're having second thoughts?'

'I just didn't think you'd really do it. In the moment.'

'We probably won't win. It's not like we can go any higher.'

'But what if we do?'

'We'll need to decide then.'

'Going once, for *one billion dollars,'* Burroughs called out.

'Jesus, Will,' Annette said. She had turned white. William was focusing on his breathing, a technique he had learned years earlier to help with moments of intolerable stress.

'Going twice,' said Burroughs.

In the front row the Clarke family were twisting around to see the person who was about to restore their family fortunes for many years and generations to come. Only Pendula looked disappointed. She had thought it might get to one and a half.

'One final time,' Burroughs said, his hammer in his hand.

Then: 'Sold! Sold! Sold!' he shouted, finally unable to maintain his composure, pounding the lectern. 'One billion dollars! Sold!'

Annette could not speak. In footage of the event she watched later, she thought she looked as if she had just been given some terrible medical news.

* * *

Donna watched the auction with Rebecca, the two girls hunched in front of the small screen in Donna's shed, so close that their arms were touching, sharing heat.

'My God,' Donna said, when the hammer fell.

'Oh my *God*,' Rebecca echoed her.

'It's just so *crazy* though.'

'Imagine destroying a billion dollars. Shooting it.'

'No-one could do it, surely?'

They talked and talked for hours until Rebecca really had to go. Donna bolted the door and looked at her bed with a sense of longing. It was late. But instead she went to her workbench. She picked up the grinder, but didn't even need to put on her protective gear or start up the tool to know she was still blocked.

This fucking story, she thought. She looked down at the unfinished piece. 'I am going to call you the *Martyr*,' she whispered to herself.

She went to bed and closed her eyes and was immediately asleep.

* * *

The media storm around William and Annette in the days after the auction was extraordinary. They hired Emily Han, a well-known PR consultant, to help. She often dealt with heads of state and movie stars and sportspeople, but she admitted privately she had never seen anything like this before. The world seemed obsessed.

The statue was delivered to Annette and William's Washington State ranch. The property remained as yet undiscovered by the online hordes, but William still hired a global security firm to make sure it was safe. Grim men and a few grim women became fixtures in their lives, at the edge of every scene. Annette had the wooden crate holding the statue brought into the barn alongside the main house. For more than a full day she could not bring herself to open it. Was it too late to go back? William was in his office, rearranging their entire net worth to pay for the statue. Annette felt sick. But William seemed unchanged, just happy as ever to be working on a complex task.

But eventually Annette ripped off the wooden siding with a crowbar, pulled out all of the protective packaging, and there was the statue. Standing silently in her barn. No eyes on it but hers. She reached out to touch it, making her hand cover the intervening space slowly, until it was flat on the statue. The marble felt cold and hard to her touch, and the silence of the barn was immutable.

Emily thought it would be best if they did one interview with someone to tell their story. Neither of them wanted to, but they also wanted the world's attention to move on from them, and Emily thought this was the best way to at least start that process. Out of the thousands of interview offers they had, they chose Oprah. She was the one they felt they knew best.

When they sat down with her, wired to microphones and slightly dazzled by the studio lights, William explained that their net assets now comprised of properties and stocks worth about 10 million dollars, and a statue worth one billion dollars.

'But your whole fortune is gone!' Oprah said, trying to understand, along with the rest of the planet, what the hell was happening.

'Well, we still have ten million dollars,' William said, gaining himself an instant bump in his online following.

'What are you going to do with the statue?' Oprah asked.

And Annette said: 'I am going to destroy it.'

* * *

The full incoherent fury of the internet was released by the interview. The hatred and bile were obscene. Annette and William became heroes and villains across the political and cultural spectra. They were philistines who were destroying art. They were out-of-touch billionaires. They were sadists. They were saviours. They should be ashamed of themselves. They should be commemorated on national coins. They were the best and worst people who had ever lived.

Once the death threats started flooding in, the FBI got involved.

For a few weeks the story dimmed – there was an impeachment, a Middle-East crisis, a trade war and a few of the other usual things – and then it came roaring back to life as the final deadline approached. December 16, 2020. One hundred years to the day.

William and Annette had built a special shooting range for the occasion, fully enclosed, a hundred yards long. Only key personnel would be there for the actual moment, but the event would be filmed from every possible angle through dozens of cameras, including some that shot one million frames per second and had been provided by the Discovery Channel.

Annette had never held a gun before the auction, and to learn to shoot over the previous few weeks she had hired a former special operations instructor who said his name was John Smith. He had no bank account and answered every non-firearms-related question vaguely. But when guns were involved he radiated calm control. 'There is no way you can get this wrong,' he said to her. 'I abso-fucking-loutely guarantee it.' But every night she dreamed of missing her shot, or of shooting only an arm or a leg off, or of simply passing out from the stress.

'How many people do you think will be watching?' she asked William, not for the first time, a few days before the deadline. They were in bed but neither of them could sleep. He was handling all the surrounding operations and logistics so she could focus on the main task.

'Some estimates put it at two billion,' he said.

'It's free, though, right?'

'Yes, free to anyone.' This was very important to Annette.

She turned to face him, and she was crying.

'I just don't know what to do,' she whispered.

He pulled her close.

'I wish we'd never bought it,' she said. 'I wish we were still ... as we were.'

He stroked her hair and said nothing.

* * *

Then the day was upon them. Annette felt she had not slept in weeks. She had thought a lot about what to wear, and settled on an outfit that would allow her to hold the gun and shoot comfortably and safely. It looked vaguely military. John approved. Hundreds of millions of people online dissected its every detail.

Oprah hosted the day. They had become friendly since the first interview. On camera they sat with her and talked about the online hate they had received, how they just wanted to complete the arc and give the artist what he wanted.

'Do you not feel guilty about the incomprehensible amount of money you've spent on this?' Oprah asked. 'So much good could have been done with it.'

'We're doing what we think is right,' Annette answered. She felt like she was delivering a pre-approved answer, and that's how it seemed to the global audience, too.

After the final interview they went to the gun range. Two FBI helicopters were chattering overhead. An unknown number of agents were stationed around the secure perimeter of the property. A 'free speech zone' set up a mile away held over ten thousand people. They were faintly audible as a dull roar even over the sound of the helicopters. Aggregators of the countless surveys that had been run both online and offline showed that the world was tied fifty-fifty on whether to preserve or destroy the statue, but the reasons for each choice exploded into fractal complexity once the surveyors asked: 'Why?'

The President of the United States had weighed in on Twitter: 'Shoot that bitch RIGHT IN THE FACE!!'

'He's a fan, apparently,' William noted, as he showed the message to his wife.

It was time. Annette went into the shooting range, William on one side, John on the other. The atmosphere was charged but muted.

When she saw the statue positioned about half way down the range she gasped audibly and tears sprang to her eyes. She looked and looked and looked, unable to move.

'When you're ready, my love,' William said to her gently.

She took a shuddering breath, then went to her position. John handed her the rifle, and she chambered the round. 'Range is hot,' John announced to the room.

Annette sighted down the gun. She thought of the billions of messages and images being exchanged at that moment out in the world, an invisible raging planetary storm.

The Martyr, beautiful and vulnerable, stood about half way down the range. The cross on her breast was the target. Esteban had specified it in his wishes.

Only a monster would shoot her.

Annette had never been more frightened. She looked over to William and he was as steady and unyielding as ever. A strange man, she thought.

'Are you sure?' she said to him, her voice almost a gasp.

'I'm sure,' he said. 'I love you.' He seemed to be focused on his breathing.

She didn't answer. Couldn't.

She settled the crosshairs on the Martyr's heart.

Around the world, millions of people were in tears. *Cold fucking bitch … Heartless … No shame …* More were shouting for her to do it: *For art … For money … For capitalism … For power … For women … For chaos …*

She looked at the statue and thought of the vast fortune she had shared with William. They had *ten million dollars* left, she kept telling herself, and yet that number seemed so small, so vulnerable.

She couldn't do it.

She loosened her grip on the gun.

'I can't do it,' she said to William, with a sob.

The world held its breath. The gun felt incredibly heavy and slippery even with her gloves. Tears streamed down her face. The barrel was bouncing around wildly, exactly as John had told her not to let happen.

'It's okay,' William said to her. 'It's okay.'

Then something slipped into place within her.

Annette took a deep breath, turned away from William, let herself sink into the moment. Then she took aim and pulled the trigger.

* * *

The howl of online outrage at the destruction of the statue (or the 'killing' of the statue, as many hundreds of millions of people thought of it) was the most intense wave of hate the internet had yet produced. The live video stream showed that Annette's shot had been true. The statue had come apart just as Esteban Clarke had intended it, the inner stone a blood red. The overall effect was unsettling. When Annette walked down to its remains, her face damp with tears, it seemed as if a real person lay destroyed at her feet, as well as a billion dollars.

Annette and William went into hiding. They were assisted by the FBI and various other people who were vague about exactly which agency they belonged to.

'I have done something terrible,' Annette said to William as they lay in a cheap motel bed not far from Topeka, Kansas, three days later. The safest thing was to keep them moving around, the FBI said, and they didn't feel they were in a position to argue.

'You closed the arc,' William answered. They were lying facing each other, a distance between them.

'And everything is gone now,' Annette said. She managed to hold back a sob. 'All our lives.'

'Mmm,' William said. He thought of what that would be like. Just building again, not worrying about what was already built.

But Annette knew that sound. 'What do you mean, 'mmm'?'

'Well, there were one point eight billion people on the stream in the end,' William said.

'But it was free!' She sat up accusingly, pulling the sheet with her to cover herself. 'You swore to me!'

'It was free, it was free,' he said. 'Just as you wanted. Anyone could watch. But there were ads and sponsorships and what have you.'

'God,' she said, closing her eyes. She wished she had paid more attention to all this, but it simply hadn't been possible. 'What was the revenue?'

'Well it's hard to say, finally, there are various …'

'How *much,* William!'

'There are all kinds of spin-offs and recreations and TV shows and reproductions. Plus the Tate has made an offer on the remains of the statue itself, if we wanted to sell. The story is still rolling. Who knows when it will end. All told, over the next few years, probably, um … Probably close to a billion dollars.'

Annette lay back down in bed and was silent for a long time.

'But the world hates us now,' she said finally.

'Some people think you're a hero,' he answered.

'What do you think?'

'Hero, of course.'

She reached out and touched his face. 'What do you think really?'

'I think it was just a statue.' He paused. 'By the way, did you see that the president has been impeached?'

She shook her head, only half listening.

'It's the first time we've not been the top trending topic on Twitter.'

'That's good,' she replied.

But what she was really thinking about was the moment when she pulled the trigger and the gun bucked and the statue disintegrated. It was such an incongruous emotion that it took her a long time to recognise it, but she knew it now. It was the feeling of being free.

* * *

Donna watched the video over and over. There was an undeniable beauty to it. Then she went to her workbench.

Four days later, at 3.30am, after a period of work more intense and productive than any other she had yet known, Donna finished her sculpture. She was exhausted and exhilarated, her face grimy, her eyes rimmed from lack of sleep. She kept a radio on in the background and the story of the statue went on and on, but it had lost its power over her. Other stories were taking over the top spot. In her sculpture, the sleek rods pierced the waves brutally, just as she had first conceived it. Not as pure as the original idea, of course, but she was proud of her execution.

She had liked the name *Martyr* as a working title, but now there was another she preferred. *Circular.*

Little Wren

Rosie Cowan

She appears every morning without fail, a fluttering scurry along the hedgerow, this wee, peat brown, field mouse of a bird. Brittle twig legs dart forth as she carries her tail straight up, a miniature, feathered ballerina en pointe. So fragile she seems, defenceless, yet she is not afraid. She knows I am waiting for her.

Jenny. Little Wren. She is eight. Only child of her parents' middle age, yearned for, well loved. A happy soul, always running, skipping, climbing, born to blossom out of doors, limbs stretching towards the sun.

There were a dozen of us in that damp, mouldy terrace, five sisters, four brothers, me, ma and da, legs sprawling, tripping over gutties everywhere. Walls you could spit through, twin tub in the scullery, wooden drop toilet in the outside shed. No place for the likes of us in the big white house on the hill.

Da delivered coal, bowed knees ploughing up steep streets, hessian-shawled shoulders sagging. Ma took in washing, when she wasn't scrubbing floors or stirring a big pot of her famous stew, potatoes, carrots, turnip, and a taste of bacon when we had it. I don't ever remember seeing her hands empty.

After school was sugar pieces, thick, chewy slices of white pan with a sprinkling of sugar, and a cup of hot, sweet tea. Friday night was a fish supper, damp, floury chips, slathered in the sharp tang of vinegar. Saturday night was the tin bath in front of the fire, scrubbed for mass in the morning, Ma saying the rosary, Hail Mary, full of grace, the Lord is with thee.

Those long, bright summers in the caravan, the morning dash across the grass to the endless carpet of bone-white sand, cradling its salty rainbow of shrimp nets, buckets and spades. She spends hours digging, patting, sculpting a fairy castle, adorning it with shells, only to be devastated at the tide's overnight desecration. But minutes later she starts to build another, determined to make it even bigger, stronger, more beautiful.

Right to the edge of the paving she comes, hovering expectantly, head cocked to one side, while I break the remains of my toast into crumbs. There is always plenty. My appetite is modest now.

A clever architect of wondrous dome nests, when the birds held a contest to see who could fly highest, she hid amid the eagle's plumage. He flagged and she soared above him, closer to heaven.

For one so tiny, she has a fine, sturdy voice, note rising over eager note. To the ancient Celts, birdsong revealed divine truths. Her clear, insistent melody brooks no falsehood.

I loved hurling, cars, working with my hands. If I could have done anything, I would have designed buildings, tall, dazzling giants of granite, marble and glass. But there was no college, no job for the likes of me. People were dragged from their homes, penned like animals, mown down in the street because they dared want better. No one was listening. There was only one way to make them listen.

She is chalking a hopscotch grid on the pavement as he parks beside her. She looks up and smiles, open, friendly. He cannot help but smile back.

My father took me fishing when I was a boy. I loved warm, idle days by the river, threading flies he had painstakingly crafted onto hooks, the flick and sweeping arc of the rod, tiny intricate whorls skittering iridescent across the shimmering surface of the water. Shoulder to shoulder, silent communion of patience.

Then, the faintest twitch on the line, a glint and gleam through the depths and the game began. Reeling in this wonderous silver creature, slowly, slowly, no sudden startle, quivering and flailing on the bank, till my father stilled it with a sharp blow.

He could shout at her, maybe scare her away. What would he say? Soft as butter with his wee brothers and sisters, voice barely raised in all his 20 years. Or just grab her, he'd have to be quick. Bundle her into the boot of the getaway car, drive out of town, throw her in a field somewhere, and race off, leaving her dazed, bruised, terrified, but still gloriously alive.

The wren brings a change of fortune, good or bad. She perched on a sentry's drum to peck a morsel of bread and beat a warning reveille with her beak. Thus Cromwell's army discovered and killed every last Irish soldier hidden in the night to ambush them. Fate is a coin with two sides, one man's victory, another's defeat.

But no, it is broad daylight, he wears no mask, she will remember his face, the car. This has been planned for months. He cannot jeopardise the operation, put his comrades at risk. He has no choice. There is always a choice. He gets out of the car and walks away, not looking back.

Wren Boys went a-hunting on St Stephen's Day. In bygone years, they would trap and stab the tiny bird with thorns. Some claim this cruel custom was vengeance for her tell-tale song betraying the martyr's hiding place. Some say she pinched the Celtic hero Fionn Mac Cumhaill's ear and his cries led his enemies straight to him. Others reckon she was slain in memory of Herod's massacre of the innocents. Whatever the case, that little being died for obscure deeds long past.

She wonders who the man is? She doesn't see many folk she doesn't know round here. She smiles because he's wearing a Liverpool shirt. She likes Liverpool, they're Daddy's favourite. He's parked his big, fancy, black car but he's getting into a smaller one down the street, must be getting a lift somewhere and coming back later.

Bomb-making is a delicate art. Those who make the bombs may well not be those who plant them. They may not even know them. It is often better that way. Large quantities of fertiliser are meticulously ground down in coffee grinders. Nails, bolts, stones, anything sharp which cannot be traced to an identifiable source, may be embedded in the surface for maximum impact.

There's this massive boom, the loudest, loudest noise she ever heard. Her ears hurt. The black car leaps apart, windows wrinkle then tumble like slow, icy waterfalls, the sky rains brick and slate, pavements rear up. Then everything just stops.

Larger cars are chosen so the downward drag on the suspension is not too obvious. Only a modest amount of accelerant is necessary. Detonators are attached to timers, which must be meticulously set. Safety is paramount.

She is not moving. The girl so full of life is utterly and terrifyingly still.

Surely she is only asleep, she has just lain down and turned away from the chaos, the blazing car, screams, blaring sirens, the smell of blood and burning flesh. But her eyes are wide open in surprise and the back of her head is split with shrapnel.

They would wreathe the small, feathered corpse with holly, string it from a stout pole and carry it door to door, stooping and swaying as though weighed down by heavy burden, all the while beating bodhrans, blowing tin whistles, begging pennies to 'bury the wran.'

The story of grief is etched on the pale faces floating on a sea of black. They are that family now, they will always be that family. Father and grandfather buckle at the knees as they shoulder the small coffin between them. Mother's banshee wail rends the silence, anguish lurches from vaulted ceiling to packed, wooden pews. At the graveside there are white roses in the shape of a teddy. In every chest, hearts pitch and tear.

English mystic William Blake wrote that 'He who shall hurt the little wren shall never be belov'd by men.' But the Irish say he who sacrifices the wren will gain its divine power and rise to become a great leader. Mutiny or freedom, the teller weaves the tale.

Two massive explosions rocked the town, claiming nine lives, the youngest an eight-year-old girl. Seven died at the scene, two more lost their battle for survival hours later in hospital. Scores more were seriously injured, several are missing limbs, others suffered horrific burns and shrapnel wounds. Some will never walk or see again.

Bloody Sunday, Loughgall, Gibraltar, Milltown, Greysteel, Loughinisland, the hunger strikers, children flayed with rubber and plastic bullets, people shot in churchyards, country pubs, at kitchen tables, in their beds. Dirty tricks, collusion, lies. Our backs were to the wall and we fought. I have buried fallen comrades, seen mothers weep, comforted brothers. Who can say, after all this time, who should have lived and who should have died? Another would have sprung up in my place, fiercer, even more ruthless. There are always more of me.

The car bombs were positioned and timed so that those trying to escape the first ran into the path of the second. No group has yet claimed responsibility but the atrocity bore all the hallmarks of a Provisional IRA attack.

How many died because of me? How many because of Churchill? Mountbatten? All your English generals? Enemies, traitors deserve to die. I never wanted other deaths but every war brings collateral damage. I did not start this. Was there another path? We will never know because we have all lived this now.

Bloody Friday, Claudy, Ballykelly, La Mon, Kingsmill, Warrenpoint, Enniskillen, Shankill, Omagh, our map of open wounds. People felled in a hail of bullets, blown up, burned alive, in the street, in a disco, going to work, at a war memorial. The luckier ones never knew what hit them, the unlucky lay screaming in the wreckage, knowing they would soon follow.

I was disciplined, kept my men in check, tolerated no dissent. Some of them drank, joked of things no joking matter, and I despised them for it. Drink loosens the grip on guns and minds, yet some said it was the only way to cope with pleading faces, charred corpses. Those who drink confess, to priests, lovers, torturers. They yearn for absolution yet to come. I keep my own counsel.

Her parents move away to live by the sea. It brings no solace, but it makes some kind of sense, the constant turmoil of the waves. Her mother tells the story over and over, but the ending never changes. Her father rarely speaks of it, it is too big for words. The hardest days are weddings and births, the pain of what could have been, should have been. That's not true. Every day is hard.

I am a strategist. I would not say I changed direction, rather I followed the road in front of me, which twisted and turned like a country lane. I called a halt when it was right to do so. I brought my army with me, every long, slow step of the way. Only I could have done so. I worked with the enemy. Only they know if they are different now. I did it for the good of the people, all our people, and I hoped others would join us. But we stayed ready always.

If only we'd been on holiday, or kept her inside. If only it had been raining, or she'd been sick, lazy, playing at a friend's. Do her killers sleep soundly? Do they dream of her? We wake and then realise that waking is the nightmare.

I felt no fear until my children were born. I never felt it for myself. Lying in ditches, derelict buildings, back seats of cars, waiting, hardly daring to breathe. Later, going about my daily life, knowing I am hated, how many want me gone. I never dared hope I would grow old.

Every night we hear her. Daddy, Daddy, in two years I'll be ten, I'll get two numbers on my cake and ten candles. Will I get a uniform for big school?

It was only when I felt a baby's finger curl around mine, saw the little blue pulse on a translucent forehead that I realised I would give anything to protect this child. I have loved and been loved. I have been a good husband, father, grandfather. That has not been difficult, given the circumstances. I am old now, I have had my time.

The years pass and still our arms ache with emptiness. Our troubles are over but our troubles are never over. We want to believe she's building her sandcastles in heaven. All we have left to hope for is that we will join her there. Do you think there's a God?

They have brought my bed near the window now that I have grown too weak to go outside or even sit up. Sometimes I see her, a fairy spirit peering through the glass, but other times I cannot turn my head, I can only hear her portent call.

'Why? Why? Why?'

I cough and there is blood on my hands again, red droplets on my fingertips, and I think of the little wren and the holly berries. My disease is genetic, a Celtic curse, civil war waged within my own body. My wife and daughters sit beside me, whispering prayers, and I know my final battle is upon me, the one I shall lose. Every time I think I have made my peace she is there again, looking up from her hopscotch grid.

'Why? Why? Why?'

I want to tell her, I do, but I have no answer. I am sorry for what I did to you, Jenny Wren. Down through the years, I told myself I never meant you harm, tried to believe you could forgive me and it would all make sense in the end. But now you are here and you fix me with that steady gaze, no longer smiling, and I am certain of nothing.

Jenny. Little Wren. She is eight. She will always be eight.

Dado

Sheila Armstrong

The air is sawdust, warm and dull, and the sweet smell of burnt timber licks up from under the buzzsaw. The old school hall is high-ceilinged and echoing, and thin metal chains drape from patchwork windows all the way to the concrete floor. A corridor wraps the main space like a curled intestine. In the bathrooms, the spit-hot rage of teenage girls lingers in black ink on the cubicle doors, and there are finely drawn scorch marks on the walls from a potassium toilet-bomb. The explosion had damaged the plumbing, just a little, but the excuse was enough to force the construction of new student prefabs further down the road, so a community centre has moved into the space.

A yoga class stretched here earlier; their purple mats have been piled in a far corner in loose, uneven rolls, like pursed lips against a window pane. Yesterday, swing dancers chose partners from a wide, rotating circle and attempted the Charleston for the third week in a row. Mondays, a cancer support circle; Fridays, a dwindling Scouts group, decimated by the early swirlings of puberty and a sci-fi program that airs at the same time as the meetings. There has been talk among the parents of rescheduling, at least until the season ends, but there are no time slots free; and anyway, the troupe leader says, a bend is as bad as a break, when it comes to children.

The builders come on Thursday evenings for two hours, but the time often flattens itself and distends further into the night. It is timetabled on the large whiteboard as a class, but there is no tutor, no students, just hands clutching plans and files and screwdrivers as if they are knots on an old rope. Metalworkers, wood-strippers, rewirers, rescuers, they work from instruction videos, phones propped up against winter jackets, although the coverage is often patchy because of the concrete walls.

Two old school friends, now middle-aged and soft-handed, are crafting a canoe, capturing memories of sparkling waves and salt-soaked skin to entomb in wood. An elderly man in paint-stained denims, boots that come up to his knees and clawmarks of white hair across his forehead; he welds without a mask, but the sparks jack-knife away from his face. A woman, grey-haired since her twenties, is making a rocking horse, and each week she smooths away at the surface with fine sandpaper. A teenage refugee comes along on foot and speaks softly; he makes nothing of his own, but carries and presses and measures for others. He smokes rolled-up cigarettes while he works and scatters paper skins like confetti. Around them, the thin September air drifts in under the half-open shutter and becomes warm, softening the whine of power tools and the twisting of clamps into a gentle purr.

Nine o'clock comes and goes; the projects are tidied away to one side of the hall to leave room for the next morning's art class, which will fill up the space with slashes of colours and sighs. The group disperses in fits and trickles, making shapes out of their hands to compare angles and lines laid down in steel and wood and rubber. On the way out, a conversation between the white-haired welder and the dislocated teenager dangles over the edge of familiarity, but it is drawn back to the solidity of a snapped drill piece.

Another man lingers behind them to fuss with an old credit card at a line of glue, teasing it, pushing each attempt at a drip back into the mass before it has a chance to stretch down onto the wood; if it spills, the trail will harden on the surface, and he will need to take a chisel to it. He is building a cabinet from plans downloaded on the lone, yellowed computer in the county library and printed for 15c per sheet. There will be four upper drawers and a cupboard below, but for now it is still skeletal and he works slowly, so slowly; measure twice, cut once, he tells the others when they will listen.

When the glue finally begins to firm and hold he is sated, rocking back on his heels and resettling his yellowing glasses on his nose. The building settles as he leaves, pulling the graffitied shutter down after himself. There is a wrist-thick chain and a padlock for the door, but it is rarely used; the community outcry a break-in would provoke would almost be worth the intrusion. Besides, the shutter is firm and heavy, and it makes a shuddering, solemn noise at it grazes and then settles on the concrete floor. The light above the entrance is motion activated; it will startle a grazing rabbit twice in the early morning and light up once for no reason at all.

The man's dark-green Peugeot is in the furthest spot in the emptied carpark, drawn up half on a pavement and half in thick grass. He had arrived late tonight, and the others were already head-bent and working by the time he arrived. Headachy-warmth from a moulding vanilla air-freshener spills out as he opens the door, and his hands sink into the padded steering wheel. He slips into gear and out off the pavement, dipping his lights in salute as the old school hall falls away in his back mirror.

The road home is narrow, but smooth; his mind sits with the cabinet he is making, exploring the hollow spaces that will be filled with drawers, shaping them with his fingers, counting the sheets of panelling remaining to be finished. Dried glue coats his fingers, and he worries at it with his teeth, pulling the skin off with the crust; the pink flesh whimpers a little at the first touch of air, but it will yellow and harden by morning.

The beams of the headlights churn gently, losing focus and breathing out into patches of autumn fog. A glow on the horizon brightens, splits into two and converges again. He veers off the tarmac onto a swelling of grass, and waits for the other car to pass; the placement of the lay-bys as familiar as the knuckles on his hand. He closes his eyes as the passing light sears his face, then pulls out again. The driver-side window is half-open; the crisp air streams in across his forehead in a wide stripe while his ankles pool in warmth from the rickety heating system. He is thinking of drips; of hard, rounded shapes slipping from the wet glue and escaping down the smooth plywood, blurring the fine, sharp joints.

And then a distant splotch of canary-yellow swoops into focus and becomes a striped high-vis vest; screaming from the dark, filmy background to the foreground, and the car screams too, although his foot has already left the pedal, screams as it rolls over rubber and spokes that break loose and stab at the heavy tyres, and air hisses and metal clatters in a dead and furious way, and he is rattled up and off his seat so hard his head hits the roof and slides sideways to stutter against the car-frame, and in his dazed fright his foot slams to the ground and the high-pitched, clanking sounds cough out once more and are left behind as he picks up whining, eager speed.

The road is still there, still somewhere, traced out in stop-motion as one shattered headlight flickers off and on, but it is memory alone that leads him home. Between his legs is a warm pool of urine, cooling rapidly and clinging to the dark hairs on the inside of his thighs, drying from the warm gusts panting out of the heater; the leather seat rejects the liquid, and it sits in the vee of his lap and washes from side to side against his groin as the car sways through the night and home.

In the morning, the red matchsticks on the clock-radio rearrange themselves and the news bells chime out. The man comes suddenly out of a drifting sleep that had crept in after an early-morning rousing, an hour vividly dream-stretched into a year. Groggy, he reaches over to the bedside table and fingers his smeared glasses, rubbing them against his belly through the creases of the salmon-coloured duvet.

He sleeps on a camp bed now; the queen-sized double mattress has been lifted and shoved up against the wall, trapped in place behind two full-length wardrobes, the bedframe dismantled. The lowness of the camp bed surprises him each morning, his feet jarring against the cold wooden floor like a slap, so he lies a little longer beneath the duvet, postponing the jolt of a new day. He thinks again of the fine, smooth lines of the cabinet, tracing its shape against the far bedroom wall for perspective, the single wall that is a garish, violent purple, because Yvonne had said it would perk them up in the mornings to see a colour so alive.

He had filled two metal skips with her things, but had kept the purple wall and a yellowed recipe for tamales pinned to the fridge, brought home from a six-day Mexican holiday they had won in a crossword competition three years ago. They had walked for hours through Cancún in awe of their luck, stopping at stalls and little shops, eating antojitos until their fingers turned damp and shiny with grease. Ankle-aching in evening restaurants, Yvonne had made lists and itineraries, and sulked when time refused to fit into her discrete packages. He had teased her about her Catalan-flavoured Spanish from a lost study year in Barcelona, and she had eaten a chilli pepper so hot she had stayed in the hotel bathroom for an hour while he watched *telenovelas*.

Her tumour had been discovered soon after in dizziness and stumbling, in words that came out sideways, and its spindly fingers had spread so far and so fast she was skin-stretched and wet-eyed in a month. He had clasped her fingers tight between his knees at night, but she was whisked away in sunlight and daffodils, in an unseasonable April heatwave that had charmed green things from the earth in proud, thick tufts. Her passing had called home children and cousins and friends from far-flung corners; the church had been an overstuffed cushion, the funeral mass spilling out into the road. Yvonne had had the knowing of small kindnesses that braided tight bonds, a knowing that had frightened him at times.

At the airport, he had held his half-Australian granddaughter's hand in his for the first time. After the burial they had coloured together with thick markers while his grown-up son and daughter discussed his health, his schedule, his future, over endless cups of tea and triangle sandwiches. His granddaughter drew great, looping flowers and cats with exactly six whiskers; tree-strung houses billowing dark smoke; circle-handed figures with spaghetti hair. He added his own creations to the page: a lobster with the head of a rabbit had made her peal with laughter, and she had begged for more and more creatures, each christened with a name set down as solemnly as a curse. His children had spoken around him, as if the great, aching gap in him was vulgar, somehow, and they were wary of tumbling down and losing themselves in the weeds of his grief. But the girl had rested her weight on him as they coloured, and had felt no fear at all.

His children had both left on the same weekend, and he had insisted on driving them to the regional airport, on hauling out a heavy black car seat from the depths of a neighbour's garage. The little one had forgotten to wave goodbye, the casual cruelty of a child, and he had sat alone on the hard, grey seats of the departures lounge for a long, long time.

Early retirement from the post office came easily then, a decision made around him, a slippage rather than a leap. For a time, he tripped over cottage pies and banana bread set at his doorstep, clasped hands with passers-by in the street; found himself caught up in a weaving of old favours. But he has always been sharp-sided, and soon the fibres split beneath the awful denseness of his weight.

Now he eats two boiled eggs for breakfast and takes brisk afternoon walks along the river, collects his weekly pension, waves and is waved to, but he is untethered and the days carry him along in their surf. His heart goes tick-tick, and sometimes tick-clank; he has pills to take to soothe its shivering. His body forgets to breathe in the night, ten heartbeats at a time, and he sits up gasping before turning over on the camp bed beneath the biting purple wall. He doesn't remember the wakenings.

This early in the morning, the headlines trickling down into the regional radio station are a day old, or detail some overnight move from Washington or the Middle East. Afterwards comes the national news and then the local, dribbled through the fingers of the guards and politicians: planning permission rows, notable social events, sports fixtures, break-ins and break-outs. Accidents, one nearly every morning: young and heartsore men slamming their feet against accelerators to doppler themselves out against tree trunks; bare, weeping car tyres slipping on patches of black ice; small hands slipping out of larger in brief, flashing moments that will be grasped after in dreams and wakefulness for years on end. And a torn high-vis vest, umbrellaed on the spokes of a bicycle wheel.

The morning newsreader finally talks herself into silence, ending awkwardly on an indrawn breath, and the presenter races to introduce a slow country song. But the breach of silence, the ugly, airy joint between the two voices, throbs through the room, across the salmon-coloured sheets, through the piles of newspapers, and presses itself up against the thick, frosted windows.

The talk of the hit-and-run is loud and strong as the news breaks across the community like the cresting of a dirty wave. There are pointed fingers and accusations, a criminal investigation ordered from above, angry letters from cyclists in the local paper, promises of cat's eyes on every road. The poor man had been a tourist; or a poacher; a delivery driver or a nurse – nobody is quite sure, although the woman in the flower shop says he was newly come to the town and had spoken to her once; he was impressed by the award-winning lilies she had nestled in an old fishing box outside her shop.

After the interviews and examinations, the body is flown across the sea to elderly parents in the south German foothills. For a time, the accident is a dark, shapeless blot on drivers' windscreens as they pass along the route. Some bless themselves or tut, and others look away from the rotting, plastic-wrapped flowers left at the base of a nearby sycamore. A white cross is left one night under the bare branches of the tree. Nobody claims responsibility; crucifixes sprout like mushrooms along the verges.

At Halloween, nervous parents confine their children to trick-or-treating along the pavements of their brightly lit housing estates. There is a well-attended firework display in a field on the outskirts of the town, and there are no reported firework injuries at the regional A&E for the first time in six years. The Scouts troupe organises a Monster Bash in the community centre. Prizes are awarded; the best pet category is won by a tan mongrel with a stuffed jockey seated on its back. Around the snacks table, the topic of boy racers and unsafe roads is raised again.

A few locals begin a campaign for streetlights to extend further out from the heart of the town, and an online petition is started; it reaches over 2,000 signatures when a campaigner does an angry interview on the local radio station comparing the infrastructure funding allocated to small towns to the aid sent overseas to an ongoing civil war in a small African country. The matter is raised at a December council meeting, and a preliminary plan is approved, but the funds are mired in an account for another six weeks due to an oversight by the secretary, whose mother hasn't been well. In his absence, he is quietly voted out of his position and the new secretary sets up a WhatsApp group for internal discussions. Somebody paints IRELAND FOR THE IRISH on the back wall of the community centre and it is a number of weeks before a power hose is found to clean it off.

Just before Christmas, a young man is taken in for questioning about the accident; his Subaru is examined thoroughly and he is released. On New Year's Eve, he takes three tablets of ecstasy and tells his friends that he has had enough; that he did hit the cunt but couldn't give two shits for him or for the whole fucking lot of them anymore. He sets off for a construction job in the city, leaving his car to rust in his mother's back garden. In a pique of frustration, she sells it in January to a local mechanic for less than it is worth. When the adrenaline subsides, she calls her son to tell him, and he swears to kill her with a baseball bat, leaving her in tears.

The village council meets again in the new year, and money is assigned to a cattle grate at the base of the bridge that crosses the river, because two lambs and a nursing mother had fallen in to the water the previous weekend and drowned. In the WhatsApp group, somebody sends around an all-caps chain message warning of data theft; another sends an off-colour cartoon.

The cyclist's mother flies over from Munich in early February for the inquest and sits quietly in the back of the high-roofed room while strangers make statements of fact about her son. Afterwards, she rattles her way down from the city on the cheapest bus to see the spot where the accident happened, but the back roads are nameless and the sycamore tree has no leaves left to identify it. She buys vinegar-sodden chips from the smaller of the two Chinese takeaways for the bus journey back. Her hips ache against the shallow commuter seats but the warmth of them throbs in time with her low and quiet rage.

The angle of the evening sun dusting the floor of the community centre has slightly changed; winter has dragged and released. The yoga mats are still piled in an uneven purple heap, and the sweat from yesterday's swing dancing class lingers in the air like oil on water. But the high windows have been cleaned and a capsule coffee machine has appeared, sponsored by a poorly attended table quiz; mugs fuzz and steep in the sink of the kitchenette. Space heaters plink in exhausted relief in the first sun-lit evening of spring.

The Thursday group filters in, taking up their tools and speaking softly, as if moving an overfull jug across a narrow bridge. Putters-together, shiners, rescuers, their numbers have swelled, slightly, by a handful of newcomers, including the mechanic, who stopped in one evening for a look and has found himself returning weekly to dispense advice on faulty connections and steady wiring. But the ancient welder has been admitted to a care home after a suspected stroke, and the teenager stepped out for a call early one December evening and has not returned. The grey-haired woman still smooths at her rocking horse.

The canoe is now finished and has been painted a brilliant, liquid green with the help of the art class and a local sponsor, and the launch will take place the first weekend of March. The town's councilman will be there, to shake hands and talk about values; he will sit in the boat for a photograph and smile for a second or two longer than is necessary. Other projects have more bones or a metal ribcage, and a couple have added flesh and electric veins, but most linger on, unfinished, as a safe anchorage in the lapping circles of conversation.

The green Peugeot comes late, and limps into the spot furthest away from the building. The mechanic, seeing it awkwardly parked, offers to have a look at the broken headlight, but the driver seems surprised when the damage is pointed out. He tells the mechanic that he doesn't drive at night anymore, and besides, the car, no more than himself, is an old dog that has had its day.

The man moves through the building, nodding at nobody in particular, and finds the corner where he stores his cabinet. It now has one completed drawer and a frame that is fully backed in plywood. The man has decided that hardwood knobs will make a pleasing accent against the lighter grain, so he is smoothing at lumps bitten from a slab of old, dark mahogany. He takes up his hand-plane and the skin on his upper knuckles becomes reddened as he works.

He sees the cabinet finished, painted a sky blue, filled with little dresses and white socks. He sees it covered with stickers; unicorns and flowers and glow-in-the-dark stars.

Billboard

David Munro

I haven't seen Clyde in a week. He stretched a blue tarp across the steel catwalk last Sunday morning, separating his half of the billboard from mine. He did it right after his morning prayer. We're in the midst of one of those ridiculous fights like you see on a sitcom, where one roommate draws a line down the middle of the room and threatens the other: *"You cross this, you die."*

He very well may be dead, too. I haven't heard his Christian radio or his heathen snoring or the sound of him vigorously brushing his teeth three times daily, the mouthwash spitting, or him talking to himself (self-inspirational pep talks in third person) or his girlfriend, Tina, who used to come around every few days to pray, whom I haven't seen for over six weeks now. From my vantage point I don't think I could even see her approach anymore. The billboard entirely blocks everything to the north and ever since Clyde strung the tarp, I can't see much to the east, either. It's like I'm living in the apex of a giant kite, the mouth of a funnel, and all I see is south and west, all trees, nothing but trees, the full green trees of late summer, and of course a relatively untraveled section of I-78, which I guess was the point of this billboard in the first place, the reason for its very being, now to gawk at idiots like us.

Let me explain. Thirteen months ago, I've lost track, let's call it thirteen months, early spring a year ago, I won my place on this billboard. So did Clyde. Or, more accurately, Clyde won his half of the billboard, and I won my half. We were the lucky finalists chosen at random (a fact I sometimes find hard to believe, given our world views) from over three hundred entrants (or so they say). WSYM conjured this contest. It's simple. Live on a billboard for as long as it takes for the other guy to quit. Last man squatting, that sort of thing, wins.

Only, neither of us are going anywhere.

Let me go back to the beginning, or near the beginning. Clyde

Marquardt was/is a good man. He's a plumber who got laid off from the company he worked at for fifteen years, until the housing industry collapsed. He's forty-seven, divorced, father of an estranged daughter named Connie, who is twenty. He was born and raised in Easton and insists he'll never live anywhere else, not in this life. He calls himself Christian though he doesn't go to church as much as he feels, or thinks, he should. He drives a Buick LeSabre, old, I972, that used to belong to his grandfather and which he's kept in mint condition. He's left-handed, a Philadelphia Eagles fan, likes to play poker. His favorite beer is Yuengling Lager. He tried a vegetarian lifestyle once, for six months, while dating a woman named Blue. This was during his post-divorce heathen days. The Republican Party has lost their way since Ronald Reagan, he insists, but it won't keep him from pulling the R-bar.

These are the circumstances that make Clyde the man. I learned them the first month up here, when this was all brand new, back when neither of us knew what we'd gotten ourselves into.

Back even further. My girlfriend and I had just broken up. I won't say her name. I won't say her name not because it's too painful, but because I determined at the time that I never would speak her name, ever again, and of all the things in life I've given in on, and have regretted ever since because I gave in, never saying or thinking her name is simple. It wasn't even a very pretty name.

So, call me vulnerable. I entered this contest on a lark, like most everything else I've done in my life. I worked at a video store and am generally ungrounded, and all I needed to be in the running was to be the fourth caller (Clyde was the seventh caller, on the day he called). This happened randomly, over many days for a month. My day was a Friday. I was on my way home from work, feeling good because it was Friday and I was heading home from work, where I had begun to feel ungrounded, when the deejay, the drive-time deejay who goes by the moniker Rocky Road, announced the fourth caller would be entered.

I dialed, on a lark, figuring what the hell. It was I-78 and the drive is boring as hell (except for the billboards!) and I was feeling complacent about things. I had a six-pack of Budweiser on the seat beside me, a pack of Garcia y Vega cigarillos, a bag of McDonald's, just feeling pretty ordinary about life.

I was the fourth caller. Some guy answered, it wasn't Rocky Road, and he said, pretty matter-of-factly, "Congratulations, you're the fourth caller."

No fanfare. Like he was bored with his job.

"Cool," I said. "I've never won anything before."

"That's what everyone says," he said.

I gave him my name and address and phone number, and he said I'd be entered into the Grand Prize Drawing, which was to happen on April 15th, tax day.

Great, I thought, what a way to stick it to the man!

And by that I mean, whoever wins, ultimately, and I am one of only two finalists now, Clyde Marquardt being the other, living on this WSYM billboard the past year or whatever, to bring attention to both a classic rock radio station and the collapsing global economy and the unfairness of it all, living in America these days, will receive a brand new house.

I've never really wanted a brand new house. I'd been living in a decent little apartment in Allentown, above a Jewish deli, ordinarily content.

It's just ... *I won*. I'd won a chance, and here I am.

I'd never won a chance before.

* * *

The past year has been hellish, starting out so hopeful as most hellish experiences do, hell not a word much appreciated by Clyde, when the novelty of the thing has you so excited you're emotionally off-guard and unsuspecting of the inherent dangers. The immediate future looks bright, naturally, but it's that glare that blinds you from the long distance view.

There was much fanfare that first day. WSYM rolled out a red carpet from the gravelly shoulder of I-78 through a clear-cut path in the woods, a path which has subsequently grown over again in a stunning example of ecological succession.

We stood, Clyde and I, at the bottom of a temporary ladder which reached up into the fixed ladder welded into the superstructure, our meager provisions and belongings at our feet, Clyde's pastor nearby to offer solace, where we shook hands for the TV stations and newspaper photographers and, of course, for the radio station executives and the regional vice-president of American Homestead Homes, a man by the name of Jim West, who shook our hands and said a few words about hopefulness and how America was exceptional and we'd all get through this together and blah-blah-blah, how American Homestead Homes (the worst company name I'd ever heard of) promised to play a big part in America's economic recovery.

They saw us off, as it were, Clyde kissing Tina goodbye and climbing up first, myself kissing no one goodbye and climbing up second, and from the top of the billboard we waved goodbye to the good folks on the ground and the small, strange crowd that had gathered out on the shoulder of I-78, and in less than an hour everyone was gone, all of the TV trucks packed up and gone, the hubbub and fanfare gone, replaced with the sound of silence blowing on the slow, eastern breeze, and Clyde and I began setting up our separate little perches in the sky.

The first weeks we had visitors. The radio station stopped by and interviewed Clyde and me to see how things were going. Clyde's pastor came by every few days and tried to get me to pray with them. Clyde tried to save me one day, our first verbal argument, and things went south between us. I am not devout about anything and Clyde prayed so hard I thought he'd burn off all the hair on his head, and he didn't have much to burn. The thing about religion and God and all that, I explained to Clyde, was that everyone always smiled all the time and was happy all the time and, well, that just seemed weird to me.

"It seems weird to you," Clyde had said, "because Satan is a silent, controlling partner in your life."

I shrugged, said "Maybe so." That began the fight, and we rarely talked much after that.

Summer ended and fall arrived, and then we were into winter and battened down hard against the wind and snow with the help of Goodwill and Salvation Army. Occasionally a car would stop on the shoulder of I-78 and someone would get out and have a look, maybe take a picture, and then drive off. Sometimes people stopped and yelled insults at us, like, why we didn't just get a life and go back to our real jobs. We didn't have real jobs.

"If it was up to me," Clyde said one day, "I wouldn't have started this.

It's gosh darned perverted if you think about it. Like when they put on those dance marathons back in the Depression, you remember the stories – make people dance until they pass out. The last one gets something like a hundred dollars? Big deal, right? Okay, because back then, maybe a hundred bucks was a heck of a lot of money."

He was generally talking to the air since we weren't really talking to one another. Six months in, halfway to a year, and I could tell Clyde's nerves were wearing thin. It is then I first started knowing I had him beat.

It was clear to me and, I think, clear to Clyde, that WSYM had been flying by the seat of their pants on this one. They'd had contests in the past where they'd given away cars or free vacations to some Pocono resort, and even once an all-expenses paid trip to the Super Bowl, including round-trip airfare, but never had they taken on a contest of this magnitude, placing two grown men on top of a billboard to see who could stand it the longest.

Looking back, there were certain contingencies they simply overlooked.

For example, how *does* one sleep safely on a narrow catwalk, three feet wide if that, eighty feet off the ground? (Tying off with a rope, of course.)

And, where and how *does* one defecate, at eighty feet off the ground, diarrheal, during a blustery three-day spring rain? (No clue.)

What exactly happens next, then, seven months out, when all of your so-called "support group", your so-called *friends*, decide they have better things to do with their lives than buy groceries and trudge them a mile through the woods to feed your sorry ass?

"They're a bunch of regular clowns if you want my honest opinion," Clyde said.

"I think you're right," I said. "Why don't you go on down and tell them that?"

Clyde looked at me sort of funny. His eyes narrowed and his mouth took on this wicked, un-Christian-like smile, as if he wanted to come over to my side and punch me in the face.

"No way," he said, wincing. "What, you think I'm stupid or something?"

"No … I was just saying –"

"You throw me off here … *then* I'll go talk to them. Until then, no way, buster."

"I'll go with you."

"And we both throw in the towel? You *are* stupid."

"That's very un-Christian of you Clyde … to say that."

"I'm sorry."

"I'm just saying it isn't right," I said, "what they're doing to us. How long do you think this thing can last? How long can we hold out?"

"Sheesh, this is nothing," Clyde said. "I'll live my whole life up here if it's what they want. It's a principle thing anymore."

"I guess what I'm saying," I said, "is you just have to hang in there. No matter what you think –"

"No you're not!"

"What?"

"That's not what you're saying at all. You want me to go down there and crap the bed so you can win the house. That's what this is. I can read you like a book!"

He stood up and started approaching my side of the billboard. His sleeping bag, however, caught around his feet and he stumbled, falling face-forward and almost spilling over the side, and the weight of his body crashing down on the catwalk made the entire superstructure lurch to my side and then sway back and forth for what seemed like half an hour.

"Jesus! Watch yourself!"

"Don't you use the Lord's name in vain, you asshole!" Clyde screamed. "How about you go down there and tell them what *you* think!"

But I was perfectly content. I had my baseball bat ready, a 34 oz. Ryan Howard given to me as a gift by my ten year old nephew for good luck, though I think his mother, my sister Meg, really meant it for protection.

I choked-up on the shaft and wielded it like I meant to use it, and Clyde scrambled back to his side of the billboard.

"Try me, Clyde," I said, "and I win."

That was six months in.

Things have gotten much worse since.

* * *

Those first few weeks I awoke with the sun, and for long stretches found myself in an unnatural, for me anyway, peaceful solitude as I watched the sun cast various shades and depths of golden orange and yellow light over the slow moving Lehigh River and the surrounding low rising hills. I even thought I believed in God for long, extended moments. I felt like a bird on a perch. I felt gratefully inhuman for a change, in a good way, if you know what I mean. By contrast the western sunset was solemn and bittersweet. I watched this play out daily, sunrise-sunset, the entire day opening and closing for me, the dumb observer, hope to gloom and back again.

Darkness on top of a billboard is pretty weird. Cars and trucks heading north to New York City never stop, making an endless chain of headlights like glittering pearls strung on a necklace. The traffic hum was a constant, too; a lullaby during the night and an unrelenting murmur during the day. We learned all we wanted to know about one another, Clyde and me, those first couple of months, before things went bad, and after that we became mean and entrenched. After six months I had grown completely tired of Clyde, tired of the entire operation. The unceasing traffic, the bird shit, the passersby who'd stop along the shoulder and call out stupid questions and insults at the top of their lungs. Men getting out of their cars and pissing. And Clyde, with his snoring and cordless electric shaver that his tittering girlfriend Tina came and retrieved every few days so she could dutifully charge it back up, the good woman, got on my nerves big time. I have always hated the sound of electric razors and had no qualms transferring that hatred to men who used them. I cared very little about Clyde as a human being. In fact, I thought poorly of God for having created him, if he was in His image. I secretly wished he'd roll over in his sleep some night, un-roped, and fall to his death.

"You suck, Clyde," are the last words I spoke to him.

"You're not so great yourself," Clyde said.

There was much praying after that, loud praying. A WSYM lawyer came by and intimated that should one of us give up, come down, make this thing go away, we would be rewarded somewhat. We didn't believe him. The pastor stopped coming by, but Tina continued, whistling through the woods like Little Red Riding Hood, her perky pertness cutting like a knife through the doom and gloom.

He threw a can of tomato soup at me.

I pissed into a rare westerly wind, spraying his sleeping bag.

The lawyer came by a final time and said some sort of settlement would be reached. "Liars lie because they like it," Clyde muttered. I agreed for the last time.

Months. We've seen no one since.

* * *

The tarp is standard blue nylon with chrome grommets. I don't know where he got it; maybe it's a gift from God. My cynicism keeps me company; these are the thoughts I have.

I have been tempted to slice through the tarp with my Buck knife just to piss him off, only that was days ago, that feeling, and now, I must admit, I'm a little worried. The silence, though deafening, though peculiarly pleasant, portends something really, really bad. I feel alone, as if I've finally won.

"Good morning, Clyde!" I call out, as I have every morning this past week, reveling in the end game. "It's a beautiful day in the neighborhood."

This probably pisses him off. For me it's just psychological warfare, a counter-strike to his fire and brimstone Christian evangelist radio. He's no longer as pleasant as he was a year ago.

"It's a beautiful day in this neighborhood, a beautiful day for a neighbor. Would you be mine? Could you be mine?"

He once accused me of being gay. I love it.

Still, no answer. The wind in the trees is such that I can't hear even the subtlest murmurings from yonder Clydedom.

"It's a neighborly day in this beauty wood, a neighborly day for a beauty. Would you be mine? Could you be mine?"

But, I'm so not gay, which pissed him off even more.

Still, nothing. "Oh, come on, Clyde! Talk to me!"

I raise my tenor.

"I've always wanted to have a neighbor just like you! I've always wanted to live in a neighborhood with you! So, let's make the most of this beautiful day, since we're together we might as well say! Would you be mine! Could you be mine! Won't you be my neighbor?"

No Clyde.

"Won't you please, Clyde? Won't you please? Clyde! *Please!* Won't you be my *neighbor?!*"

I think I hear movement, a distant crackling. It's treacherous to move too close to the tarp, the Demilitarized Zone, but I can't not do it at this point. We must put an end to this. If I've won, let me win! Something occurs to me. He might be dead, it has occurred, this thought, numerous times, in fact, and I can no longer ignore it when even the slightest sound … a feeling of *hope*?

Yes, hope.

"Clyde. *Psst*. It's Tina. I see Tina coming back."

Crunching through the woods from a direction I can actually see is, miraculously, coincidentally, Tina.

We have loved each other from a distance, Tina and me. She is perky but beautiful, with an ordinary mouth and eyes and I have seen her naked in my thoughts. We've had long discussions about important, sensitive things, and Tina understands me in ways no other of God'd people have understood me, ever. She is my dream of dreams, and I could get a better job for her, even though she wouldn't want me to, wouldn't ask anything of me above what I barely want for myself. Clyde and I are lucky, lucky men.

Today, she's wearing a hunter's flannel shirt, puffy international orange vest and tight jeans, which I love, but her hair is tied back severely in that style that makes her look like a regal bitch, which I hate. It troubles me I've come to think these mean thoughts, but there it is. If she were my real and not imaginary girlfriend I wouldn't think this. Oh, well. I haven't had sexual relations in a year.

"Billy!"

She is calling my name! She's carrying a camo-backpack full of provisions, I imagine, or medical supplies, a first responder, perhaps, coming to rescue her boyfriend who's attempted suicide by slitting his wrists and is now bleeding to death, drip by drip, on the other side of the blue tarp.

"Billy!" Tina calls again.

She's calling me, which I don't understand!

Over the past year my interactions with this woman have been fleeting and unimpressive, for both of us. Tina is the most Tina-like woman I have ever known, diminutive in every aspect, from her teeny feet to her teeny nose, to her teeny hi-pitched, glass-breaking voice that would never in a million years attract delicate song birds, but scatters them from the trees in mad, blustering flocks. She is not Little Red Riding Hood. She is the opposite of Little Red Riding Hood, and I hate her, although she is beautiful.

"Billy! Have you seen Clyde?"

"I think he killed himself!" I say. "He's gone to meet his Maker!"

Tina reels, palm of hand slapping her mouth, aghast.

I cackle. "Have you come to give him missionary position? Pray, thee, with thy Clyde-ness?"

"Oh, shut up, Billy. His mother died. Clyde! Where are you?"

"He has a mother? *Had* a mother?"

"Billy. Please. Show a little respect."

Eighty feet below is tiny but beautiful Tina. The fog in my head of months of being trammeled by the elements, the isolation, the brittle anger between Clyde and me is difficult to break through.

"Why do you have to wear your hair so tight?"

"Huh?"

"It makes you look severe."

The vertiginous height prompts me to sit down. I dangle my legs over the edge.

"If I don't it's just a frizz-mop. I can't see him from here. Can't you just take that tarp down?"

"He threatened to shoot me if I tried. I suspect he has a gun."

"He does have a gun, Billy. But he wouldn't shoot you. He's too much talk for that."

"A part of me wants him to be dead. Does that make you think I'm a bad person?"

"It's just stress, Billy. Our thoughts are fleeting. Always remember that."

"I love you."

"It's the stress. Take the tarp down. I have a bad feeling here."

"Me too."

But I arise. I am risen. Keeping one hand to the rail I step ever so gingerly toward the blue tarp as if newborn. There is no sound but for the wind and my heart thumping inside my chest. As I finally touch the tarp I feel I am touching a membrane of some sort, a divide or meniscus between two entirely separate realms. I remove my Buck Knife from my pocket, open it, flash the blade toward Tina below for confirmation to proceed and she nods, gives me the go-ahead, as it were, this God-woman. The slice is smooth as butter. I stretch the gap and step through, herniating myself into Clyde's Realm.

He is dead.

I know the stillness of his sleeping bag and the gray pallor of what little of his face I can see peeking out of the zipper. I have seen it in movies but never in real life and yet there's no mistaking Death.

"Billy! What do you see?"

I turn toward Tina.

"I see that I've won," I say. "Clyde's dead. I won a house."

My words act as an invisible hand that reaches down, removing a cork from the top of Tina's head and she deflates, a heavy gut-punched breath escaping her mouth.

Her knees buckle; she folds to the earth.

"I'm sorry," I say. The wind is strangely quiet for my words. "That was a terrible thing to say. It must be the stress."

Tina is sobbing. I can hear her and see her head bob up and down, her chest-cracking sobs scattering songbirds to the far corners of the earth.

I find Clyde's wrist for his pulse. I place my finger below his nose to feel breath. He is dead as dead ever was, his soul emptied out, his body a vacant cask.

I win.

* * *

I do not cry, because I do not cry as a rule.

Assured Clyde is dead, I climb down from the billboard assured of victory, and knowing that my victory is tainted. I am not a competitive man by nature, so this victory is bittersweet, a bit melancholy, like kissing your sister. Nothing I've ever done, mind you.

"Perhaps you should call his pastor," I say, dangling by one arm from the final rung, poised to fall the remaining eight feet or so to my new home, my new life. The brush appears soft enough to break my fall.

I drop.

"He was a good man," I say.

Tina looks up at me. Her eyes are wet and red and that tight hair of hers has pulled slightly loose. "He *was* a good man," she says. Her emphasis on *was* I take as one of two ways; either she wants all of this immediate nature to know it, the plants and trees and birds, or she wants to make herself believe it. She nods her head enthusiastically, pummeling herself with this notion over and over.

I have not been much of a social human being in over a year and so I find myself standing dumbly, as if hat in hand, but I have no hat, wondering what to say or do next. Tina smells nice. She is even more beautiful to me this close than I remember from way back when we were standing around so hopeful with all the cameras rolling and the people clapping.

I feel my face and my dog's age beard. My hair is below my shoulders and I've lost weight, I'm certain, and my legs wobble like Neil Armstrong back on earth.

But, still, I step gingerly and place my right hand upon her left shoulder, and pat her once, then twice, then three times so robotically that it's obvious I have a long way to go to being human again.

"It's okay," I say. "You and me … we'll get through this."

The Sorry Business

Róisín McPhilemy

Sarah O'Prey was fair, freckled – skin so white you could see the veins in it. And for a mortuary assistant, Matt Anderson decided, too small and slight by half. Every morning, he'd walk into the prep room, head already thumping, and have to screw up his ageing eyes just to see her, wraithlike in all that gloom. But he knew she was there. She was always there.

At first the arrival of a young, single woman in Warburra caused a flurry of interest, among the men under fifty anyhow. But Sarah kept to herself, and soon only the no-hopers over the way in Harris's pub would stir themselves to call after her.

'Hey Sarah, is it true that it looks even bigger when you're dead?'

If Sarah heard the hoots of laughter and jeering, she paid no attention. As far as Matt could see, Sarah just went about her own business as if she wasn't half time in this world.

She was a quick learner, mind you, quicker even than Colby. Took to the business as if she'd been at it for years. She listened quietly to his instructions, did them to the letter. And the place generally became cleaner, organised. More like it used to be. He couldn't bring himself to think it. *A woman's touch*. When he refused to let her order fresh flowers for the window display, she went outside to the remains of the garden. He'd caught sight of her on her knees in the dirt, cutting and pulling at stems and grasses. He'd chewed her face proper then – *this is a funeral parlour not a bloody florist's*. But for days the window was filled with spikes of red bottlebrush, pompoms of yellow wattle.

'Don't think you'll be doing any of the important stuff,' he'd warned her the day she started. 'And I can't pay you much. You'll be a bit of a dogsbody, is the truth – not much of a step up from Colby over here.'

She'd looked over then at Colby, who was brushing the dust on the porch into new arrangements.

'Pleased to meet you,' she'd said, her accent musical and strange.

Colby looked up then. He didn't smile, just tipped his head in acknowledgement, holding the brush in his large, dust covered hands. Looking at them, Matt saw some kind of comical inversion, a theme park mirror's tricks. Colby must have been a foot taller than Sarah, taller than most blackfellas anyhow. Sarah looked like a stick of straw beside him.

But as the weeks went by, he could see the ease with which they worked silently in each other's presence, washing the prep room, replacing the utensils in drawers. When the day cooled, they'd sit for a short while out the back, and she'd calmly open a beer, pass it to Colby as if he was just another bloke. Matt wondered should he say anything to Sarah, point out the law against serving blackfellas, warn her against Colby's colour, his creed. His randiness. But by that stage his tongue would be hanging out of his head. He'd climb upstairs to his room, to the chair by the window and the bottle of Scotch, pour a glass and slowly swallow. The dusk would settle, and the day retreat to the rim of rock on the skyline, and the stars dim up. Later, he'd see Colby slope off to the outhouse. Then the soft click of bottles and jars from below as Sarah gave the basement prep room one last clean with the large antiseptic wipes he'd stockpiled from Silverton. He never asked. But she did it anyway.

Sarah let the last drawer slide closed, and gave the steel handle a final wipe. Air that moved through the vents during the day had become trapped, drugged with heat. She took a fresh wipe, pressing it to her forehead and neck, avoiding contact with her eyes. Untying her surgical gown, she dropped it into the neck of a bin bag, tying it swiftly with a knot. Matt had finally agreed to disposable gowns after she had patiently showed him the cost of laundering. Her first victory. She flicked the light switch, the fluorescent tubes hissing before falling silent. Climbing the darkened stairs, she locked the door and hung the key in the recess below the kitchen sink. She poured a glass of water and swung open the door to the porch.

Outside, the air was muggy. Sarah sat on the steps of the porch, placing the cool glass against her cheek. The colours of the plants and outhouses took on a surreal cast in the dim porch light. Yakka, mint bushes and honey myrtles spiked shadows on the concrete walls of the outbuilding where Colby slept. In all this time, Sarah had never seen where he slept. She wondered if he was in there, now. She imagined his long, thin body angled into a narrow bunk, arms folded over his head.

It was late. She swallowed the water in gulps, draining the glass and pushed back through the porch door, rinsing the glass in the kitchen sink before going upstairs. The door to Matt's room was closed, and no light showed beneath the door. Sarah moved silently to the other end of the corridor, down the few steps that led to the annexe room. Any awkwardness she had felt in sharing the house with Matt had long disappeared. He rarely spoke to her outside working hours, and the few times they passed each other in a corridor or the kitchen, he was businesslike, curtly so. They did not eat together or talk over the day's events. And it suited her, the distance. Not caring about somebody's fate.

She changed into a cotton shirt and lay on the bed, her faced turned towards the window with its protective mesh. She was used to the night sounds now. The daytime blur of cicadas and crickets sharpened into focus. Spiny legs of beetles, knocked from flight by the porch lamp, scratched frantically against unfamiliar floorboards. At home in Ireland it was early autumn and the boys would be back at school. She imagined her mother placing the latest postcard behind the clock on the mantelpiece. A picture of a kookaburra, perhaps. A bush kangaroo. Long sandy beaches and pictures of jewel fish that Sarah had never seen. Her mother does not read it. She calls the boys for their tea. The table is set for the three of them. Upstairs, their school uniforms are folded over the banisters, the arms of jumpers hanging, like gangling teenage bodies. A year or two, and they'll be out of there like a shot, like they've escaped a fate worse than death.

Frogs made whistling *wheep wheep* calls from the moist crevices in which they had taken refuge from the heat. Sarah closed her eyes. Dams, ditches, ponds and streamside pools. The boys as kids, their fat little legs mottled with purple as the cold waves scudded over their feet, wetting pants and T-shirts. Her mother scolding, *look at the state of them.*

Colby once told her that the ghosts of gum-trees in the dry creek beds had been brought down by floods. But it never rained.

There was no shocking either of them – Matt had to give them that. When he'd shown Sarah how to leave an infant's mouth slightly open to make it look more lifelike, she'd nodded, her forehead puckered in concentration. And Colby had been helping him for years without batting an eye. Business was steady, in spite of *Brown's Funeral Parlour* in nearby Silverton. Matt knew that in Warburra he was a prized commodity. He-who-cannot-judge. They came to him with the shameful cases – the suicides, the alcoholics, the still-born – knowing that he would accord each corpse the same attention. Matt didn't advertise the fact that as a teenager Colby had helped undress and wash and dress again the stiffened corpses of the men, women and babies of Warburra. And at first the business was as simple as that – the viewing time was short, and interference with the remains was as unwelcome as it was unnecessary.

Things were different now. Matt was preparing decent folk for funerals they couldn't afford in Silverton. His equipment might not be the fanciest, but he prided himself in thinking that he could do most things. He began each day in Sullivan's diner, dressed in a dark suit, in spite of the heat, drinking black coffee. He was careful to hold himself apart, a slight nod to those who greeted him by name. He looked the soul of propriety, all the more impressive because people knew he was not. Over the past few years, he had harnessed his drinking to the nights only, and those who came to *Anderson's Undertaker's, Warburra* gradually expected more of his services, and Matt was willing and able to oblige.

Sarah's arrival added to his standing – not that he'd ever admit it. How she ended up here, in the arsehole of nowhere, Matt did not know and never asked. Perhaps she thought he'd be a soft touch. She'd been in Silverton, and maybe someone there had told the Irish bluey about Mad Dog Anderson, and his do-it-yourself funeral parlour. His half-breed boy. Sure could do with a woman around the place since …

Since.

His wife left him the moment she heard the truth. Afterwards, he'd cursed the boy for the bastard he was, maybe he hit him. He drank four days solid. When he woke, his suit was folded on the chair in the bedroom, his boots set side by side. Colby was a dog you could kick.

He'd lick his wounds instead of howling.

Colby told Sarah that the period of mourning for the Koori was known as the 'Sorry Business'. They sat on the porch, Sarah on the bench, Colby on the steps below. When he spoke he tucked his beer against his chest with one long hand, and gestured with the other into the night, towards some other place.

'All the people show their loss for those who pass. They wail and cut themselves. Paint their faces white.' His face gleamed like polished slate, like wet rock.

He told her how they burned the houses of the dead so that no-one else could live in them, not even the spirit. They no longer can say the name out loud. The line of mourners that filed past Matt's open caskets must seem uncaring to Colby, Sarah had thought. The process of mourning indecently short.

The sorry business. The business of being sorry.

One night, earlier on, they listened to thunder clouds roll up, a crack of lightning. He asked her what Ireland was like. She told him she missed the rain. She missed the clouds piling up over the Atlantic and smelling the rain on the wind. She missed being a big sister. The heat turned into mugginess. Pellets of rain thudded into the earth, then stopped. The storm would pass on to the coast, he told her. But the weather would break, he said. Not this time, but soon. He turned and looked at her then. A promise.

Matt needed both Colby and Sarah to help with preparing the body delivered from Silverton morgue in the afternoon. Sarah could assist under his careful watch. Three of the regular occupants of Harris's helped him heave the casket, red-faced and sweating, down steps to the basement. They looked around them as they left, curiosity overcoming a vague repugnance. If they were looking for signs of alchemy, there were none: the room was tiled, the chemicals off to the side behind a curtain, the slab covered with a pristine sheet – Sarah's touch, Matt thought grimly. Sarah and Colby hovered until, irritated, Matt told them he'd things to do first, and to come down when he hollered.

Their client, as Matt insisted he was called – *he paid me himself, a little over a year ago, a real gentleman* – was in his sixties, and had succumbed finally to a weak heart. They'd done a post-mortem in Silverton anyway, the scar surprisingly livid against his puckered skin. Matt had placed a cloth over the privates, and the corpse on the slab was featureless, drained. Before he began, Matt felt for a moment a sense of authority, as he stood at the head of the corpse, Sarah to his left, Colby to his right. Both silently waiting their instructions.

He lifted up a grey arm close to his face, screwed up his eyes. Placed it gently down. Cleared his throat.

'Mr Petersen here – he's of the generation that knew just what this godforsaken country does to a body – living or dead.'

He lifted a scalpel from the tray Sarah held, and made a cut near the shrivelled armpit. He inserted the tube and thickened blood seeped out morosely.

'That's why he came to me to tell me what he wanted. Exactly what he wanted. Said he remembered taking the door off the room in which his father died, so's they could lay him out straight.'

He rattled in the instrument tray, his fingernails scraping slightly on the steel, then pressed the blunt end of a knife on the thick tubing, where the blood had gathered like glue.

'By the time they got the body to Silverton on the back of the cart, a cloud of blowies had already settled on him. Them fancy undertakers said they'd do the best for him but …'

Another slit, then Colby was instructed to wheel over a copper bin and the embalming fluids were pumped in. With a sudden lurch, the outgoing blood slid down the tubing, sucking softly and insistently into the drain.

'… when the family got to see him, they just couldn't recognise him. His face was smooth, like it had been plastered, and the heat just made him shiny, like you'd touch him, and flesh and all would just slide off. Old Jim here, he didn't want that shit. Looked me in the eye he did. Gave me eight hundred dollars right there and then. Said he wanted whoever was left to mourn him to have somebody left to mourn. That's what he said.'

Here Matt almost smiled. Then he straightened up, wiped his hands on a piece of clean cloth.

'"Jim Petersen," I said, "you've come to the right place."' Lobbing the cloth expertly into a large bin lined with plastic sheeting, he moved efficiently around, fingering tubing, tightening connections. Sarah stood still with the tray of instruments in her hands, while Colby moved silently out of Matt's way.

'Denying a man a decent corpse is one of the most spiteful ways in which disrespect can be shown to a person. That's why our enemies hang our guts out for all to see. And that's what makes them boongs out in the bush so bloody uncivilised – hold this, Sarah – they treat the body with – '

Glasses on the end of his nose, he crouched down, so that the top of his head was level with that of the corpse.

'– absolute disrespect.' The remnant of his words made a soft 'tuh', glancing off steel receptacles and glass bottles on the shelves. Straightening, he motioned to Sarah to show him the tray, and selected a clean scalpel.

'The next cut is the belly, to get at the organs inside. So for chrissakes, hold your noses if you think you're going to barf.'

More tubing, chemicals pumped in, bits of Jim Petersen pumped out. Matt surveyed the process with satisfaction, watching the skin plump slightly, a hint of a bloom.

'And he understood exactly, Jim here. Said he'd never forgiven those bastards in Silverton for what they did to his father. Of course, that was before refrigeration – but there's no excuse for denying the dead. That's one sure way to get yourself a ghost.'

Matt stood back from the slab to survey the results. Couldn't resist a bit of a show in front of them.

'Here lieth Jim Petersen – husband, father … and grandfather to a passel of brats that are no longer his responsibility. May he rest in peace.'

Satisfied, he moved behind the table and leant closer to inspect the face.

'Shit.'

He pincered a piece of gauze from the shelf behind, positioned himself back at the head of the table, hands hovering over the dead man's face.

'Do you see that?' His thumbs moved slowly downwards until they rested on the eyelids. He peered over the top of the head like a dentist, neck craning up, head craning down.

Sarah leant in. Matt's right thumb pressed gently but insistently on the right eye. He held himself still, as if waiting for the glued edges of a toy to stick together. When he took his hands carefully away, she saw with a shock the crescent gleam of an eyeball.

'That should have been closed before the embalming.'

Matt turned suddenly and stalked in the direction of the curtained store. He called over his shoulder to Colby and Sarah.

'Go. I don't need you anymore.'

Sometimes in the evening they would ride out, head straight for the low hills outside of town. They'd climb to the top, sit down, watch the colour leach out of the sky. They'd sit until the sky was lighter than the land around. Dogs barked, ferocious even at this distance. The traffic on the highway rumbled gently behind them, a conveyor belt to the coast. Side by side, they watched the shadows grow. When it was dark, he'd pull her to him, slip his hands beneath her shirt, spread his fingers across her breasts, her sides. Sarah laid a blanket on the ground and Colby would reach for her as she smoothed out the corners.

He never knew his mother. He was too young when she died. He had no memory of being sent to Matt, only of having to do chores. No brothers. No sisters. She would have to be all things to him, he told her – lover, mother, family. When he laughed, his stomach clenched beneath her head, the sound muffled and rich. The nights they sat on the porch, a careful distance between them, she would remember this, the warmth of him beneath her, the gurgling of blood in his belly.

He remembers his first day at school, how the teacher told him he'd be given pencils to write with and books to read, and hope for all eternity. He stayed at the school night and day. Then one day the yellow school bus took him to Warburra. He remembers the driver's voice as if he wanted to laugh, asking if it was his old man's place. The house was big and run down. He remembers a man opening the door, then turning, without waiting. Inside was dark and cool and smelt of disinfectant.

Colby's voice was quiet, dreaming. She was beautiful, his mother. She would have lain until her flesh was gone and those that loved her would have carried her bones and left them in sacred places. Her spirit was housed, at peace. He'd find the place, marked by a rose bush or a carved young tree. That's what they told him at those meetings he went to in the community hall. Sarah should come with him sometime, maybe. Or he could tell her, like he was doing now, on nights like this.

Matt heard the *phut* of the moped stop some way away, then moments later Sarah's light footstep above. Stupid buggers. As if he didn't know. As if he hadn't known for months now. It sickened him, the thought of her and him, coupling like bush pigs. He drank deeply, a long, burning swallow. He refilled his glass.

Sarah reminded him too much of her, the way she quietly went about the place, shifting this and adjusting that, fixing things just the way she wanted them. Between the pair of them, she and Colby moved like ghosts, organising and clearing and arranging. He wished they'd both just fuck off, back to the bush, back to Ireland – imagine the looks they'd get there!

'What are you doing?'

A click, and the basement flooded with forensic light. Matt looked at the cloth covering his hand, the blood blooming through it. The empty whiskey bottle stood on the stainless steel of the draining board. The corpse lay on the slab, sewn, washed and pitifully naked. One eye slightly, stubbornly open. Sarah stopped only for a fraction. Then she fetched a sheet from the store, shook it as if it was laundry, floating it gently down. She went back into the store. The acrid fumes of surgical spirit stung his nose, his eyes.

'Give me your hand.'

Her voice was quiet. He hesitated, held out the injured hand. She unwrapped the cloth as if his hand was a parcel.

'A clean cut, at least.'

She quickly tipped out the contents of the bottle, the spirit running over her wrist. With a howl, Matt jerked his hand away.

'Would you get the fuck away from that!'

His voice broke, tears scalding his throat. Colby's feet appeared on the steps above. He reached the bottom, looking from one to the other.

Sarah unwrapped the cellophane from a bandage and motioned Colby to come over.

'She left me.'

Matt's head swum with pain and drink.

'My wife left me. Because of you. I …'

'Hold your finger here.'

Colby placed his finger on the bandage. Matt felt the tug of the knot being made. His head was close to Sarah's, closer to Colby's.

'I *told* her. When she found out, I *told* her – it was a mistake. You –'

His face was sweating, leering at Colby.

'– were a *mistake*.'

He lashed out drunkenly when Colby tried to place an arm around his shoulders and the younger man had to hold him by the upper arms from behind, pushing him firmly but gently towards the steps, the hallway, tightening his grip when Matt stumbled, up the stairs, down the corridor, into the bedroom. Matt lay down heavily on the bed, and felt a blanket loosely tucked in around him. The light switch clicked softly, plunging him into darkness.

The viewing of the corpse was the following day at three. Matt woke to the heat of midday. He opened the shutters to see Colby raking dead leaves from the drains of the outhouse. In the centre of the yard, he could see a pile ready to be burned, dampened with water to prevent sparks. The leaves shone with moisture, resurrected. Matt washed in cold water and dressed in the black suit and tie Colby had hung on the back of the door. He looked in the mirror. His face was pasty, darkness under his eyes. His mouth was sour and dry.

He went down to the kitchen and poured himself a lukewarm coffee from the percolator. In the basement, Sarah looked as if she had been waiting for him.

'I managed to glue the eye closed. I've cleaned the cut on the eyelid as best I can and we can cover it with make up.'

Taking his time, Matt leaned over the head of the corpse, inspecting. He quickly saw she'd done a good job, a damn good job. He straightened up.

'Get me the cream make-up. Not the powder – that'll stick to the glue.

Something you might remember for the future.'

He used a sponge to lightly stroke the lid, building up the make-up in layers until the cut was hidden and there was a faint warmth to the lid. He handed the sponge to Sarah.

'Now do that with the other lid. And be careful. Lids are delicate, especially on a corpse. Don't mess up.'

The Petersen family began arriving just before three. In the viewing room, on a small table covered with a cloth, Sarah had placed a vase full of black-eyed susans, stripping away the green foliage to reveal soft stems and heads of yellow. Through the open window came the faint smell of smoke from the burning leaves. Colby's rake was propped against the outbuilding, but he was nowhere to be seen.

Matt stood just at the doorway to the viewing room, his tall frame filling the corridor. He kept his head bowed, and shook the hand of each of the mourners.

'I'm sorry for your loss,' he said.

Walnut

Bruce Meyer

Greg waited three hours to be seen at the walk-in clinic. His eyes were burning, his joints aching, and the collar of his shirt was soaked in sweat. Thirsty, dizzy, exhausted, he tried to read the book he'd brought with him to pass the time, but the mask he had been issued at the triage desk caused his glasses to fog. He felt like hell.

When his name was finally called, he raised himself from the waiting room chair, careful not to step on the feverish child who lay on the floor in front of him. At least the kid hadn't cried. He felt sorry for the toddler. He'd seen children stricken during his time overseas as a journalist – children with matted eyes and runny noses, their eyelids caked in flies. This child, who lived in another world from the children Greg had witnessed, was next. He was going to get help.

The nurse called Greg's name a second time, and with his coat over one arm and his book in the other hand, he ambled into the treatment room and sat down on the examining table. After a few moments he felt faint, dropped his coat to the floor, and lay down on the shelf-paper carpet that ran in a narrow white road the length of the black leatherette.

The doctor came in, a blond woman about his age, attired in the requisite white lab coat. Greg sat up. He didn't catch her name. She listened to his chest.

"Do I still have a heart?" he asked as she unhooked the rubber tips from her ears and put the stethoscope in her pocket. She took out a light and shone it down his throat, then reached over to a jar beside the sink and pulled out a tongue depressor. He was getting the full treatment. He made an 'aww' sound for her.

"Don't say 'aww'," she said in a matter of fact way.

She stared at him, felt his neck glands, and took his pulse. She was not to be humored. She looked in his ears, took his temperature with an ear thermometer and told him he had the flu. He knew that already. She merely confirmed the obvious, and he wondered why he had waited three hours on a snowy winter evening in a room packed with other sick people and a difficult drive home in a blizzard to learn what he already knew.

"I knew you were going to tell me I have the flu," Greg said, hopelessly. Still no response.

"Bed rest, fluids, at least three days off work. There's not much else to do for it. Antibiotics only work on infections so I'm not prescribing them."

Greg nodded. He had received his instructions, a set of imagined ideograph images in his mind as if he was a piece of furniture to be assembled – instructions where a universal round-headed man lay in bed. An ideograph of a glass of liquid. Three suns, three moons. By then, he would be assembled. By then, wellness, or at least wellness with weakness, would provide him with enough information to share around the coffee machine at the newspaper with his colleagues, small facts he'd look up on-line when he felt well enough about how not to cure the flu, how the flu spreads, and why everyone gets it eventually. Everyone has a war story about the flu. As an annual event, it makes for comparative conversation.

The doctor stepped toward the examining room door but paused as she reached for the handle, and in afterthought stared at Greg.

"I waited as long as I could, and you never showed up. Now that you're here, now that we're in the same place, I'm moving on. I've joined Doctors Without Borders and I'm leaving on Friday." She shook her head then looked at Greg, "It's a shame. It could have been a good life for us." She opened the door of the examining room and was gone.

For a few minutes, Greg sat in silence on the examination altar, his stocking feet dangling over a chrome and black step stool. Had he just hallucinated the doctor's words? Did she know him? Had he known her? She didn't look familiar. He thought he'd seen her, perhaps once, long ago, but she was a piece of flotsam in the addled mess of his fevered brain. Why did she think they could have been happy? Did he look unhappy? He didn't feel unhappy. He just felt like shit, and he was going to go home to his wife who would tuck him in bed and make him feel as if there was something other than merely shit happening to him and the world. The doctor's remark bothered him. He remained motionless.

The nurse came in to change the paper for the next patient. "You're finished. You can go now," she said to Greg, over-pronouncing each word as if he was deaf or had difficulty understanding simple statements through his fever fog. She helped Greg down from the table. "Are you steady enough to get home?" the nurse asked. Greg nodded. "Okay to drive?" Greg shrugged. He put on his overcoat.

"What was that doctor's name?" he asked the nurse as he slipped his arms into his overcoat and adjusted his mask into place – he felt he needed to have the mask on. It was his badge of suffering. He reached for the door handle.

"That's Dr. Auchlyn. This is her last night at the walk-in. She's leaving in a day or two for Africa."

"Auchlyn," Greg repeated, trying to memorize the name. "Would you mind writing it down for me, please?"

The nurse looked puzzled but grabbed a notepad and scribbled the letters on it, then drew a line through the clinic's address at the top of the small sheet so the paper could not be used for a forged script.

Greg made it home, removed his tie and trousers, and fell into bed with his shirt still on. His wife came into the bedroom.

"So, flu, eh? You got your shot, but I guess it hasn't kicked in yet, or this is some unexpected brand you've picked up. I'm sleeping in the spare room tonight. Stay away from the kids, too. Here's some juice I brought you. It's cranberry. I know you like cranberry. I'd mix it with a bit of orange, but we've got just enough for breakfast."

"Fucking flu," Greg said. He wanted to tell his wife about the doctor's odd parting remark but decided against it. It would require too much explaining, and Greg didn't have an explanation handy or the energy to discuss it.

"Poor Poo-poo," said Susan. "Want the light on?" she asked as she drew up the blankets around Greg's chest.

"Turn it off. I'm going to sleep. I feel like I've turned to shit. I feel like I've gone missing in my body."

Even though he closed his eyes, even though he tried to abandon himself to the fever and the sleep that lay on the other side of it, he could not get the doctor or her remark out of his mind. They must have met before, somewhere. Life is long and a person crosses paths with millions of people. They could have passed in an airport when Greg was running to catch a plane. They might have been on the same university campus. There is a medical school there, and the medsies made fun of the artsies and painted the grassy quadrangle of his college with bleach. The message was "Artsy Virgins". But the longer Greg lay in the dark, bubbling with fire as if he had become a crucible, the more he was certain he had met the doctor or, at least, seen her when they were younger. The world is a small place, a place where people know each other but don't know each other; but if they had, it must have been long ago. Maybe she thought he was someone else. Maybe he was someone else when they had been in the same place at the same time and she remembered Greg as he was then but not as he was now. People change. They lead lives. They go their separate directions, and as Greg drifted to sleep the idea rattled in his head that life is not what one does but the infinite possibilities that reside in what one does not do. Did she know him from a life that could have been but that they never led?

Greg had grown up in the small town of Walnut, an old, Victorian community. The town was bisected by the Grand River – the older parts on one side, the newer subdivisions on the other. Every other year, the river overflowed its banks and submerged the portions of the town nearest the floodplain. Greg had grown up in the new section. Maybe he had met the doctor while sandbagging a street. He'd had a good childhood, done all the things a boy in suburbia should do – gone to school, made friends, rode a bicycle, played road hockey on a dead-end cul-de-sac where his best friend Tom had lived, fallen in love for the first time with a little brown-haired girl in his grade twelve geography class and fallen out of love when he moved on to university. He'd had a past and he'd left his past behind in as many ways and as many times as he could. The past is meant to be that way. It is the movie in the rearview mirror.

In his mind, in that out-of-focus zone that is neither sleep nor wakefulness, Greg was back walking the streets of Walnut. When he was very young, he'd go for walks with his grandfather. One day, an early autumn day when the walnuts were falling from the trees, the old man stopped, bent down, and picked one of the nuts off the sidewalk.

"Walnuts have the hardest shells of any nuts." His grandfather demonstrated by throwing the nut as hard as he could on the pavement. The wrinkled shell bounced but it did not break. Greg looked at the lawn of a house. A squirrel was gnawing on a shell, but it wouldn't crack.

"Now, watch this," the old guy said as he bent down beside Greg. "It's all in how you open it. There's a million ways you could open a walnut, but only one way to unlock it whole. See this seam running between the two halves?" His grandfather pressed the seam between his thumb and his forefinger. "It takes a bit of strength and a bit of skill, but watch."

And with that the nut opened as if his grandfather had said a magic word, and by spell the shell of the nut opened. When the shell split, his grandfather blew the dusty insides away and lifted out the meat – a pair of praying hands joined delicately at their imaginary wrists, each a mirror image of the other. "It only works if you do it right and there's only one way to do it right."

Why did Greg remember that moment? His grandfather had passed away the next year, just as the walnuts were falling on the sidewalk. Shards of shells lay everywhere – on the lawns, on the boulevard, and on the street, each part of a nut the hard fruit of a hardwood tree opened the wrong way.

Walnut, the town, had no time in his mind. He was twenty again, was standing in front of Tom's house, watching as people in black filed in and out, wanting to go in but not knowing what to say if he had gone in. Tom had committed suicide.

Then, he was younger, maybe eight or nine. He and Tom were laughing, replaying in slow motion a pretty goal scored by Bobby Hull or Gordie Howe. If it was a Howe goal, the raising of the stick was punctuated by an elbow in the face of whoever was tending the net. Those had been good times. Those had been nights beneath a purple, dusky sky, when it was so cold as the stars came out that their pantlegs froze with the snow that had woven itself into the furrows of their corduroys.

When they were walking home from school along streets banked with shoveled snow on either side, sliding when they hit a patch of ice, or jumping up to balance on the peaks and claiming they were Tenzing

Norgay or Edmund Hillary, they'd break their imaginary moments by talking about the girls they knew, who was hot, who was not, and who they'd like to ask to the after-school dance in the gymnasium. They had their whole lives ahead of them. Tom wanted to be an underwater welder, a Jacques Cousteau of acetylene. Greg said he didn't know what he'd do, didn't want to be a teacher because that would be a betrayal of the strength and courage they showed each day as they endured the hours of classroom tedium. Maybe, Greg said, he'd become a newspaper writer. Tom told him they get drunk a lot. He'd heard that from an uncle. Greg imagined asking questions or sitting in a smoky bar with Ernest Hemingway.

One lucky assignment led to another for Greg, and soon he was an established foreign correspondent. He hated travel, but every time he landed safely, whether in London or Lagos, he knew there had to be only one way to land. As long as the safe landings continued, the small, thin avenue of possibilities that made up his life continued to unwind before him, and in doing so eliminated all the other possibilities of what his existence could have been.

But in his fluish state between sleep and reality, in the dark both beyond his burning eyes and behind them, he thought he caught sight in his memories of a blond girl who was framed by a window. She was sitting at a desk. She kept smiling at him. Where was the window? And the name Auchlyn. He'd heard it somewhere before. "Dr. Auchlyn will see you now."

Four doctors in Walnut shared an old, gabled Victorian house on Cherrington Street. The street had once been the fashionable area of town where homes with stained glass windows and gothic cathedral dormers lined the street where the town got its name: sentries of walnut trees met over the road, and on a summer day the light through the trees was dappled in bright coins. One of the doctors, not Greg's doctor, had been named Auchlyn.

Auchlyn – it was coming back to him now – lived down the street from his medical offices. He had six children, all of them blond, tall like he was, though none of them had inherited his Scottish brogue, the roll of his r's, or the saunter in his step when the doctor walked down the street on a house call, his black medical bag in-hand.

The summer Greg was twelve, he got mono. Mono was serious in those days, more so than it is now. Greg's mother was afraid he wouldn't be able to give her grandchildren, though he had, with Susan, his second wife. They'd had three. Greg thought about what mono was like. It struck in June just as school was getting out. He'd had a paper route lined up for the summer. He was to be the replacement for the regular boy, George, who was off to camp and would likely outgrow the job and leave it to Greg the following autumn. Greg's room had been stifling. His father didn't believe in air conditioning. His mother brought in electric fans and bowls of ice she placed in the air stream of cowled sets of blades. His glands swelled. He couldn't turn his head. He had slept through the first two weeks. Mono was called "the sleeping sickness". Greg thought he was dying in Africa when he overheard his own doctor, a grey-haired man named Bovaird, say, "It's a sleeping sickness. We'll let him lie there for a while. In a week or so I'll need more blood."

Greg's white count must have been high. The familiar sleep that had embraced him and erased what could have been the first fine summer of his life made him doze off in the waiting room of the Cherrington Street practice. What had been the home's living room was lined with modern plastic chairs that didn't fit with the carved fireplace. The arch of the dining room had been sealed off except for a window, and behind that were banks of shelves with hundreds of file folders, each tabbed with letters. There was a blond girl in the dining room. She was bent over an appointments book. A nurse walked to her on the other side of the glass window and the girl handed her a file before sliding the window across its track and calling Greg's name. As she said "Greg", the girl smiled at him.

Was that all there was to the doctor's odd remark – "I waited for you as long as I could?" Was she going to say something else, perhaps explain her cryptic statement? The next morning as Greg sat up in bed, his fever broken, he downed the last mouthful of cranberry juice from the glass on the night table. He tried to reconstruct his summer of sleep as his brain had retraced it when he drifted off to sleep.

The mono summer was the year his parents rented a cottage at Cape Cod. They thought time on the beach, in the sun, though with swimming restricted to days when the shallows were warm and calm, would be good for Greg. He slept all the way south to Albany and through the Berkshires in Massachusetts, waking only to see the humped-back bridge of Sagamore rising over the tops of white pines and the blue edge of the sea beyond it. The beach was, indeed, a place to fall asleep, but because he was pale his mother had to cover him in towels and beach blankets. The sound of the sea was soothing in his ears. The rhythm of the waves was hypnotic. That is when he had the dream.

He was pushing a shopping cart through a crowded grocery store. All the wickets but two had long line-ups. He paused first at the checkout of a brown-haired woman, but at the last moment turned away and approached a young blond cashier. He was certain he'd seen her before, but he wasn't sure where. Then, he spoke to her, "And when I return, we'll be married."

The next thing he saw in his mono dream he was in uniform. In reality, the summer of mono was the height of the Viet Nam War. On the thruways and the turnpikes his family had passed convoys of young men in trucks, all almost identical in their green uniforms and helmets, seated with rifles between their legs. More than anything, Greg feared being caught up in a war. His mother said that his father had turned down lucrative job offers in the States because he was afraid of Greg getting drafted. Resident aliens were the first to go; but in the dream, after the tender moment with the blond cashier, he was in army fatigues. He was running to get up a beach then falling hard and pressing his body against a sand dune for cover when he heard an explosion, and then a voice, clear and distinct leaning over him, saying, "He's dead." Greg woke, his body drenched in sweat. He drew a beach towel over his chest to dry off.

There was an older woman wearing a caftan and broad-brimmed sunhat in the parking lot at the beach who had set up a small, folding table. On the front of the table, a sign fluttered back and forth in the wind. *Fortunes read. $5*. Greg walked up to her. She peered between the brim of her hat and the top of her oversized sunglasses.

"Honey, you're too young. I'm not permitted to read anyone's fortune until they're eighteen. State law. Besides, when you're young, your future is all jumbled up. What's going to happen could happen a million ways from Sunday and right now not even heaven knows." She shuffled her tarot deck and pushed her sunglasses up on her nose.

"Do you interpret dreams?"

"Dreams, honey? Dreams are just stuff in your head, but if you need someone to talk to and no one else wants to listen, then maybe I can give you a freebee if you hand out some of my leaflets to folks on the beach. Deal? Fire away."

Greg took the Gestetnered yellow leaflets from her and he told the woman his dream.

"That's a bad trip, honey, bad trip. But here's the thing, it's like I said. Your future ain't cooked yet. Anything could happen, but if I were you, I'd avoid blondies until you sort things out."

"Why?" he asked.

"Cuz, honey, it probably means that if you find that girl of your dreams there's going to be a big war and you're going to die in it. Maybe that ain't so, but I'm just saying ..."

Greg walked up and down the beach with the leaflets. No one was interested. When he returned to the parking lot with the extras, the woman was gone. He took the handful of papers and buried them in a dune behind where the fortune-teller had been seated. If she returned the next day, he could fish them out of the sand. She didn't return.

By the time school was back in session, Greg was still weak from the mono. His mother picked him up every afternoon and he would sleep until dinner time. There were blond girls in his classes, many of them cute, some of them beautiful. Greg wasn't interested in them. Tom said that one of them, Shirley, liked him, and Greg replied his preference was for brunettes. And though he probably passed her on the streets of Walnut countless times and stood in the same theatre line-up on Friday night at the Bijou, and though he went to the clinic for various maladies from broken fingers to migraines, he never noticed Jane Auchlyn. She went to a school on her side of the river, and the river that flowed between them rose and fell with the seasons. Greg graduated from high school, was accepted to university in Toronto, and told his father that he had no desire to follow in his father's business or remain in Walnut. Greg wanted to be a journalist.

After paying his dues on the night desk of *The Toronto Star* and walking back to his apartment, bleary-eyed one morning, Greg stopped at the corner of Yonge and Front, looked to the east, and decided it was time to put some adventure in his life. Ethiopia was in crisis. Millions were going hungry. Untold numbers were dying of starvation each day. There were warlords with their personal armies fighting for control of the shattered country, and aid workers struggling to keep up with the hopeless task of holding back a deluge of catastrophe. In a bar at Heathrow on his way home from his foreign service, he met a Norwegian who had heard of Walnut.

"You wouldn't know Jane Auchlyn, would you? She's from the same town and she mentioned, when I met her at a convention in Geneva, there was this guy named Greg she always hoped to catch up with. We were discussing destiny and such."

Greg was surprised. "Did she say where she was headed next?"

The Norwegian shrugged. "People go anywhere if they are looking for something."

He didn't tell the man that Jane Auchlyn had popped into a dream he'd had as a teenager, or that he had been advised by a fortune-teller in a beach parking lot to avoid the girl of his dreams. He could not even say he had forgotten his dreams. Dreams were not part of Greg's work.

His work was, at last, bringing him home to report on Federal politics. He would start a new life, a new marriage, and a new beat. Years later, his experience called him back to Africa though Susan, his second wife, wondered why it had to be him and not some rising star willing to risk life and limb in a war zone.

He wanted to see how Ethiopia had changed, if at all. When he landed in Addis Ababa, the air was dry and hot. He felt as if he had walked into an oven. He could feel his skin becoming brittle in the heat. His thoughts wandered and he realized, after only half an hour in the open Jeep that would take him into the war zone, that he had forgotten to buy water before leaving the city and the berbere factories, low and anonymous, in the Jeep's dusty wake.

The trip out was not the perilous journey he had anticipated except for the roadblock where a valley intersected with the scant highway that traced its way south through the desert. Checkpoints were the norm. There were government men at the crossroad. They were suspicious of Greg. They questioned what he was doing in that part of the country. Why a Canadian doctor? Why not a Swedish physician or a Swiss nurse? The soldiers gathered in a huddle in front of the Jeep. They spent an hour and a half going through his papers, pointing at him, first with their hands, then with their weapons. Greg was hungry and tired. It was dinner time and he hadn't eaten since he boarded the connecting flight in London. He never trusted airline food.

His research had pointed him to one camp where the aid agency had told him he might find and interview a Canadian doctor named Auchlyn. She had established a reputation as the angel of the famine camps. As he approached, the perimeter looked desperate.

Blue plastic tarpaulins, the kind he might throw over a barbecue or patio table to keep the ice off during a long winter, were flapping and fluttering in the wind. Dust spun in circles where invisible, fiery angels chased each other from nowhere to nowhere. He heard the sound of children crying. He could see children cradled in their mothers´ arms as swarms of flies clustered around their mouths and eyes. At the center of it all a medical tent. The tattered Red Cross flag was flying at half-mast.

As Greg stepped from the vehicle and reached in back to gather his bag from the rear seat an Irish voice called to him from the crowd that gathered at the treatment tent.

"We can use your help here," the Irishman said.

"Is Jane Auchlyn here?" he asked.

"She was looking forward to your visit."

Greg paused. He looked up at the night sky as it spread its stars above him. The Irishman shook his head.

"Where did she go?"

"You're knackered man. Get some rest. That's Jane's," said the Irishman pointing to an empty cot. "You can put down there for the night."

Yes, it would be a good idea to lie down. He'd get some rest and have breakfast with Jane and tell her he'd been blind, that they had played a game of hide-and-seek throughout their homeland, ducking in and out of places, always missing each other, and only together in dreams, but life had a way of keeping people apart and no matter what destiny they might have shared they were both on their own paths now and had been for years.

He lay down on the cot and closed his eyes. He was certain he saw her. She was emerging from the medical tent, her forehead drenched in sweat as she wiped a bare forearm above her eyes and blew back a strand of her blond hair that had dropped toward her mouth.

Before dawn Greg woke and walked to the edge of the camp. He could smell death everywhere. A silence hovered over the ground as if all the life within its invisible boundaries had exhausted itself and cried itself to sleep and no one heard. The sun was just breaking in a grey-green streak to the east. He looked out over the empty ground, the flat, cool vista where the moon sat waiting on the far horizon for the sun to chase it away. The Irishman came up behind him.

"You're taking your chances standing here. This is where the jackals hunt. They'll drag off anything rather than go home empty-handed after a long night. And there's the animals, too, not just the rebels."

"I came looking for Dr. Auchlyn," Greg said, almost in a whisper, as if speaking would break the impenetrable stillness and shatter the frail calm of the moment between night and day.

The Irishman put his hand on Greg's shoulder.

"She knew you were coming. She wanted to be remembered to you. Here it is in a nutshell, lad. You just missed her. You came all this way, but it will be a different story than the one she thought you'd write. She was expecting you but, as she said, she had to move on. You were probably already on the road by then. Was she someone you knew well or just a topic for your journalism? I'll tell you, everyone here thought the world of her. You'd have to go a long way to find anyone her equal. I hope you will write about what she did. She gave her life searching for what she loved, though we always knew her first love was right here in the thick of the fight for life."

Flash Fiction

Morning Routine

Kim Catanzarite

I opened a can of cat food and grabbed a saucer and one of the forks nobody likes and scooped out the food and gave the fat one the fork to lick and gave the kitten the full saucer and lifted their water dishes from the floor and filled them up and then turned the lights on in the living room and raised the blinds in the eating area and made my way to the fridge and put the bread in the toaster and grabbed the butter before tapping out the allergy medicine and her ADHD medicine and her other allergy medicine and pouring her glass of water. Then I put the kettle on and grabbed the brush and dustpan and picked up some mud that tracked in on her shoes the night before, and then the toast popped and I buttered it and she came in and said "good morning" and asked me if her socks matched her outfit and I said yes and she told me it was cold outside and that she was going to freeze her ass off at the bus stop if I didn't drive her there, and I told her that she would live, and she breathed out a cloud of disgust and said that if the puddle down the road was enormous like it was the other day I would have to drive her because she couldn't get around it, it was so big, and I stared at her and said nothing because that's often the best response, and then she looked out the window and also said nothing, so I knew the puddle was gone.

Blink

Mary McClarey

I lick a fingertip and run it around the salty rim of my Margarita, enjoying the squeak, as I watch, across the open air rooftop cocktail bar, the young couple fussing over a baby.

With sticky finger I suck, mesmerised, as she clicks and he cradles. The fronds of the palm trees move gently in the sundowner breeze.

Sweet pink bootees on floppy little legs. Sweet pink family. Well known rather than famous. Well, known to me anyway.

She stops clicking, seeing me watching. She sips from a cardboard coffee cup. I sip in reply. He sinks his mouth onto the downy hair of the little one's head. Holding her close, he stands nearer the edge of the hotel balcony parapet, pointing out the palm treetops, the water glistening just across the road.

'One more,' she asks. 'Hold her up so I can see her face.'

He turns, lifts the floppy body up for the photo, then walks slowly back to the parapet again. The traffic humming gently, far below. He's a New Man Dad, the best he can be.

I close my eyes, washed by the memory of my own small babies. They were dependent but perfect. I never coped with disability, pain or illness. Grown, gone now.

Time for another sip. I open my eyes, blinking, shading with my hand as the sunset blurs my vision. Sudden screams shatter the idyll, the traffic below a mass of honking, brakes squealing, a siren wails.

And they are gone. Off the balcony. The man and his baby are gone. I blink. I look again, to make sure. They are still gone. I see her leaving, putting her phone in her bag, and the used coffee cup. Our eyes meet. I raise an eyebrow, a question, she nods, I nod, I sip.

Bog People

Anne Cullen

She met him at the museum. He was sequestered behind glass when she leaned in for a better glimpse. Their heads so close they could have shared a pillow. Her breath temporarily fogging the view before she stepped back to read the tiny card affixed near the display.

Bog Man
Found: 1951
Age: Approx. 2300 years

And there he lay, or what was left of him, the head and torso of him, eerily intact, like a perfect, freakish cast rendered in what resembled smooth chestnut leather, as though the half of him had somehow wandered in from his bog bed to finish his nap in a climate controlled box. His hands curled closed, the nails still visible, calm fists each as big as the human heart. She admired his symmetry, his serenity, such beauty preserved in deep slumber, placid and pain free, and yet the rope around his neck meant otherwise. A face not unlike that French film actor she used to fancy before his career went south and those cheek bones were lost amid a puffy train wreck, a face she'd fall for again were it out in the world, say across from her on the train or standing next to her at the bookstore. She couldn't stop staring. He looked so alive, and she waited for a rise and fall, an inhale, an exhale, a twitch, a blink, a somnambulant murmur, a whisper of the voice that matched the face. A thief? A martyr? She wanted him to tell her the how and why, the secrets he learned while hidden beneath a blanket of earth, about the magic preservation of youth in the alchemy of pH, alkali and calcium, and to tell her about the quiet, the natural history of peace.

Domesticity

Claire Powell

A woman waits for the kettle to boil. As she waits, she stares at her ghostly reflection in the dark pane of window, and she thinks about some mistakes she's made, or some regrets she has.

A woman waits for the kettle to boil. As she waits, the phone rings. The person on the other end of the line is the man she once had an affair with, or the woman her husband had an affair with. Hello? she says. Who's there?

A woman waits for the kettle to boil. As she waits, she absent-mindedly slips her hand inside her towelling dressing gown and discovers a lump on her right breast.

A woman waits for the kettle to boil. As she waits, she prepares a plate of biscuits for the two detectives in her living room. The detectives are here to talk about her missing daughter, or her missing husband, or the money missing from her employer's account. Her hands tremble as she arranges the Custard Creams.

A woman waits for the kettle to boil. As she waits, she opens the fridge, changes her mind, takes out a bottle of wine.

A woman waits for the kettle to boil. As she waits, she explains to the woman at the table – her sister or her neighbour or her colleague – that she slipped down the stairs, or walked into a door, or that she accidently fell out of bed. The woman at the table says nothing.

A woman waits for the kettle to boil. As she waits, she steps into the spotlight of sunshine in front of the fridge, and she closes her eyes, sees pink.

A woman waits for the kettle to boil. As she waits, she feels a deep sense of sadness, or unease, or loneliness, or weariness, or thirst.

Recipe for Disaster by Jan Kaneen

Ingredients

1 small child (aged 5 is best)

1 tender parent completely out of their psychological depth

1 unexpected death, a fatal accident or lethal illness will do, a pulmonary embolism is ideal

Lashings of raw grief

Packets of emotional naivety

2 shakes of trying to do what's right for all the wrong reasons

A dash of collusive silence lightly tossed in a dressing of complete and utter denial

Preparation Time: This is an organic dish that to all intents and purposes preps itself

Cooking Time: As long as it takes to properly stew, but a lifetime is not unusual

Method

1) Following unexpected loss of parent, surviving parent should attempt to reduce/cure terrible grief by re-marrying as soon as possible, ideally to dead parent's best friend

2) New family unit should re-hash dead parent's passing making it step parent's tragedy, not child's

3) All contact with deceased parent's parents should be dissolved then permanently scrambled so no unsavoury grand-mothers or fathers are left to sour already sticky situation

4) After short resting period, existence of dead parent should be thoroughly reconstituted. Step-parent should poach elements of dead parent's backstory and blend them into their own to make new concoction

5) Carefully burn all photos of dead parent and scorch stories about them from familial narrative

6) Cook up reason why new step-parent must only ever be called mum/dad

7) Clarify to child that new narrative is what really happened. This may be difficult for them to process at first so roast, reduce, sweat and grind as often as is necessary. (Occasional sweetening and coddling might also be beneficial.)

8) Leave to simmer

Reclining Nude

Stella Klein

Stretched out before your hungry gaze, your puking cough and hashish-brandy pallor, that palette of flesh tones tells me all I need to know of what you see in me: the ripe curves of my haunches, my sweet cherry nipples, my soft and dimpled thighs. I have heard such longings a thousand times, beneath the lanterns, between the sheets, from the lips of the prowling gentlemen on the streets of Montparnasse.

You look away to choke and wheeze, then, raising your nervous brush, you turn to stroke and dab and feast on me again. Too bad my lips turn down for you. Too bad I am not charmed by these airy apartments of your slavering Zbrowski. Well, let me tell you, Monsieur Amedeo Modigliani, Prince of Vagabonds, or whatever it is they call you: you mistake these angry cheeks of mine for blushing modesty.

Try all you want to paint a smile and hide your shame. But when you've finished with my pubes and rosy hues, be sure to blacken my eyes as you have done to the rest, your cellist, your gardener, your gypsy boy. Then, at least, down the centuries they cannot say I was a doting muse.

The Abnormal Normal – Belfast 1970

Jennifer O'Reilly

You're walking up the street, your file of lecture notes under your arm. From behind, a heaviness throws you to the ground, sending waves of exaggerated confetti fluttering above. Heaviness weighs on your back and a hard, calloused hand presses your cheek into the gritty cold pavement. Pressure vice-like, you cannot move save for your eyes. They dart and look and see, see splatters of gravel splutter into the air. Ricochet. The unseen shooting at the unseen. Ideology and recklessness as one, spitting through the air. And then silence. Tentatively, people reappear. Heaviness releases his grip and you move to kneel, picking up scattered Camus, Sartre and Descartes. "Sorry," heaviness says and you say, "thank you" without looking. And when you look you see the man you saw at the sale, a sale organised to raise money for war-torn Cambodia. You remember him because he was alone and you sold him a rusted tin of tomatoes that nobody else wanted. And for days after, guilt haunted you. What was a man alone going to do with a rusted tin of tomatoes that nobody else wanted in those pre-bolognese, pre-lasagne days? And as he turns to move away from you, you say "sorry," and you watch him disappear through the gates of the Morning Star home for homeless men. And you turn to walk up the now busy street, your file of tattered philosophers tucked firmly under your arm.

The Other Flight of Icarus

James Wise

Icarus straightens his aviator's cap and marches through the hanger's gaping maw onto the gaslit airstrip. People seem content to keep telling Daedalus' story but, he supposes, if they find a moral about obedience useful, who is he to argue? The breeze is up and crew hang all their weight on guy-ropes, boots slipping across slick grass. The airship's hydrogen sack bulges and strains and its bow swings wildly.

Icarus pities it, destined to be moored, helmed and controlled. Forced to observe strict altitude regulations, with only Manhattan's dizzying maze to look forward to. Why they still believe his father's version, though, is somewhat of a mystery. To be fair, not many had flown before, so how could they know it doesn't get hotter the higher you go, but colder? Among the queueing passengers, sparks fly from the fingertips of a man in a wax jacket and feathered fedora when he taps his cigarette. Icarus tuts and strides past him. He waits for the stairs to swing his way and climbs them without even grasping the handrail.

In the control car there is frost on the windows and Icarus' breath escapes into the air. He fires up the engines, grabs the radio, opens the port hatch and calls down, pointing to the microphone, that there's been an emergency and he's needed upstate. The men look at each other, shrug and let go of the ropes. Icarus watches the smoking man shouting and shaking his fist as the ground falls away. He will not navigate this clueless cretin's demands, nor tiptoe round his trapdoor smile avoiding the naked anger at his centre. He'd done that once before, and couldn't understand how no one could see it wasn't just his father's stone labyrinth he was fleeing, nor merely the minotaur he feared.

When you look down the throat of a doll there's nothing inside

Rosie Garland

As a child, you ask for dolls. You line them up along the headboard, their arms held out for hugging. While other girls dress and undress, you learn the endurance of toy bodies and what goes on beneath clothes at night when people pretend it's too dark to hear.

What a waste to hurl your dolls away and let a wall have the pleasure of the crack and shatter. Foolish, to scrawl out their eyes with ballpoint pen when there's so much to learn from the study of the retina. You recall the sharp rush of that first time, when you discovered it is possible to detect the splintering of a heart in the opening and closing of an eye.

It is impractical to retain them all. You keep the ones who are easiest to break, who keep returning to be broken. They would resist if they didn't want it. Now you have put aside childish things, you savour challenges. The complex flavour of those who think themselves cleverer than you, who dance escape and capture, forgetting that any doll can be brought to heel if you snap it at the knee.

All those tiny footprints leading to your bed; none departing. You wonder how people can't see the tracks face in one direction. You wonder why people don't despise themselves. It's not like you pretend. There's no way to apologise for the mindless trust of lovers, the way they throw something as crisp and valuable as love down wells, off the stern of ships, into the face of storms.

Throwing Cockerels

Alan Passey

His mind was wandering when the string broke. A final discordant note skimming the chatter and the glasses. The string swinging loose like a snapped tendon.

He winced his smile and returned his guitar to its stand, took his bow with a luxuriant sweep. Left to right, right to left. I am done with these, he thought. Few noticed.

He pulled his glass closer, feeling the click in his thumb, the pain he accepted, and raising the glass high peered through the clear liquid at his misshaped hand, taking in the curve and rise of a Lilliputian mountain.

Alone, lying on his berth, he threw crooked shadow cockerels at the wall. Role playing overheards and profanity transported to the farm yard. He threw another and squawked "BB King called his Lucille. You," pointing at the inept instrument "are Madge."

He replayed an assignation. A lonely cruiser amongst the strangers and the sea. He'd been gentle with his hands. She'd enjoyed the blue.

The bar would usually empty at six and the poultry dressed for dinner. Sometimes he joined them mingling in the buffet queue. Chasing hens. Cockerels crowing. The weary repetition.

His stillness went unnoticed to this new flock. He closed his eyes, behind his drink, a solitary finger twitching to the soundtrack in his head, rising to the thunderous applause of his pain free melody. A smile and sweeping bow. Encore and fade.

Walking the evening deck he occupied his mind with views of water. The cold rail cooling his taut fingers like an ice pack.

Later, when looking at the photographs, they would comment on his manicure.

Lockdown

POCKET PROSE

Out For A Duck

Paul McGranaghan

The only ashes to be taken are those that have been taken before; electronic ghosts in the scrying glass, batting and catching where now there is only the slow silent growth of the grass. Perhaps dandelions are gleaming in the out-field, daisies in the slip.

Re-runs, indeed. There are no overs, no byes; just a front room fossil bed of sixes and innings, while mirthless squares go for the wrong sort of run by the cricket ground. The sun shines down on emptiness. Where is the worth in the glories that were, when measured against those that could have been?

Six Feet Away

Shamini Sriskandarajah

We check the small print: graveyards aren't an exception, even if you keep six feet away.

So we cut spring flowers from the garden, arrange them in vases, and share photos with each other.

The flowers intended for the ones we love who will always be six feet away.

My Pawn Gently Sleeps

Shamini Sriskandarajah

Easter weekend. The weather's gorgeous and my disabled sister has been in an uncharacteristically good mood for the last few days. In a fit of optimism, I dig out the old chess set from the garage and start to set it up.

She takes over, putting the white pieces on black squares and the black pieces on white squares in an aesthetically-pleasing, social distancing pattern. I move a pawn one place forward. She does the same. What a miracle! She instinctively knows how to play.

Then she turns every piece on its side, as if it's bedtime.

HAIKU

corporate fallout
the merger of Office Wear
and Pyjamas

by Lee Nash

Stretching out
from dry wood,
a new leaf.

April *by Julia Travers*

Leaving this lockdown
will be as my dentist leaves my teeth:
numbingly well-drilled.

by James Allan Kennedy

Self-isolation
is not a four-letter word.
It's longer than that.

by James Allan Kennedy

Fran Lebowitz is not happy

Emma Gallagher

Fran Lebowitz is not happy about not leaving New York.

Fran Lebowitz is not happy about that other New Yorker leaving New York to ruin.
'Sloth,' she says, 'recognises sloth.'

Fran Lebowitz does not have a mobile phone, a microwave or a love of technology,
she is knee-deep in books, peeling cucumbers for salads that someone else should be making.

Fran Lebowitz doesn't care for cooking, she cares for eating.

Fran Lebowitz is smoking cigarettes and missing tourists.
Fran Lebowitz hates tourists, but tourists are better than no tourists.
In the no-one else of her existence, Fran Lebowitz is the worst tourist she has ever had.

If a tree falls in Times Square, does a butterfly flap its wings in Wuhan?

'Contagious unfettered capitalism,' she says, 'closed culture quicker than Corona.'

Fran Lebowitz's concierge desk is a glimpse behind a velvet rope,
see, New York society distanced before it was cool.

Fran Lebowitz says that the president is the stupidest person you could ever know
and love to him is the algebra equation of someone who cannot add.

'A smart woman,' she says, 'never had much of a chance.'

Fran Lebowitz loved Toni Morrison because Toni Morrison loved everyone she met,
and made two days out of one; wise and brilliant, she could teach you to think differently.

There are books she expects to finish but she's at very high risk (of not finishing books).

Lost Connection

Jennie Ensor

Now we are all small squares on a screen. I can't tell which one is me
till I move my hand. I dream of looking into the mirror, seeing someone else.

Now we are adept at keeping our distance. A friend at my front door;
we cringe apart. I want to grip her hand, crush her to me.

We ask each other who's died, who's survived. We queue, alone,
wait for what's next. The hardware shop man bare-hands me a roll of bin bags.

I stare into lit windows, listen for splinters of conversation, yearn for ten
minutes
of someone else's life. Consolation in silk-soft baths, dance of early morning light.

Now we speak through panes of glass, smile through pain of separation.
Many slip away unheard, unseen. We'll meet again? I don't know when.

I sing behind my screen, muted. Memories of altos rehearsing for Easter,
shoulder to shoulder, not knowing this would be our last song. Our laughter
at that odd phrase *When death takes off the mask* – its sudden, unexpected fit.

Small blossoms drift into my lap, gifts from the horse chestnut. I touch a frail,
yellow-dusted petal. For days I watch the halo of hopeful cones, their slow sway
as if gathered in contemplation or prayer, each stubbornly pointing to the sky.

Safekeeping
(or Schrödinger's Lunchbox)

Gráinne Murphy

My daughter's lunchbox is not empty. Though it holds no banana peel or
sandwich crusts,
no pips from grapes or the half-licked lid of a yogurt carton. No air-
softened cracker crumbs
or rubbery carrot sticks, cut late last night with too much grumbling and
too little gratitude.

I gather into the beeswrap, instead, the crumbs of resolve that remain
after the nightly horse-trading of screens and stories,
the weary backdrop of homeschooled tears and pleas for *five more minutes*
for the important things forgotten all the rest of the day.
A hug. A biscuit. The hind leg of the dog left unfondled.

Stay safe. Stay healthy. Stay positive. Above all, stay.
(We must succeed in this or miss the point entirely.)
With endless hours in endless days, the stretch in the evening
is one more judgement. Conditioned to believe the necessary is contained
by the time available, we are betrayed when time becomes infinite.

Walking to other voices, I learn that our internal clocks are governed
by the eye. Absorbing daylight, godlike it smooths our rhythms. I live with
the knowledge that simply keeping my eyes open holds us on course.

There's a strange alchemy in the word *daughter*. Say it aloud. Hear its
soul of wish and regret.
Hear its *both*-ness. It is a promise, a vigil for and against. My daughter's
lunchbox is not empty:
it houses my wide-eyed hopes for her, neatly folded and placed in the
cupboard for safekeeping.

POEMS

Change

"Cocoon" they said –
if such miracles are possible
I might grow wings.

Once I kept a caterpillar.
It nibbled privet leaves
and walked around – accordion style,
a shrinking and expanding bar of bright green music

which stopped the day it lost its skin –
    – the way you might forget a tune,
and closed itself
in a hard brown lacquer case.

"It might die" they said,
knowing more than I did
how hard it is to change.
I kept it warm and safe
                                        in case.

Rachel Parry

NOTE: During Lockdown the Irish Government advised the elderly and medically vulnerable to "cocoon", meaning they should not leave their homes.

Daughter

I loved you like a pandemic,
like an emergency –
you, running naked in everyone's yard.
Loving you started like an acid trip: one day,
you emerged from my body like a slippery fish
and the world breathed.
Things were always burning around you,
collapsing in a store because you got what you wanted,
laughing at the neighbors with sauce on your face.
You taught me to say hello to the moon.
I met you and forgot who I was, or I gave it up
to run my fingers through the knots of your bedhead.
I loved you on the brink of something,
and then one day, the doors opened,
and you walked through.

Ash Adams

a measurement of silence in one hundred words

in-utero/ underwater length/ a night's sleep/ tabula-rasa/ dog whistle to the human ear/ reading a chapter/ listening/ silent movie/ hesitation/ bake for 8-10 minutes at 180ºC/ quiet/ Harpocrates/ the silent treatment/ power-cut/ outage scheduled for 3.15 to 3.45am/ 1000 piece jigsaw/ one minute's silence/ texting/ a penny for your thoughts/ secret/ radio-silence/ a bath/ prayer/ meditation/ video conference awkward pause/ mime/ knitting 82 inch scarf/ shock/ the right to silence/ mute/ forty winks/ shhhhh/ conversation turn-taking indicator/ ghosting/ loneliness/ inaudible/ writing letters/ fear/ a comfortable silence/ 11 down seven-letter crossword clue/ peace/ a rest in music/ the rest/ ex silentio/ death

Rosaleen Lynch

Short Memoirs

Buck Rabbit

Noelle McCarthy

"Get in 'til you see what we got you. This is my daughter." Mammy is loud, showing off for the driver. The cab smells of drink and Estee Lauder. Wherever they've been, they've been there all morning. Angela is jammed in the back, the big cardboard box on her knees shaking violently.

"You'll have to mind him, give him curly green cabbage." Mammy taps the side of the box. It lifts a few centimetres up into the air, sides bulging. Angela throws herself forward over it, Medusa curls flying, the ash from her fag goes all over the seat in front of her. I reach for the seat belt. It's way too long for me. "Up past the crucifixion please." Mammy sounds haughty. His knuckles are white on the steering wheel. They'd have kept him outside The Chimes a good half hour. There's loud scrabbling from the back, the witchy sound of long nails scraping. The statues blur past: dying Christ, his weeping mother. "Father, Son and Holy Spirit. Come on, girl!" Mammy blesses herself theatrically, insists I do the same. The driver thumps his chest three times with a vengeance.

The worst is not when she keeps them waiting, the worst is when she won't pay them. A guy the other night pulled into the Guards Station. She got out with the glass still in her hand: vodka and lime. Dwarves, Angela calls them. We pretended to be asleep when the Guard came out, me and John Paul in our school uniforms. Something cold pressed up against my leg, the bag with the crispy pancakes. They put her back in the car eventually. The Guard must have told the driver to bring us home. Daddy gave him some money and flung the crispy pancakes all over the hall on top of her.

Passing the asylum, the box flies open. A savage kick, a flash of fur, thrilling and alien. Angela tries to jam the flap back down. "For fuck's sake, hold onto him!" Mammy is high, triumphant. Children's allowance day, maybe. Not The Chimes, The Raven. Up to Sullivan's afterwards, the clock running down on them, buoyed by dwarves, unusually monied. Past the soft green glow of the fish tanks, up the back to the long rows of biscuity-smelling cages lined with sawdust. Fluffy piles of fawn, grey, tortoiseshell. Five pounds for a guinea pig, rabbits for a tenner. Three brothers own it, or four. Country people, they all look identical. The mice are only eighty-five pence, but I'm not allowed them anymore, after the last time. I am deeply excited about whatever is in the box, even though it's Angela holding it. Her son catches pigeons when we're outside The Chimes, just throws his jacket over them. I don't know what happens to them afterwards. She's trying to keep the box steady. Whatever's inside is trying to tunnel through the bottom.

Mammy makes the driver wait for his money, counting out coppers. Her bag is all over the back seat, Silvermints and tissues, Granda's mass card; she refuses to gather it up in any kind of hurry. She wants to provoke him, there's a perceived lack of deference in all of these encounters that infuriates her. Many years later I am back in Ireland. In a cab late one night, the driver points at the house. "The one who lives in there, she's a fucking bitch, I'll tell you. A fucking demon." It's the same man, bit greyer, still weaselly. I get out three houses down and keep the five euro I was going to tip him.

She doesn't have a key but the side gate is open. Released from its box, the rabbit is enormous. Grey and mangy with massive hind legs, it quivers all over. "A buck," says Mammy approvingly. Crazed from the journey, it runs straight at the garden wall and finds a too-small hole to jam itself into. When I try to pull it out, it makes a thin wailing noise like a baby. "Don't go into her, boy, she'd fucking eat you." Catherine next door. Mammy says she is a whore, that her children are possessed by the devil. The middle boy called her an alkie once when she took his ball off him. She puts Daddy's big metal toolbox under the window ledge and stands up on it. Angela stays by the washing line, smoking. Her black clip-on earrings have streams of crystals that reach down to her shoulders. Her eyes are panda'ed with kohl. She narrows them at me through the cigarette smoke: "You'd want to mind that rabbit your mother got you." I turn my back on her. I was very young when I realised they'd get kicked out of places if I started roaring. Angela would glare as I flung my crisps on the floor. "She knows exactly what she's doing." Eventually the barman would say no as soon as he saw the buggy. I am the least compliant of my siblings. They used to sit my sister on a high stool and she'd polish the darts trophies.

"Christ's sake, help me Angela, I don't want to knock the Busy Lizzie." My mother is pushing against the glass like a cat, her fingers working the catch on the window. Last time, she cut her hand open. Blood all over her good blue dress, must have been a wedding they were at, or a christening. Angela braces her leg and she pulls herself up and into the kitchen. The rabbit is trying to dig its way under the fuchsia by the back wall, white cotton tail in the air, hind legs pumping furiously. There's room in the hutch after the guinea pigs got eaten but I'll have to catch it. I imagine Daddy coming in from work, Angela sitting in the kitchen, the bottle with the blue label on the table in front of them. The next time I see the rabbit, he's on the main road, we left the side gate open. Mammy breaks ice cubes out of their tray. "He'll come back, he's only exploring."

* * *

It's my first time. The ceiling feels lower than it should be. There's a row of coffee tables running down the centre of the room, spindly legged, peeling wood-coloured laminate. On them are clear plastic jars of biscuits, chocolate-chip, the cheap ones, and a big pile of dark blue hardback books in the middle. Two rows of chairs along opposite walls, old-fashioned recliners upholstered in grimy florals. The books are handed round. I have real problems; it's going to take more than fucking *book club* – but the familiar weight of a book in my hand is reassuring. At the top of the room, sitting at a table under a large ugly painting of cart horses, is a man who looks like John the Baptist. He picks up a laminated sheet. "Welcome everyone to Wednesday night Young Ones Meeting." His voice is high and nasal, weirdly at odds with his burning eyes and spiritual cheekbones. The name of the meeting is confusing – I'm clearly the only one here under forty, but everyone goes ahead and stands up with him, we say a short prayer in awkward, arrhythmic unison. "God grant me the serenity to accept the things I cannot change ..." My chair is an old recliner; when we sit back down, my feet fly out to nearly eye level. I won't be able to get up again unless someone pulls me. My shoes are yellow, I've been wearing them all winter. Beat up leather high heels, $20 from the Paperbag Princess. They go with everything, my lilac tights, the tartan coat I'm wearing. I wish I hadn't worn it. It's too loud, the check is blaring. And the round brass buttons. I look like Sergeant Pepper, with my ass on the floor and my legs in the air. My face is red, I can feel it. I'm ashamed of myself. In general, not for any special reason, although I could take my pick if I had to choose.

There's a homeless man asleep in the chair opposite me, furry dreadlocks wrapped around his neck, lap full of chocolate chip cookies. I know him from the strip I think, from sitting outside SPQR with Jarrad and Jeremy. Home with $10 bottles, rolling in through Jarrad's bedroom window, we lost the front door key months ago. Not long after that, I took a taxi driver home with me. I made him take me to the Countdown in Grey Lynn for a box of Corona first and then brought him in to watch Shortland Street. I had a week of episodes taped on the Sky box. He went out and took the sign off the cab at 3am when I said he could stay over. He said his wife was dead, maybe? In Bulgaria. He was very hairy. Jarrad thought it was hilarious. Fuck Rebecca for putting "who sleeps with a cab driver?" as her Facebook status. And writing it in Spanish, thinking I wouldn't translate. I've been dreaming about planes falling out of the sky lately. I asked the therapist about it. "Sounds self-explanatory," she said, not giving me much to work with. She has coarse skin and a wide flat nose. Nice brown eyes. She writes me out receipts in an old-fashioned invoice book like I'm going to file them away carefully. After we finish every Wednesday, I walk down the narrow stairs in my yellow heels and I go into her dank little toilet and put on more lipstick. Lady Danger.

I'm rereading Dracula. Over and over, late at night, early morning, lying on my bed, smoking out the window in my yellow dress with the blue daisies and wine stains on it, the same maudlin Cat Power song playing over and over. Jonathan Harker uses a diary to try to keep his mind in order. I write things down, but I can't read my handwriting the next morning. There's a scrap in my make-up bag in shouting capitals NO ONE IS GOING TO RESCUE YOU. No one rescued Jonathan Harker. He came down that wall himself, hanging on by his fingernails, nearly lost his mind doing it. I walked over the bridge by the motorway in my yellow shoes, into an AA meeting. It looked like a club I wanted nothing to do with. But they do not go out alone, Mina and Van Helsing, Arthur, Quincy, Dr Seward and Jonathan Harker. The Crew of Light. They band together, bare their shameful secrets (those sexy vampire ladies in the castle, Jonathan!) It is only by helping and receiving help in return from one another that they are able to defeat the monster. The thing that wants to eat them up, destroy them. John the Baptist is on my team now. And the sleeping dreads guy, if he wants to be. And the woman sitting opposite, with the hiking boots, who brought her own muesli.

* * *

The archaeologist meets me off the train. He's younger than I thought but his hair is prematurely receding. We drive through the town, vague shapes loom in the rain. He is friendly and chatty, used to questions now the site's achieved notoriety. I still feel guilty. He doesn't ask what kind of article it's going to be. I'm relieved, I haven't thought of anything. We pull up at an overgrown boreen – I'd never have found this place – walk along a path and then step off it into the long grass of the field. My city shoes are soaked through in seconds. It isn't much to look at – sodden, green, dotted with cow pats and tiny hillocks. This ground holds hundreds, if not thousands, of dead people, two of whom interest me especially.

"They were here." He walks me over to a low tangle of brambles. "One was on his back, facing the sky, the other had his head turned – the stone in his mouth had been jammed in so hard, his jaw was dislocated." Deviant burials is the technical term. I'd been careful in my email not to mention vampires. "Both of them were bound hand and foot. We don't know if they went in the ground at the same time. One was a lot older than the other." No, it wasn't possible to see the skeletons at the university. I have a feeling he's used to answering that one. I walk where he leads, look where he points obediently, playing at being an interested reporter. The field is open to the river on one side, "a sort of medieval motorway", it would have been used to ferry goods and people from the south and a connection to the bigger waterway of the Shannon. It is a strategic place to put a church – anyone standing here would have a clear view of horsemen streaming down the hills that surround us. This was O'Connor country, part of their stronghold in Connaught a long time before the churches. The big rock a few yards away from the deviants was possibly a place where leaders were invested, crowned, whatever they did with them. Maybe a place where they made sacrifices too, he says, further back. I don't ask who 'they' were. His answer would be archaeologically accurate; I prefer figments of my imagination.

He takes me to the top corner of the field. Under dripping whitethorns, I feel a raised outline beneath my wet feet; the foundations of the church from the 13th century. It would have served the township, it's mentioned in various annals. I take photos of grass, pretending they're necessary. I feel like such an absolute fraud getting this tour, he came all the way to the train to get me. In that corner over there – he points – we found many infant skeletons. It wouldn't have been unusual for the ones who died unbaptised to be buried together. After they were dug up, the farmer who owns this field arranged a blessing. I have a sudden flashback – my aunt taking me out to the coast one night, after she moved back to Kerry. We stood on a stone wall and she pointed at a rocky patch in front of the shoreline. That was where they put the newborns she said, the ones in purgatory. That sort of graveyard has a special name in Irish she said, but her Gaelic accent was terrible, and I forget it.

We walk along the perimeter of the church, me trying to ask intelligent questions and not step on any babies. How many different churches on the site, from how many different centuries? Did they date the bodies? How many were there? Well, it's certainly a lot busier than we thought initially, he laughs, waving his hand over, for all I know, thousands of skeletons. Occasionally he says things that bring me out in goose pimples. One of the ones with the rock in his mouth was very tall, abnormally so, for that time in history. The O'Connor connection. Connor. Conn-er. I'd thought I was so clever calling him that. My trickster. I don't know why I don't just say I'm researching a novel – it's a thing people do, it's perfectly legitimate. I don't think he'd be out here for that, I don't think he'd think it the best use of his time, providing me with a backstory for a vampire. But what a perfect spot for the birth of a revenant. A dreeping field in an obscure corner of Connaught, an open grave next to a big black rock overlooking a sullen brown river.

On the train home, I turn the river silver. I tint the edges of the rock blood red in the setting sun. They push him against it, hands and feet bound, chest open to meet the spear. I write it all out long-hand, half-eaten Twix and a green paper cup of tea on the table in front of me. The seats smell of wet hair, the windows are steaming. "I went to the place where they killed you." It's the heroine talking, Hanna, named for my grandmother who carried gin in her handbag and looks like a bag of bones with eyes in photographs. She used to let me stay up all night and gave me lemonade and Maltesers. Poor Hanna, obsessed with the vampire who maimed her. I went all the way up to a wet field in Roscommon to find the start of a story and then lost the nerve to finish it. Stones in mouths beneath the ground, babies under the dirt alongside them. Mammy's second one nearly killed her. He's down in Blackrock somewhere, a pauper's grave she called it. The day we went for my communion shoes she told me about him and his sister, her other, not-us children. I sat opposite her in The Left Bank bar, a glass of red lemonade and the shoe box on the table in front of me. The shoes were Clarks, cut-out flower designs in the toes, a little golden key in the heel of the left one. "We'll think of them now, girl," raising her glass of Carling.

"All that pauper's grave shit was completely unnecessary." My aunt in Jury's years later, drunk, sounding very American. "I'd have paid for a grave, no big deal, I was working. But it was always the same with her. She did it her own way. Terrible thing, I'm not saying it wasn't. But eighteen months later wasn't she married with you?"

* * *

On the train we drink tea from green cardboard cups and eat muesli bars. I do anyway, I'm breastfeeding. When we rang my mother from the hospital, her scream was high and thin, like someone had left the world, instead of coming into it. "Is she OK? Is she OK?" I laughed and laughed, wasted on fentanyl. "Of course she is. She's perfect." Filling out the departure cards, there was a big fat toad of fear in my belly. I held her the whole way to Dubai, terrified she'd scream the plane down. But she just slept and fed; tiny fingernails scrabbling on my chest, the steady insistent pull on the nipple. 17 hours later, I was like one of those desiccated Pharaohs dug up by Victorian Englishmen.

Mallow. They will be waiting. They are too early for everything. A familiar clench of frustration. "You know what today is?" He must have noticed the change in my expression. Lately my cheeks have hollowed; when I'm annoyed I look 300. "Today is the day you took your daughter to meet your parents." It's too much, placing me in the middle of a lineage. They're not ready for it, I'm not either. "Mother" is confusing too, I think of having one, not being one. For a second, I want to look fabulous getting off the train, be effortlessly perfect with her. I get hold of myself. I have carried her all the way here from New Zealand. If that is not enough, they can fuck off. It's not about me anymore anyway; I'm the support act now. I will be for the rest of my life. It's like loosening a collar, I feel myself relaxing, receding. Something new has been added. I should have done this years ago, I can't believe it's this easy.

They're waiting at the barrier. They're all crying. My mother is holding half a dozen helium balloons. They look like they're going to lift her into the air and out over the open roof of the station. My sister is covering her mouth with her hand and sobbing. Her nails are very long, with square white tips, like a porn star. As we get closer she cries harder. My mother is trying to cheer, but it comes out as wailing. Her hair is the same colour purple as the biggest balloon, which says EVE ALEXANDRA HERO in swirly gold writing. Her ski jacket matches her lipstick: Rimmel Heather Shimmer. Sudden flashback to her redoing it in The Chimes, while the taxi driver waited outside, beeping. My dad says very little, shakes John's hand, smiles at everyone, and nobody in particular. They try to take our bags, but they're disoriented, cack-handed, we're all tangled up in suitcases and the balloon ribbons. My mother is on top of me, clawing at the sling. "Let me bless her. Let me bless her." My coat is soaked. She is shaking around a small plastic bottle in the shape of a mountain grotto with a statue of the Virgin Mary on it. The baby sleeps, oblivious. "This is Eve …" I pull down the front of the pack, trying not to sound too smug or too proud, fail completely. "God bless her. God bless her" – my mother kisses the air a few inches above Eve's head, throwing more water. A few drops land in the cradle cap on the open bit of her skull, where the brain pulses when I'm feeding her. "Stop that will you, she's blessed now, put that away for fuck sake!" She steps back, impressed by the aggression. The following year, when she is dying and I am back in New Zealand, I'll look at the photographs; standing on her own in front of the departure board, balloons about to bear her off, a tiny purple mascot, pink-haired, ("Karolina from the B&B showed me how to do it, two packets of dye, five euros from the Polish supermarket") eye teeth bared in a furious determination to celebrate, whether or not anyone wants it. Another one, me beside her, hefty post-birth, poleaxed from jet lag, the baby in a sling, presented for the camera, not hidden, not taken away like hers was. 40 years between those two children, maybe longer. I don't know how old she is now, Mammy's daughter. She got the same train as I did, down from Dublin. She came back alone, no sleeping weight strapped to the front of her. Her mother told people she was up there for kidney stones.

In the car later I put their fingers alongside each other, my mother and my daughter. I look more like my father's side, but you can't tell my hands and Mammy's apart in a photo. The baby's are the same, long, and wrinkled and elegant. "'Piano fingers' Han called it," I could hear Mammy whispering to Eve about my grandmother. I looked back at them through the driver's mirror, Mammy's flamingo head leaning into the car seat, Eve's jack o'lantern grin back up at her.

"We're going to have the best time, you and me girl."

Inner Core

Miki Lentin

I never admitted it to my wife Anne-Marie, but I really wanted the boy with the toothy grin to pull the trigger, and shoot the French woman who was standing a few steps from us. I had nothing against her, I didn't want her to die. But at that moment, I wanted everything to pause, so I could hear the crack of a gun blast, smell the gunpowder, and see if I could follow the bullet spinning through the air. I even considered what it would be like to lick the spattered blood from my face, wipe Anne-Marie's jacket down, and go for dinner on the Asian side of Istanbul, just as we'd planned.

Lying awake back home in Dublin a few months later, I pondered this as images of that evening flickered in my mind like a strobe light. Dizzy, my breath shallow, the small of my back tight, I fumbled in the dark for my watch, just like I did every night, knocking my hand into a book and a glass of water. It wasn't there, of course it wasn't.

I was sure that my watch had been stolen from our hotel room in Istanbul, on the last day of a city break Anne-Marie and me had taken. I knew that I'd wound the silver winder, which kept the mechanism faintly ticking just before I'd gone to bed. I knew that I'd placed it by the side of my bed, the strap doubled over, so I could see the watch face. I knew that I'd reached for it first thing in the morning, but for some reason hadn't put it on. I knew after breakfast that it was gone.

"Anne-Marie?" I'd yelled, my heart palpitating with panic.

"What?" she'd shouted from the shower.

"My watch, have you seen it?"

"Didn't you leave it by the bed?"

I spent what seemed like hours tossing clothes, opening cupboard doors, rummaging in bags, chucking sofa cushions, and retracing my steps around the hotel. While I searched, I kept touching my wrist, as if I could still feel the silver strap pinching the hairs on my arm.

It had been my father's Tissot, the watch my mother had placed on my wrist the day after he'd died. The hotel manager shrugged when I suggested that it may have been stolen, I didn't want to spoil Anne-Marie's birthday trip, and at some stage she held me tight and told me to stop, "just bloody stop looking." Reluctantly, I called the search off. "It's only a watch, these things are replaceable," I'd said, trying to convince myself.

Eyes wide open in Dublin, my spine pinching the nerves in my back like a bulldog clip, I looked at the LED alarm clock that Anne-Marie had bought me. It lit my pillow. Four am. She'd told me that it softened the light in the room, and was scientifically proven to assist sleep. I'd thanked her as I knelt down to plug it in, unable to bend my stiff spine, but I hated the digital display, and couldn't fathom why it also needed to show the room temperature.

I had woken at the same time every night for the past three or four months, but had lost track of just how long it had been. My head, like an alarm clock, was set on repeat. Automatically it switched on a light in my mind, dropped the stylus of a record player onto a vinyl disc and started to play *'breathe, breathe in the air …'*, that song by Pink Floyd, and filled my ears with the ticking of the kitchen clock. I put my lack of sleep down to age, nearing my fifties, and theorised that even though I might never get used to it, the older I got the less sleep I needed.

A few weeks before over curry and pints of lager, my friends all bemoaned their sleeplessness, citing anxious children, work worries and marriage difficulties, as they snapped poppadums and drenched them in chutney. I listened in, encouraged that I wasn't the only one not sleeping. I nodded in agreement, and took long gulps of beer. "Sure I read the other day that a pint every night actually helps you sleep," I said. We laughed, clinked glasses, and slapped each other on the back. I went home tipsy and happy, believing my lack of sleep was a phase. It would pass.

When Anne-Marie asked if I was tired, I'd shrug. Tired was not a word I used anymore. Resigned maybe. Pissed off perhaps. Scared, a little. I let my beard grow heavy, hoping it would mask my puffy eyes that squinted permanently. My left eyelid often twitched uncontrollably, and horseshoes circled my sockets like burn marks.

Some sleep guru called Yoram Schultz, who featured on a sleep masterclass app I'd bought, confidently informed me in a Californian drawl that a human can function fine on five or even four hours sleep a night. It was all in the "quality of the sleep you get," Yoram would say, "not the quantity." Every class would end with a mantra, "fill your whole being with breath, stay afloat, come home," and my favourite, "ride the mysterious sea," as if I had any idea what that meant.

Needing eight hours of shuteye was a myth, I was informed, perpetuated by marketing people who didn't understand the deep physiological science behind sleep. Everything was scientific these days. Maybe I just didn't understand the science. That was the problem. I had to become better informed. I read a bestseller about sleep that warned of early dementia if I didn't go to bed early, that I'd lose weight if I slept properly, and that more sleep would improve my looks. I listened to podcasts and read articles, did a mindfulness course, and an hour of hot yoga looking at some fella's sweaty arse bent over in front of me every Wednesday morning. But I kept putting the milk in the larder, had to strain my eyes wide when I drove to the supermarket, and couldn't concentrate when I read, often falling asleep at my desk at work. And then there was the time I drove into the back of another car. "What the fuck! Like what the actual fuck!" the other driver screamed through the window as I nervously got out of the car to inspect the damage. "I'm really sorry, is, everyone ok?" I asked, even though I knew full well that there was barely anything wrong with her car, I was only going three miles an hour, and why was she being so obnoxious, and sure these things happen all the time, and I'd only closed my eyes for a split second before impact, so there was no way she could blame me for being negligent, and couldn't she just leave me alone and not make a fuss on the main road for God's sake, it was only a scratch.

I'd cower in a corner of the train every day on my way to work, my body battered with exhaustion. Fuelled on coffee, I was bombarded with adverts selling the ultimate spring-loaded mattress with added this and that membrane which improved the airflow in bed, foam pillows that memorised the shape of my head, silk stitched eye masks and silicone ear plugs that blocked out the world. Every night I put on the eye mask and ear plugs that came free with my new mattress topper. "Now then," I'd look at them eagerly before listening to an eleven o'clock sleep story on the app, "please help me sleep tonight." But when I wore them, I felt as if I was floating awake underwater, my heartbeat the only audible sound reverberating inside my hollow body.

It was jeans and t-shirt weather in Istanbul when Anne-Marie and I had visited, even though it was November. Wearing my cowboy hat and sunglasses, I held Anne-Marie's hand as we roamed the antique shops and cafes of Kadiköy, drank muddy Turkish coffee, smoked like teenagers, drank a bit too much, and listened to schmaltzy jazz in a bar into the small hours. For those few days a lightness swept over me, like I was experiencing it for the first time.

The afternoon before we left for our last supper, we visited the Museum of Innocence, which was based on a book with the same name by the author Orhan Pamuk. I found the heaviness of historic museums tiring. I didn't always know where to start, and couldn't resist my childhood tendency to just look at the biggest and oldest pieces. The Museum of Innocence was different; four floors in a narrow house packed with objects all touched at one time by Fusun, a woman the narrator Kemal was obsessed with.

1,593 lipstick stained cigarette butts nailed to a board, smoked by Fusun and collected by Kemal, faded family photos in plastic albums, birth and death certificates written in curly handwriting, chipped wine glasses, the nibbled lids of pens, tarnished ornate silver cutlery, airmail letters with yellowing stamps, souvenir fridge magnets, empty bottles of perfume, crystal ashtrays, receipts stapled to accountancy booklets, floral dresses and shirts on hangers, an airgun, a set of rusty kitchen knives. Fusun's whole life, everything she had ever touched in one house.

The soothing voice of the narrator on the audio guide told stories of Kemal's daily visits to Fusun's house. I liked the way every item had a place, a role in the story. Nothing was wasted. I could press pause on the audio guide, and stop inside Kemal's head at any moment in his life and his relationship with Fusun, and know what was going on. Each scene was documented in detail, with a beginning, middle and end. I wished I could pause and look into my own life like this. Chop it up, divide it, day by day, hour by hour, second by second, unblended.

Along the fourth-floor banister of the museum staircase, from where I could look down into the atrium, was a display unit with dozens of watches all collected by Fusun. Wrist watches, pocket watches, flip watches, alarm clocks. Some worked, some didn't. I spotted a silver watch that looked like my father's. It had those Roman numerals that glowed in the dark, which even at my age I thought was cool. My eyes looked up to the corners of the gallery to see if the security cameras were on me. I was almost sick with desire for the watch. I placed my elbows firmly on the glass of the cabinet hoping it might crack. An empty retch pulled inside my guts. Maybe I could grab the watch. Maybe I could clip it onto my wrist. Maybe I could walk out without anyone noticing. I licked my lips in anticipation. Why, I thought, if Kemal needed to obsessively collect Fusun's belongings, couldn't I also take something that wasn't mine?

"Come on, let's go for dinner," Anne-Marie said, startling me as she walked up alongside.

"One minute," I said, and just before I left, I knelt down, put my ear to the glass, and concentrated on listening to the watch faintly ticking in the background.

I'd planned that we should visit the Asian side for our last dinner in Istanbul. We ran onto the passenger boat from the European port of Beyoğlu just as the barriers went up, sat on the side deck, shared a cigarette, and watched as a blue darkness enveloped the Bosphorus bay, silhouetting the minarets. The boat gurgled white frothy foam from its rear. I thought that it looked like an inviting bubble bath. The sea was now oily black and container ships and tankers blocked the view north to the Black Sea, and south to the Sea of Marmara. I liked the word Marmara. I liked trying to roll the r's. It sounded faraway and exotic.

We'd run out of mobile phone data and stood by the ticket machines in Kadiköy harbour on the Asian side, trying to connect to wifi so we could find somewhere to eat. Passenger boats came and went, moorings and gangways thrashed on piers, and people gathered and dispersed in the square around us. Anne-Marie said she was cold, so I slung my jacket over her shoulders. I fidgeted in the pockets of my jeans. It was getting late. As we scrolled through our mobile phones, out of the corner of my eye, I saw a teenage boy approach a couple who were standing in front of the ticket machines for the boats. The boy was wearing tracksuit bottoms and a black hoodie with sleeves that had been ripped off at the elbow. He had a goofy smile on his face, was nibbling his fingernails, and seemed to be bouncing on his feet.

Four thirty am in Dublin. My bloated bladder ached. The toilet was en-suite, and even though I never woke Anne-Marie, I didn't want to move. She slept like the dead. Her sleep ebbed and flowed like a calm river. Flicks of her arm after she dropped off, then a bit of chatting away to herself, the odd grunt and heavy breathing and then, absolutely nothing. I felt calm looking at her while she slept, a picture of stillness, beauty, sculpture-like. I was desperate though, and sat on the toilet, my belly hanging over my waist, my spine throbbing with pain, and peed in the dark.

I turned onto my side and tried to hold my stomach in so it didn't flop onto the mattress. Aiden, my physiotherapist, had told me to clench my core. An MRI scan had shown that I had a bulging disc in my spine. My hip flexors screamed, the small of my back stretched, like a tight-fitting jumper. Some days I hobbled straight-legged around the house, my legs with a mind of their own, holding onto the sink as I brushed my teeth, and kneeling on the floor to stack the dishwasher.

"Hold it now Jerry. Holding it will protect your core, but Jesus, don't forget to breathe now," Aiden laughed. "You can't do much if you don't breathe." I nodded as I forcefully exhaled.

"Protect your inner core," Aiden repeated, opening his mouth wide as he spoke, so I could see his uvula swinging like a jelly bean at the back of his throat.

Aiden instructed how I should hold my pelvic floor muscle, "ten percent now, and don't hold your breath," so that my stomach didn't bulge. "Just a little now, concentrate now, slow down those exercises, it's all in the quality, not the quantity, that's what I want to see."

As Aiden used his pointy fingers to rub some oily muck into the small of my back, he gave me a running commentary of his drive to the gym in his new BMW. I didn't care. "Now remember, those deep inner connected muscles hold everything together," Aiden said.

I lay face down wincing through the hole in the ripped paper sheet on the massage table. As I counted the tiles on the floor, the voices of the couple who stood next to Anne-Marie and me in Istanbul filled my head. They'd been arguing in French about which boat to get. She was striking and tall, long-legged and wearing high heels. Her hair waved onto her face in the breeze, and she was wearing what looked like a man's work shirt with a pink collar. Her companion was shorter than her. His white creased trousers stood out in the dark light and I noticed an ivory tooth pendant hanging from his neck.

It was five am in Dublin. My mouth was parched, my lips dry. I knew that if I wasn't asleep by five thirty, my chances of sleeping that night were low and even if I did, I'd wake suddenly again at seven and feel like a bomb had detonated in my head.

I bent my knees on my side of the bed and dropped my hips to one side, then the other, as Aiden had taught me. Lying still, my sore body now didn't want to move, as if the memory foam mattress topper remembered that I couldn't sleep. The brittle vertebrae of my spine rubbed together like stones, and my sciatic nerve shot spasms into my thighs and buttocks. Sometimes I visualised a scalpel slicing my flesh, and a doctor pouring liquid painkiller into my body to numb the pain.

I lifted my buttocks into a bridge position. Anne-Marie turned to face me. Making her out in the dark, I looked at her closely, my arse in the air, wondering if she was looking at me. Her eyes were closed, the curls of her hair resting playfully on her forehead. Trying to loosen the tension in my back, I tucked my pelvis forward and back, holding my inner core as I worked.

"Can't you sleep hon?" Anne-Marie asked sleepily.

"What?" Was I dreaming? "I thought you were asleep," I whispered.

"I am," she said, and reached out her hand to my body. It was warm, like a bowl heated by soup. She rested it on my shoulder for a few moments and turned over, taking the duvet with her.

´Breathe, breathe in the air …´ that bloody song. I was breathing, but not deeply. I didn't breathe deeply anymore. Breathe, I told myself, breathe, concentrate on your breath, just like Elaine, the mindfulness teacher with the twinkly braces on her teeth had taught me. "Be gentle with yourself," she said. "Quality of the breath now Jerry, quality, not quantity. Slow down. Inhale Jer." I hated being called Jer. "One, two, three, pause," she enunciated each word exactingly. "Hold it there Jer. Exhale, three, two, one. Don't force it," her smile lingering on me.

I practised my new breathing exercises every morning on my way to work, sometimes when I got home, when I went to the toilet, at my desk at work, often in the car and when I was watching television next to Anne-Marie on the sofa. But my breath was syrupy and thick, and even when I forcefully inhaled, it would get stuck half-way down my lungs, as if my windpipe was blocked.

I wriggled and twisted, turned over my pillows and threw away my side of the duvet. I turned my head to face the LED alarm clock. Five thirty am. I stared for what seemed like minutes at the circular lampshade that hung from the ceiling, until I thought I was floating from the ceiling looking at myself.

Thinking some fresh air would help I got out of bed, opened the sliding doors to the garden, and let my feet freeze on the paving stones. Lying down, the cold stone numbed my back as a few drops of rain dribbled down my bare chest and dotted my boxer shorts. I looked up at the red sky, but all I could see were images of the teenage boy in Istanbul nonchalantly remove the gun from the pocket of his hoodie. The boy slowly straightened his right arm, held the gun at shoulder height and placed his left arm onto his right shoulder. Wrapping his forefinger around the trigger, his thumb rested lightly on the hammer as he bent his head slightly to the right so that he was now looking down the length of his arm, the barrel pointed directly towards the head of the woman.

A wailing siren nearby broke the silence in the garden. Empty and bereft I looked at the skeletons of dead plants in pots spread around the patio, broken and battered from the winter chill. I wanted to cry, but as I tried, my head blisteringly cold, the rain got heavier, so I laboured up, and returned to the soothing warmth of lying next to Anne-Marie's body.

I closed my eyes. My head danced and spun around my bedroom. Could I smell roasted chestnuts from the Istanbul seafront? Tiny flashbulbs exploded in my mind. I felt as if my body was being knocked by people pushing past Anne-Marie and me to get to the ticket machines. Yoram appeared in a science lab coat bouncing on my bed singing *'breathe, breathe in the air …'* The boy with the gun came into focus. "Ride the mysterious sea," Yoram read to me from an over-sized science manual. Aiden pushed Yoram out of the way. The boy moved stealthily closer to the French woman. "Protect your inner core Jer, quality, not quantity … " Aiden cackled and shrieked. The boy didn't flinch, a broad grin across his face. The ticking of the kitchen clock got louder. The boy's arm was steady and strong. I covered my ears. The boy's legs shuffled sideways closer to the woman. I knelt next to the watch display in the museum. Nails dug into my back. The boy cocked his gun, just as the watches from the display cabinet in the Museum of Innocence all started to tick out of time in different tones to the beat of the song that never ended. "Go on," I muttered, willing the boy on, as if he was in my bedroom, "go on."

I opened my eyes. I dared not look at the alarm clock. I dared not look at the temperature of the room. I dared not look at Anne-Marie.

"Jesus, Jerry!" It was Anne-Marie who screamed first. The boy now stood directly in front of the couple.

"Anne-Marie, I can't sleep," I said, gripping the duvet to my chin.

"What is it?"

"I know love, I hear you getting up every night."

"That fella, there, he's got a fucking gun!"

"Sorry, I don't mean to wake you."

"Don't, please!" the French woman shouted.

"You don't, not every night. Are you still finding it hard to sleep?"

"Please, put it down, it's no joke, OK?"

"I've tried everything."

"Help!"

"Can I do anything to help Jerry?"

"Please. Please. Don't."

"I don't know what to do anymore Anne-Marie."

"Do you want money? Here, I'll give you my watch, please …"

"Are you still thinking about your father's watch?"

The Road to Salamanca

John Martin Johnson

Downstairs, the phone was ringing.

Who do I know rings at 7 a.m.? Nobody. I'm a screenwriter. People I know don't ring at 7 a.m. They don't know 7 a.m. even *exists*.

It was January 10th 2008 and I was brimming with optimism. The previous decade had been the happiest and most successful of my life; I was now an in-demand writer of television drama, I'd had ten great years of marriage to my long time partner, and we'd moved into a pretty, detached stone cottage in the Yorkshire Dales. Now as my sixtieth birthday approached, I was sure things could only get better.

Judi handed me the phone, bewildered: "It's Pam."

Pam? I don't know any Pam. Pam *who? Pam ...* Christ. *That* Pam. *Pam*. My first wife, who I hadn't seen since. Since I walked out on her. For someone else. Nineteen seventy-eight? Never seen her since, apart from that one time at my mother's eightieth.

"Hello?"

"Your mother's had a fall. In the garden."

How I got there I'm not sure, into that drab hospital corridor. There was no information. There was machine coffee in brown plastic cups with cream insides. There was a whip-round for change. There weren't enough chairs. Someone had to stand. There was confusion. Disbelief.

And there was my dad, sitting quietly, eighty-seven years old, still tall, trim and poised, dressed in a shirt and pullover, his old RAF scarf knotted round his neck and a green winter jacket with plentiful zips and press studs which he always kept fastened. His disreputable trilby sat at a sporting angle.

"What happened?" I asked him.

"How the hell should I know?" he snapped. His gaze slowly uncoupled from mine and slid back to the floor beyond his feet.

Eventually a door off the corridor opened and we were ushered inside. I had no idea what I should say to my mother after she had just tried to kill herself. And me a writer. She always told people; *Johnny writes for tv.* I made her proud then.

Dad stood at the foot of the bed asking, "What are you doing in bed?" Over and over, "What the hell are you *doing*?" Mum hid her head from his bewildered, hopeless interrogation. My safe and familiar world had cracked open, its insides spilling out at my feet.

* * *

"I am shrinking," I said, my words lightly scrambled by red wine. "The nurse told me, 'Five-five and a half', she said. I told her I'd always thought of myself as five-six actually. She said, 'Well you're sixty-five. People shrink. See you in six months'."

If there's anything left of me.

This was one night in late March, six years after my mother's suicide attempt. Judi and I were walking back to our hotel after a party with friends where the conversation had turned to grandchildren, ailments and pensions, and back again. And again. I have no grandchildren, no ailments worth mentioning and have made no particular provision for my retirement. This is because writers don't retire; they die. Writers don't need a pension, just a funeral plan.

"If all my future conversation is to be about grandchildren, ailments and pensions, I will have to kill myself," I told Judi, "instead of which, I am going to learn to ride a motorbike. A big one!" I added for extra emphasis.

This had been bubbling under. Five years earlier I'd ridden pillion behind my stepson, Oliver, on a big, red Honda through Richmond Park. It was thrilling, terrifying. It was like low flying, not aircraft-low but low like a hawk, predatory, skimming the ground. I was hooked. The idea when previously mooted had met with stony silence. This time, after a long delay, Judi said:

"If you must, you must."

I never underestimate how much courage that must have taken.

* * *

I turned onto the steep driveway and set the handbrake. Dad carried on foraging in the glove box for what urgent purpose he had long since forgotten. Six hours earlier his wife of sixty years had lain broken, sobbing and muttering, on the flagstones in front of us. He'd forgotten that too.

In the dead January air I scanned the familiar view across field and dale to the distant moorland. This panorama was my dad's great love, and the badge of his proudest achievement; that he had taken his family out of the cramped inner-city, roadside terrace house, a couple of streets from where he and my mother were both born, and had brought us to this. I was thirteen then; I thought it was paradise.

Inside, Mum's absence was palpable; a thick, prickling silence, a dense cloud of loss which settled in every corner and lay there like dust. Dad, still zipped and buttoned against the cold, headed straight for his favourite armchair in the window overlooking the valley.

Upstairs to my sister's teenage bedroom, all tidy these days, the bed neatly made, the small, hardwood chair tucked up to the dressing table where she put on her make-up for her first date. But now the chair was over by the window. Her mother, our mother, barefoot in her nightdress, had climbed onto it, then onto the narrow wooden ledge. She had opened the window, and was gone.

Downstairs I set a mug of coffee at my dad's elbow and handed him a plate with a couple of biscuits, for which he thanked me fulsomely. He was wrestling with his mind, trying to drag something forward out of the darkness. Finally he turned to me, politely requesting clarification, as from a stranger:

"Who are you?"

"Johnny, your son."

"Oh, *yes*."

He turned his attention back to the view.

* * *

"This will sound ridiculous, but I'm sixty-five years old, and I want to learn to ride a motorbike." I had needed a few days following the Party of the Pensions to screw up my courage.

"That's not ridiculous at all! Come down and have a go, see if you like it!"

Tim, a professional Welshman and incurable enthusiast, had retired from the Army and set up a motorbike training school on Army property a half hour drive from my home. There were two guards on duty when I arrived. I explained my business, they raised the barrier and I drove in. Then I saw the machines, crouching there, lined up on the tarmac like bare metal hunting dogs. They turned my mouth to dust, they made my heart pound.

Safety-briefed and kitted out with three other hopefuls, I climbed aboard my designated machine, cleared the sidestand as instructed and pressed the starter. The engine gipped and whined, shook with annoyance, then fired. The helmet was crushing my ears, blocking all sound but the aggressive bark of the engine and my own breathing. I squinted through the visor, a prisoner in a letterbox set around by alien smells and sounds and unknown perils, straddling a tank of highly flammable liquid bolted to a metal box packed with exploding gases.

"Get off, walk away, do not be so pathetic. Look at these people, you are three times their age. You look ridiculous, you feel ridiculous, you will fall off and break something! Go home, you silly old fool, make a coffee, read a book ..."

* * *

Dad ate supper that first night in silence, apart from the occasional "This is lovely!" or "Have you made this?" I said no, it was Judi.

Judi had driven down after work, having called in home to pick up food for supper for the three of us, overnight things for us both and clothes to last me a few days. Moments later:

"Have you made this?"

"No, it was Judi."

"Who?"

After supper, with Dad watching television, Judi and I weighed our options. We would have to handle this. My sister lived two hours away and had a full time university teaching job. I lived one hour away, and was a freelance writer. For all we knew, Mum could recover enough one day to come home. In the meantime, I would move in with Dad, and drive him into Leeds every day for visiting. The three of us would share weekends between our house in Wensleydale and the house on the hill. That was going to be our life for as long as my mother was alive.

I was privately dreading that she might recover.

That night I lay awake in the dark in my sister's old room, listening to night noises: a door opening, a drawer closing, the rattle of cutlery, footsteps moving restlessly from room to room. Like random clips from a sound effects library they made no sense.

Suddenly the bedroom door burst open and there my father stood, silhouetted in the doorway, wearing the battered trilby, the green waterproof jacket and his RAF scarf. Underneath he had on his pyjamas and wore slippers on his bare feet. He clutched his walking stick at a jaunty angle, like Fred Astaire.

"What the hell are you doing?" he snapped.

"We're sleeping, Dad. It's the middle of the night."

"Don't be ridiculous. I'm off."

"Off where?"

"Where do you think?" he sneered at my ignorance of his plans.

When a man dresses in a trilby and slippers, there's no telling what he will do next. I was sharing a house with a complete stranger. There was no history between us any more, only this grotesque, crackpot present.

* * *

I didn't go home to make a coffee, or to read a book. Instead, I opened the throttle and eased out the clutch and the bike set off across the tarmac, with me on its back, feet groping for the footpegs, my body, legs and arms rigid with fear. But, finally, I was riding a motorbike. I was terrified, excited too; even fifteen miles an hour feels fast, the tarmac fairly whizzes by beneath your feet. But I was *riding a motor bike*, and although I was not exactly flying like a hawk I hoped that somehow, some day, I might be able to do just that.

* * *

I walked Dad in to the Day Care Centre and found the person I'd spoken to on the phone, Rose, one of the volunteers who would look after Dad for an hour and give me my first break in the long days since I moved in. Dad turned on all the old charm, and waved me away imperiously.

I found a quiet table in a local cafe, ordered coffee and opened my laptop. My agent would have to know what had happened. I made the call.

I was desperate to get working again, to get writing; to get paid, yes, of course, but more for the kudos – the validation which comes from seeing a hundred people on a film set, each with a copy of your script under their arm.

But writing prime-time involves brutal deadlines and twenty-four-seven commitment. At the time an hour's drama cost three quarters of a million pounds to make, so you can't involve a writer if there's a chance they won't deliver. There was now a very strong chance I wouldn't and I knew it, we both did. For now, my writing career was done.

I'd just finished that call when my phone rang. I hurried back to the Day Care Centre.

"He's been ever so rude," said Rose. "He's made one lady cry."

"He's got Alzheimer's," I reminded her.

"I have not," Dad chimed in. "Are we going?"

We walked back to the car. He was tetchy.

"Where the hell have you been?"

"I was hoping to get some work done."

"What about my work? Huh? What about me?"

"Dad, you've been retired twenty years."

"Don't be ridiculous."

So ended the first of many failed attempts to find an hour's peace among the madness.

* * *

To get a big bike licence, you must now take your test on one, and I now owned a 600cc Yamaha. I failed my first road test with a mistake on the indicators. On the second attempt, I got the indicators right, but failed on a slight in-lane wobble. After my third test, I told Tim, "That was a perfect ride, I'll never get it that good again. So how could I stall a bike going downhill?" Fail, fail, fail again.

In the six months since the Party of the Pensions I'd parted with over ten thousand pounds on buying a bike, on safety equipment and many hours of training, yet I was still not considered fit to be on the road. How could I fail a test that thousands of teenagers sail through every year? *Three times?* I was desolate.

* * *

"Your Mum's ready to come home," trilled one of her care team, "We're discharging her today."

"You can't do that. I can't look after them both."

"We need the bed, and she's well enough to go home."

"Well, I can't take her, she's determined to kill herself, look!"

I had kept a small rectangle of white card which Mum had left behind, on which she had carved her final confession of self-loathing. It was my trump card and I played it now. Her doctors caved and my mother was detained under Section Two of the Mental Health Act of 1983.

Our daily visits now moved to the Mental Health Unit, a former maternity hospital where, sixty years before and in the cruellest of ironies, Mum had given birth to her first child, my sister. It was a dispiriting place now. Day and night came the anguished cries of the lost and mentally unwired, the terminally confused.

The full circle she had travelled within this building, from optimism and joy to the end of all optimism and joy, broke my heart. The leading role I had played in condemning her to this miserable ending crushed me utterly.

Shortly afterwards, on a May afternoon, Dad was sitting in his favourite armchair, a cup of tea at his elbow, watching the shadows of small white clouds chase across the distant moors. Closer by, the trees and meadows were painted in the fresh greens of a perfect early summer's day in Wharfedale. A couple of ponies, whose names he had once known, grazed contentedly in the field opposite.

"Ready for off?" I said.

"Where?"

"I told you. We've got a new place for you. Just till Mum comes home."

"Nonsense."

"You like it. You said so."

Slowly he grasped the significance of our visits to the bright new building with the pretty garden, and of the people in blue tunics who made such a fuss of him. I was dragging him out of the world he loved, and he would never be back. He suddenly knew it, and fought like an animal to stop it happening. We were both exhausted when I finally led him, in silence, and helped him into the car. My once gentle and loving father, my childhood hero, my dad turned to me, choosing his words carefully.

"You're a ... you're a *cunt*," he said.

We drove away from our house on the hill, Dad for the very last time.

By October, he was dead. They both were.

Neither bereavement lacked a single moment on which to focus my grief. My mother had died that night in early January; the following months were spent waiting for her death to become official. As for my dad, the death of *him* predated his death on paper by many months also. Loss wasn't, in either case, an event; it was a process, and a slow and painful one at that. But once the funerals were over and the loose ends of their lives together ravelled up, I thought I was home clear. That chapter of my life was over. I was back.

I turned to my ideas stash; every writer has one, because few people realise just how many frogs a writer has to kiss before one turns into Prince Charming. I needed one of them to turn into a Prince, right now.

Instead, every one of them turned to dust. Day after day, the characters I created refused to come alive, they had no heart, no fight, no spark, they had no love. In the early hours I would wake with a sinking sense of foreboding. I would sit on the edge of the bed staring into a black, bottomless crater where all my plans were shown to be futile, my stories unbelievable and all my characters empty shells. Once it got light, I would have to go and face them all again. But I had to write, because writing was what I did. Writing was all I was.

If I didn't write, what was the point of me?

The night terrors grew more desperate; I sat on the rim of my abyss, unable to move, close to tears, dreading the dawn, wanting it to be over and, yes, in the blackest moments, wanting to die.

It was a year, almost to the day, after burying my parents' ashes when my inkjet printer suddenly flew across my workroom and smashed against a window. I heard somebody sobbing loudly.

It was me.

"You are suffering from Clinical Depression," said Jane, the brisk and business-like Mental Health Nurse to whom a sympathetic GP had referred me (after I'd walked into his office, told him how lucky my life was, then burst into tears).

Clinical Depression. *The Black Dog.*

Jane sent me home that first day with a blizzard of handouts and a pile of homework. Cognitive Behavioural Therapy, the road I was now on, is mainly about self-help, so I cleared my desk and began to write: 'Sleeping poorly. Churning stomach on waking. Adding weight.' That was my list of Warning Signs under the heading 'Physical'. Under 'Thoughts', I started with: 'Everyone else knows more than I do.'

That is the certainty which has dogged me all my life, through school and work and in every corner of my existence, dominant, pervasive, unquestioned:

'Everyone else knows more than I do.'

* * *

I chose a clear and sunny autumn day when Tim had no pupils. The Yamaha, which had been my chief accuser ("Do you know how much I cost? Are you ever going to pass your test and make me worth having?") looked beautiful in the afternoon sun. It was a machine which appeared to be moving even when it was still, like a big cat, frozen mid-leap, sculpted in white and black by the props team on Star Wars. It was lovely, it was mine and, whatever came next, we were going to enjoy our afternoon together.

I started to do lazy, second gear arcs, left and right, letting the bike get warm as I loosened up myself. I pushed the visor up to feel the heat of the sun, took my left hand off the bars, let my head and neck relax, my shoulders fall, my left arm hang loose. We lazed around like that for a while, a couple of friends, comfortable in each other's company, bunking off in the sun.

In my head, I went through another of Jane's hand-outs, her Personal Bill of Rights, still fresh in my mind after half a decade. 'I have the right to ask for what I want' was one of them, and to 'say no to demands I can't meet' was another. 'I have the right to change my mind', I remembered, then, finally, the one I was searching my mind for:

'I have the right to make mistakes; I do not have to be perfect.'

I stopped the bike, took off my helmet and hung it on the wing mirror. Hang on ...

I have the right to make mistakes; *I do not have to be perfect*. I felt a great weight of expectation slide from my shoulders and onto the tarmac. I pulled on my helmet, kicked the bike into gear, and roared away.

After my fourth road test, the Examiner strolled over, removing his helmet.

"Pass or fail," I told him, "I really enjoyed that."

"Yeah, me too," he said, "and take those bloody L-plates off. You can ride."

* * *

My brand new, one hundred and fifteen horse-power racing-red Ducati is purring beneath me, and rural France is spinning past my visor, rocketing away into the mirrored distance. The road is a blur beneath my feet, the air a cooling stream through the helmet vents, and this is the very best of times to be alive, and on two wheels. Flanders sweeps by in vivid colour, three dimensional, unmoderated, raw.

A kestrel rises alongside and momentarily we are skimming along together. With a jolt, I'm back in Richmond Park with Oliver on the big red Honda, when I flew like a hawk and was hooked. I glimpse the pale underside of the kestrel, then he climbs and banks, showing me his rusty top feathers before returning to his hunting and leaving me to mine.

There is no cure for depression. I live with it and do my best to control it. For as long as I succeed, I remain free of its disabling symptoms, but I will never be free of the illness itself. Everything is a coping strategy, none of it a cure.

At the heart of my own condition remains that phrase, 'everyone else knows more than I do.' It is the devil which perches on my shoulder, its voice drowning out every other opinion, too loud, too long and too damn practised to be shouted down. But now there is another sound which answers back; the roar of a motorcycle engine.

How could I imagine, when I'm on board this quarter tonne of explosive power, able to make it do my exact bidding, that everyone – that *anyone* – knows more than I do?

I hunker down, tuck in, twist the throttle, watch the rev counter climb, feel the speed and let the blistering howl of the engine flood my soul.

The Black Dog will never catch me now.

I turn into a shady square and kill the engine. A white van follows me in and stops right behind, engine revving irritably. Through my mirrors I can see the driver, a young guy in his twenties, scowling behind an explosion of red hair and beard, making it noisily clear that he *always* parks his van in this square, at this hour, and in the very spot now occupied by some old guy on a flash bike. And, know what? Screw him. Two thousand miles since home, I've earned this moment. I set the kickstand, pull off my helmet and sit in the silence, listening to the familiar tick-tock of hot metal cooling after a long day on the road.

Salamanca was always going to be journey's end; home of Spain's first university, a city of wide open squares and sunlit avenues, of shady cafés and endless tapas. Sitting here, in this modest little square, I'm in love with it already.

Redbeard throws his van onto the pavement behind me with all the noise and bluster he can manage, then slams out and disappears across the square carrying a tray of produce. I give the bike a little pat. We showed him. Nobody pushes us around.

Judi appears at the opposite corner of the square, holding up the key to our apartment for the week with a welcoming smile. I get off the bike and walk to meet her.

* * *

It's now almost a decade since my mum wrote her goodbyes on a small rectangle of white card. I hope in time to forgive myself for all that came next.

Roman Quartet

Tom Finnigan

1) Ave!

Mrs Paccini gave my mother a chicken – a cooked chicken roasted in her rotisserie and clad in silver foil. "For 'is journey to Roma," she explained. "Chicken Roman style."

In October 1966 – the year England won the Soccer World Cup – a London train took me from Manchester on the first stage of a journey to study for priesthood at the Venerable English College in Rome. Snug in my suitcase, the chicken crouched between black Wolsey stockings and white collarless shirts. Embarrassed by this juicy hen, I thought it brash to produce a whole chicken when others in my carriage ate sandwiches and apples, so she remained hidden and I hungry. She spent the night in London sleeping at the luggage office by Victoria Station. The following morning, despite an aroma of cooked meat fighting the salty winds in the English Channel, my chicken stayed as secret as a sin whispered in confession.

On the Paris to Rome express, we met Alexander McKenzie Hay, a fellow church student from Westminster Diocese. Dressed in black suit and white clerical collar, he swept back a mane of yellow hair and opened Homer's 'Odyssey'. Whilst the train swayed through the vineyards of Burgundy, Alex stood in the corridor and proclaimed the story of Odysseus marooned in the arms of the demi-goddess Calypso to a bemused French ticket collector.

"The wine-dark sea," he chanted to the clanking of iron wheels. "You Poseidon, god of the wine-dark sea, you are the shaker of the world."

Jealous of this Greek god, I feared to expose the breasts of my companion and kept her cosseted in my shirts lest he violate her chic chastity. She missed the glint of snow on the Alps and the orange dawn creeping through the Apennines. At Stazione Termini in Rome, we tumbled into a taxi leaving Alex to argue with a porter – England versus Italy: a World Cup of words. Nymphs frolicked in Fontana Esedra and trams whistled in Piazza Venezia. A red-lipped flower seller stood embedded in scarlet gladioli when we stopped on the Corso. *"Porca miseria,"* the taxi-driver swore. Whether he was exasperated by traffic or the smell from my luggage, I could not tell.

On the steps of the Venerabile in Via Monserrato, bathed in the heat of Roman autumn, my luggage stank. A chubby-faced cleric dressed in a black soutane and white plimsoles greeted me.

"Hullo! I'm Brendan Howling." Behind National Health spectacles, two humorous eyes smiled a welcome. "They call me Wubbles. Do come in."

He lifted my case and sniffed, eyebrows tightening. Inside the building, he pointed to a chapel. A smell of incense lingered – balm to the odour of my shameless bird. I followed Wubbles up marble staircases, past portraits of cardinals and down a corridor cool with tiles.

"This is the Old Nunnery and here's your room," he gasped and released my suitcase, nose wrinkled in disgust, eyes no longer smiling. Then he was gone, leaving me in a place unchanged since Napoleon captured Rome.

The room was dark and hot: a desk took shape, a bed, some empty bookcases, a ewer and basin. Tall shutters covered the window. I tossed my case on the bed and flung them open. Light leapt at me from blue sky – a cascade of brightness that made me blink and rub my eyes. Terracotta roof-tiles stretched to the dome of a church. Pink knickers and black bras hung from balconies. A radio blared. Bells chimed. Outside an open door, an old man in blue shorts and white vest poured water on red geraniums. He waved. *"Ciao!"* I shouted. Heat pricked my eyes. I smelt hot plaster and rancid flesh.

She lay in my opened suitcase, shimmering in foil – Cleopatra in her burnished barge. I lifted her up. Together we strolled along tiled corridors, skipped down Renaissance stairs and evaded the curious eyes of painted cardinals. Ten minutes into my priestly training, I strolled through Via Monserrato with a chick on my arm. Vespas buzzed. A cabinet maker hammered at wood. The smell of varnish challenged the stink of putrid flesh. We sauntered into Via Giulia. Wisteria drooped from an archway. A fountain dribbled and beside it lurked a litter bin. I placed her there – decayed, but intact, still virginal as befitted the female companion of a celibate. Rotting lettuce leaves served as a shroud; water from the fountain blessed her. A blown kiss marked our parting. *Ciao cara!*

Dazed by heat, I walked back towards the English College and stopped at the church of Santa Caterina della Rota. This tiny, shadow-filled place smelt of incense. I dropped coins into a box and lit two candles: one for my grieving mother, the other for Mrs Paccini. Wicks flickered and wax spluttered. Head bowed in prayer I asked my Lord's forgiveness for fowl behaviour.

A door clicked and light flooded the floor like an invitation to dance. The art, history and beauty of Rome beckoned. Seduced, I stood up and marched towards priesthood, my Manchester bird forgotten.

2) Salve!

In 43BC, the orator Cicero was proscribed an enemy of the Roman state by the Triumvir Octavian and assassinated. His hands and head were displayed on the Rostra in the Roman Forum – a bloody example of intolerance by authority at a place where orators spoke. I stopped here in December 1967, pausing in my stroll along the Via Sacra with my hands and head engrossed in the text of 'Luther' – a play written by John Osborne. Like Cicero, Martin Luther was dangerous to know. My college was putting on the play at Christmas. The director had chosen me to play the lead and I'd come to the Forum to learn my lines.

"… the language is urgent and sinewy, packed with images that derive from bone, blood and marrow …" Alan Brien wrote in a review of the original production for the Sunday Times. I was in the right place!

I glanced along Via Sacra towards the church of San Francesca. Nothing stirred this cold winter morning apart from a few swifts pirouetting in clear, winter sky. In my imagination, the poet Horace meandered by, scratching his head, trying to rid himself of a boring companion. Text in my pocket and shoulders leaning on the rostra, the cold marble, stained by Cicero's bloodied hands and head chilled my bones. I pulled my woollen cloak tight and declaimed to history and an attentive rabbit:

"We are living in a dangerous time. You may not think so, but it could be that this is the most dangerous time since the light first broke upon the earth."

"Er ..." My fingers clutched the book in my pocket. No, leave the text alone. Something about truth ... Right ... got it:

"It may not be true, but it's very probably true – but, what's most important is that it's an assumption we are obliged to make." Standing away from the Rostra, my hands gestured dramatically towards the Temple of the Vestal Virgins and Osborne's lines came from my mouth roaring in spirals of breath: *"We Christians seem to be wise outwardly and mad inwardly, and in this Jerusalem ..."*

Behind me someone was coughing – not loudly but in that quiet, polite way some English folk adopt when they wish to interrupt. Then a voice – precise, clipped and deliberate:

"How interesting! I was coming down from the Capitol, having evaded the blandishments of Castor and Pollux, when I saw you emerge from behind the Rostra and throw your hands in the air. For a moment I thought dear Cicero had come back from death to chastise me. But lo, you seem to be a clerical student in a state of some excitement. Rome never ceases to surprise one, don't you think?"

Speaking to me was a tall English priest, enveloped in an ancient black overcoat. Around his neck a white scarf writhed in layers – Arab fashion. Above that, a pair of rimless spectacles and amused, watery eyes – all topped with a black beret. Plumes of air rose from his mouth as he spoke. Despite the scarf covering his chin, I knew him. That face and those spectacles looked at me most days from the backs of books: volumes of 'A History of Philosophy' by Frederick Copleston SJ – *"the most considerable work of English Scholastic scholarship in our day",* the blurb proclaimed.

"Why, Father Copleston, I'm sorry if I startled you."

Two English speakers conversed alone on the Via Sacra, breath clouding our mouths, like smoke rising from Roman sacrifices. He knew more about the history of ideas than I could imagine in an eternity of trying. I dared to recall themes in the drama of 'Luther' that illustrated the break-up of Europe. As if to applaud our meeting, bells pealed the hour from the church of San Teodoro and a couple of pigeons waddled towards us, nodding vigorously.

"I saw Albert Finney in your role at the Theatre Royal in Nottingham in the summer of 1961. An Oxford colleague acquired some tickets. That line – now, how does it go?" and he frowned. "Ah yes, it's where Martin describes himself as *'the lost body of a child, hanging on a mother's breast'.* Quite memorable the way Finney enunciated it. Like a scream out of darkness. Vivid and startling. I'm sure you'll be just as effective."

"'Tit', Father."

"I beg your pardon."

"Osborne wrote 'tit' not 'breast'."

I had corrected Professor Copleston. Fifty-two years later, I hold my tattered copy of 'Luther' – covered in pencilled emphases and underlining, disfigured by yellowing tape and smelling of dust, its spine collapsed – and marvel at my cheek. A second-year philosophy student had corrected on a point of fact a man of profound learning, whose books stand behind me even now: 'Late Mediaeval and Renaissance Philosophy', 'Bentham to Russell', 'Contemporary Philosophy'.

Professor and student laughed. Low sunlight cast our shadows along the Via Sacra where victorious generals had paraded captives on their way to the Capitol Hill. Much blood was shed in the Tullianum prison behind us where Jugurtha, King of Numidia, was strangled and Saints Peter and Paul were imprisoned. I hadn't drawn blood. It didn't seem like a triumph but it was 'tit' and not 'breast'. A miniscule adjustment in philosophical discourse between master and pupil, a dot in a milky way of words.

Father Copleston tightened his scarf, bade me good luck and walked on past the Basilica Emilia towards the Temple of Antoninus and Faustina. I climbed the Capitol, clutching my play and whispering lines. Below me was Piazza Venezia, noisy with Vespas and trotting ponies. An aroma of coffee lured me down the magisterial steps designed by Michelangelo for the visit of the Holy Roman Emperor, Charles the Fifth.

Two thousand years ago, Cicero had opposed Octavian and lost his hands and head. In the sixteenth century, Martin Luther had challenged the Holy Roman Emperor and thousands were killed. Half an hour ago, something impertinent had happened on the Via Sacra, he on his way, I on mine, but I still had hands to pay for coffee and a tongue in my head to taste it.

3) Cave!

For a time, bells and Beethoven woke me in the mornings: the solemn toll of San Andrea della Valle pealing from the Corso and the brook-like murmurings of the Pastoral Symphony linked to my alarm clock. Such are the morning sounds of Rome that haunt me. I cannot listen to the andante movement in that sixth symphony without feeling the curve of shallow Renaissance steps under my shoes as I fly down to my Cardinal at six o'clock on an October morning, my soutane like wings, my twenty-two-year-old feet as nimble as Fred Astaire seeking his Ginger.

Cold water, splashed on my face from a tin ewer and basin, chaffed a chin raw after shaving with cold soap. Twenty-three black buttons fastened my soutane and concealed khaki shorts, white tee shirt and long black stockings. A stud twisted in my Roman collar brought me breathless into the hot chapel of his Eminence Cardinal William Heard, Dean Emeritus of the Holy Roman Rota, retired Chief Justice of the Roman Catholic Church.

He is hunched at his prie-dieu, a frail Edinburgh priest of eighty-six years, scarlet skullcap askew on a bony, hairless head, fingers scrunched with arthritis. Dawn comes through a window behind him and finds his ruby ring, making it gleam like a sanctuary lamp. I want to fix that cap but touching is anathema to a man whose life is governed by a line from John's gospel – *Noli me tangere – don't touch me* – his rule for sixty years of celibacy. I clear my throat and his eyes open.

"Good morning, Mr Finnigan."

"*Eminenza*, it's a fine day."

Rheumy eyes peer at me. He sighs and tries to sit back – a trial for a man who used to row for Balliol College in Oxford.

"Have you prayed yet, son?"

"On my way, *Eminenza*."

We both know that this early call is to check that *he* is praying and not dead. He's been at it an hour – his life divided between prayer and reading Latin briefs: the latter punctuated with dozens of Dunhill cigarettes; evenings eased with a glass of Chivas Regal whiskey.

Meditation done, I return half an hour later and we celebrate Mass, whistling and wheezing through the Latin.

"*Sursum corda!* Lift up your hearts!"

"Habemus ad Dominum. We lift them up to the Lord."

One morning in mid-October of 1970, the Cardinal's Mass over and vestments put away, I walked down Via Monserrato, past the fountains in Piazza Farnese and into Via Baullari. An early lecture was scheduled at the Gregorian University. I'd be back for ten o'clock. Visitors from Manchester were coming to be shown around.

Narrow streets, crowded with people and vehicles, stank of exhaust fumes. A Vespa scooter chugged around an old lady tugging the lead of a poodle. Taxi-drivers blared klaxons at tourists ambling towards the market in Campo dei Fiori. Fishmongers' stalls reeked of mussels, langoustines and oysters; shoulders of lamb rimmed with fat hung above veal cutlets; slabs of Casareccio bread riddled with holes squatted behind wheels of Pecorino cheese.

"Vuole? Vuole?" a swarthy girl yelled, shoving a bunch of yellow chrysanthemums at a couple of Americans. "D'ye want to buy?" Me she ignored. Students didn't buy flowers for their girls, especially clerical *bagarozzi* in black skirts and sashes.

The building bricks on the Church of the Twelve Apostles were warm to my hands when I leaned close to read a poster from the Communist Party. It advertised a rally in Piazza del Popolo to protest against the visit of the American President, Richard Nixon. He'd passed close to me at the Victor Emmanuel monument the day before, face tanned by Californian sunshine, arms raised as he paraded through the Imperial Forum in an open-topped Chevrolet.

Nixon, Julius Caesar, Garibaldi, Mussolini – was I not fortunate to live on the streets where they had strutted; to gawp at pictures by Raphael and Caravaggio; feel marble carved by Michelangelo; hear Puccini's music; eat pasta, drink wine and have the sun on my face for nine months of the year? There was a Sicilian woman without legs who begged in Piazza Pilotta and a blind Somalian kid who tapped his way round the Trevi Fountain. They stabbed my conscience. There was the terrorism of the Red Brigades and the corruption of the Christian Democrats. This was the environment in which I had to study and learn to pray so that I might minister to all without favour. Here I had to learn to love – and do it in a society where I couldn't get married. No lips to kiss, no pillow to share. So what? That was the deal. As my Cardinal said: "no touching, no problem." "Alleluia!!" I shouted. "Alleluia!!"

That morning, Father Alfaro had lectured on faith, saying that theology was faith seeking understanding – *fides quaerens intellectum,* as Saint Anselm wrote. You had to believe before you understood or the world was nothing but nonsense. I pondered this on my way back to Via Monserrata. The Campo was emptying, the daily market over. A vegetable seller coaxed debris from crevices in the pavement, tangling lettuce leaves and onion skins with discarded pink carnations – the freshness of morning wilting under his broom's touch. Cats scavenged, tails stiff in anticipation of nourishment. The flower sellers wrapped irises and roses in squeaky cellophane sheets. At the news-stand in the Corso I saw President Nixon meeting with Pope Paul on the cover of *Time* magazine.

Back in College, I shared Anselm's words of wisdom with the visitors as I showed them the chapel with its scenes of writhing English martyrs executed for their faith. One of the pilgrims was a girl of my age: hair long and dark; face serene, exquisite as a Giotto Madonna.

"Your brother told me to come and find you. He said you'd show us this place."

I showed them the tomb of Cardinal Christopher Bainbridge and encouraged them to run their fingers over his marble effigy and feel his fine nose. We walked along the Cardinals' Corridor past the portraits of Thomas Wolsey, the butcher's son from York who became Henry the Eighth's Chancellor, and John Henry Newman, a former luminary of the Church of England. At the end of the corridor, there was a smell of cigarette smoke.

"What's in there?" the girl asked, pointing to a red baize door.

"That's Cardinal Heard's apartment," I answered. "He's ancient, retired now. I serve his Mass each morning."

She smiled. I blushed. Embarrassed, I fumbled with the latch on the library door.

"Lots of these books are four and five hundred years old. Some older ones belonged to the English Hospice which was opened here in the thirteen-hundreds."

I led them deeper, where the air was musty with old vellum. I took a heavy volume from a glass display cabinet, annoyed that my hands were shaking.

"This one we call the *Liber Ruber* – the Red Book – it lists all the students who have enrolled since the foundation of the college."

I opened it, turning the pages with difficulty.

"Smell that leather and ink."

They gathered round, cooing in appreciation.

"Look. Here's Ralph Sherwin who's just been made a saint. He was a martyr – hung, drawn and quartered at the time of the Reformation."

"Could you be a martyr?" the girl asked.

I laughed and put the book onto a table without answering. I opened one of the last pages.

"And here's me, four years ago: *Thomas Finnigan, Diocese of Salford, enrolled in October 1966*."

She bent to look and I caught her perfume – like roses. She turned to me and I was startled when her hair brushed my hand.

We ate sandwiches in the garden, sitting by the pond and teasing the goldfish with crumbs. Watching swifts do their pirouettes around the college chimneys, the girl's hair seemed to dance with them. Her friends remarked on the smell of lamb cooking, the sound of dishes clattering. She kept looking at the sky. Light caught her lips, her eyes, her skin. When I took them to *Lungotevere* for their bus, the sun had dipped and our shadows merged. I shook hands. My fists were clenched when I waved goodbye.

Back in my room, after checking my Cardinal, the chatter of the Roman evening tumbled through the window. I hurled ´The Confessions´ of Saint Augustine onto my bed, lit a cigarette and watched lights glimmer below the dome of San Andrea. A breeze ruffled the curtain. I thought I smelt roses. A bell tolled the half hour and tobacco smoke floated, soft through the night, like the fall of a girl's hair on the back of your hand.

4) Vale!

My Rector, Monsignor Alston, fiddled with a packet of Lucky Strike cigarettes. "Well, Mr Finnigan," he mumbled. "You had better go home." I winced. I would not become a priest. Arrivederci Roma!

I closed the door of his study. It was dusk. From Via Capellari came the sound of hammering. The furniture restorers were working on the Sabbath. That smell of varnish! Always seeping through the red curtains on the Cardinals' corridor. The shield of Henry the Fourth and the Plantagenet coat of arms looked down on me. The English had been here since 1362. I'd survived for four years.

In the garden, swifts dived. There was just enough light to see the water lilies nodding under the fountain's spray. Windows in the kitchen were open: a clatter of dishes, girls laughing. The bells of San Andrea della Valle sounded the Angelus. *Angelus Domini annuntiavit Maria* – the angel of the Lord declared unto Mary. What news to announce to my parents!

"Dear Mum and Dad, I shall be home on Friday."

I folded my letter. It was Sunday evening. Air mail from Italy to Manchester took three days. They'd have it by Thursday. The college motto was stamped on the envelope. ´*Ignem veni mittere in terram* – I came to light a fire on earth.´ Some fire I was lighting.

On my bookshelves – O'Farrell's 'Metaphysica', the Jerome Biblical Commentary, Thomas Merton, Council documents. No time to take all my books; just my clothes and the Jerusalem Bible ... maybe Georgina Masson's 'Companion Guide to Rome'. My pal Joe Moore would pack the rest. I'd send a cheque from England for postage. What about the piano accordion I never learned to play? My surplice? Clerical collars?

The bell rang for Compline. I buttoned my soutane, pulled up my black socks, fastened my collar and ran. There was the usual smell of wax from the sacristy. The church door still creaked. The martyrs continued to writhe amidst flaming mosaics. The organ boomed. In the middle of the second psalm, I remembered my essay on the prophet Amos – how I must check some Hebrew phrases. Father Moriarty was expecting it on Friday morning. I lowered my missal. I would be in Manchester on Friday …

The Rector gave his final blessing. Smoke drifted from quenched candles. I recalled our earlier interview.

"I don't think I can remain celibate, Sir."

"And I don't think you can," he muttered.

I lingered in chapel, listening to the creak of the door. My mouth was dry. What about a job? New friends? Those I loved were here in Rome. I felt isolated, cast off, like something unclean. The sacristan put out the lights. I dipped a shaking finger in the font and blessed myself

They were singing *Salve Regina* – the last prayer of the day – standing on the stairs, in the dark, under the statue of the Virgin. Their voices soared and fell, now loud, now soft, modulated and measured in the ancient Gregorian chant which I cherished: "*gementes et flentes in hac lacrimarum valle* – mourning and weeping in this valley of tears …"

Catch Me If You Can

Julia Motyka

The first summer my dad was dying I started running. I built up such speed on the treadmill that when I stepped onto the floor, my body felt propelled forward; as if thrust toward a destination I could not alter.

To have AIDS in 1998 meant a swift but torturous death, and AIDS is what my dad had. He entered the hospital on June 28th with pneumocystis pneumonia. He was blue-lipped from lack of oxygen, with a T-cell count in the twenties. There was little to do – the doctors told me – but wait for his life to end, so every day on that treadmill I pictured his memorial and imagined delivering his eulogy. When the words moved me to tears, I wrote them down. It comforted me to wrap up his complicated life and put it in my pocket, a finished thing on a piece of paper.

"You were a remarkable man. You'll never know what you meant to me," his friend Pat said one afternoon, through tears.

He'd come to say goodbye, they all did, the remaining members of his New York City community of downtown gay men. Each visit was an obligatory viewing of a common end and the farewell was always polished. Unlike me, they knew what to say and didn't need repeated attempts at goodbye. They'd had a lot of practice.

That summer, everyone spoke of my father in the past tense, even when speaking to him. Pretending his death had already happened was a comfort to us all. It cushioned the fall somehow, to imagine we'd already fallen. As Pat left the hospital room that day, my dad – too sick to respond, or perhaps not knowing how – stared after him.

In September, when the medicinal cocktail was successfully mixed and he was still – surprisingly – alive, I lived uptown not far from his nursing home and near a local university. One morning, on my daily walk to see him, I fell in step behind a group of freshman girls en route to class. We were the same age – eighteen – and so, for a few blocks, I put my arms into the sleeves of a normal life and wore it, pretending to be one of them. They were easy and affectionate with each other, joyful and unlimited. *This should be me,* I thought. I wanted college; camaraderie; freedom. I'd taken a gap year before his illness; worked in a restaurant, explored what it might mean to be an artist. When he got sick, what had been optional became mandatory. One year had extended to two, but my dad was 120 pounds; could not walk; could barely speak. The medication was a temporary reprieve. We were on a lily pad. This was not solid ground.

They continued straight, toward campus. I turned right, toward him.

There will be plenty of time for normal, I thought, *soon enough*.

The fourth summer my dad was dying I stopped sleeping. I lay awake for hours each night and when sleep descended, I dreamt my own death and woke within the hour, sweaty and panicked. Dad had moved from the nursing home to an apartment by then, and was planning his commitment ceremony to a longhaired Latin pianist named Louis. Every night for thirty nights around one a.m., I put on my sneakers and ran a loop around the small park near my apartment downtown.

"Is that safe?" my roommate Sari asked one night, curled up on the living room couch.

"Of course not," I said.

I was out the door before she could respond. If she didn't understand that danger was part of the reason to run, I didn't know how to explain it. My father shouldn't be alive, but was. I was alive, but should I be? As I ran, I delivered imagined eulogies for everyone I loved. I also wrote my own.

At the commitment ceremony they both wore caftans. My father spoke beautifully. He walked through the day with ease. Later that year, after that relationship ended, from a new apartment overlooking the wreckage of 9/11, he told me his leg might need to be amputated. He would not live like that, he said, and shared his plan for death. How and when it would happen (pills). How he would notify me (by voicemail) so that I could wait an appropriate period (twelve hours) before calling the police. I couldn't imagine being involved, but neither of us could stand the idea of his body lying unfound for an unknown interval.

"The smell would be horrible, darling," he said, "and no one wants that."

And so we planned his suicide.

I was a sprinter for one semester, my freshman year of high school. Each time I raced, I sprang from the blocks. In less than fifteen seconds – before my body registered its own movement – the run would be over. During the last week of the season, I was asked to substitute on a longer race I'd never tried. *Just an extended sprint,* I thought. So I agreed. Halfway through, my breath became ragged, my lungs raged, and my legs grew so tired I could only drag my feet forward under me. I had no experience of distance running. I had paced myself for a much shorter race.

The fourteenth summer my dad was dying he had blood clots that swelled his legs and turned them purple. He could barely walk and I was about to get married. To willfully choose a legally binding agreement in which the best-case scenario ends in death made me want to flee. Instead of flight, each morning for a month I woke early, put on my sneakers, and ran a single fast loop around the reservoir near my apartment uptown. As I ran I wrote my fiancé's eulogy and wondered if my dad would finally die on my wedding day.

When I was small my father and I played a game. I'd put on my best dress and say, "Ya wanna run?" He'd nod, smiling, and we'd dash to the stereo and put on the section of music from Disney's Cinderella at the point when the bell is about to toll midnight; when everyone will see that she is not a princess, but a girl covered in ash with mice for friends. It is the moment of escape. While the music played, we'd run the long hallway in our apartment again and again, a prince chasing his princess. It has always been the two of us racing each other somewhere.

On my wedding day in early September, as we waited for the processional, my father smiled, looked at me sideways, and said, "We could make a break for it. There's still time." To him, my dress probably resembled a straightjacket. He had not fared well in marriage to my mother – or in the partnerships that followed – and had talked of leaving as liberation, an escape from madness. To me, wearing that dress summoned the normal life I'd been waiting so long to have. I never got to college – I still look at freshman girls with awe and envy – but my commitment to this kind and gentle man was something I could ground myself in; our home was a place where at last, perhaps, I could rest. I said none of this. I just looked at him sideways and smiled back. The music started and, together, we walked down the aisle.

The nineteenth summer my dad was dying I had a child. After thirty-six hours of labor my daughter emerged, small chubby legs kicking from the sprint out of my body. She curled onto my chest where I felt her heartbeat, like the sound of infinity. I held her and experienced peace in an unknown future for the first time since the onset of his illness. Her legs slowed, then stilled. Curled together, we slept. It was June twenty-ninth. Just one day after he had gone into the hospital all those years ago. Eighteen years. And one day.

I'd say, *from death comes life*, but he's still not dead.

I'd say, *everything's a circle*, but some things are scribbles and lines.

The summer my daughter turned one, I stopped writing eulogies and began writing birthday letters. After twenty years of waiting for loss and honoring death, I began to choose life. I put that letter to her in an envelope, where it will stay sealed until her eighteenth birthday. I'll write one every year. I want her to hold the proof of my love in her hands, to trust my presence in her life.

My dad didn't come to her birthday party. He stopped by that morning but wouldn't come upstairs, so I brought her down instead for a short walk.

"Are you sure you don't want to join us?" I asked, as we said goodbye.

He took a breath and looked briefly toward my apartment windows before shaking his head.

"No, darling. It's better this way. Just the three of us."

He smiled, looked at me sideways and walked off alone. I watched until he disappeared around the corner.

When someone is dying for twenty years, you never grieve.

When someone is dying for twenty years, you are always grieving.

I am built like a runner. With long lean limbs that are graceful and quick, my body excels in solitary motion, but I do not enjoy it. The hard feeling of bone on bone; of bone in shoe on pavement; the inevitable stitch in the ribs; the unending fire in the lungs: No, I do not like it. I never have.

My daughter loves to run. She is two now and her body is still learning what it means to have muscles. “Say Go girl, go!” she says. And I do. And she runs, laughing. She runs because she can. Because it is freeing. Because to feel the wind in her face fills her with breath and her body in motion is a joyful thing. I am the only thing behind her, cheering. She looks back, smiles, and continues on.

Brief Notes to My Brother's Other Sisters

Lisa K Buchanan

To My Brother's No-Nonsense Sister

You were raised to think of your family as a choir in which singular voices did not ring out for individual recognition but were prized for their ability to harmonize and blend. Therefore, when your brother develops a disease that will ruin both of his kidneys, slowly and painfully, you volunteer, at age fifty-two, to donate one of yours for a transplant. Nor are you the least bit disturbed by the hospital donation coordinator who refuses to send you the consent form because "it might freak you out." You do not linger over the years-long waiting list and the people who die on it every day. You do not fuss or ruminate or wait to be asked. You have never used nitrous oxide for a dental cleaning, acetaminophen for a mammogram. You have never, even once, taken a sleeping pill. So much wussy twaddle.

Sadly, you are an alternative-reality sister and do not exist in corporeal form. And your brother – our brother – is still on the list. Waiting.

To My Brother's Glass-Full Sister

Unlike No-Nonsense, you've combed the websites of numerous transplant centers and kidney foundations. Studies about safety are quoted. Glowing smiles accompany glowing stories. Donors and recipients reap mutual benefits. In transplant forums, donors say the experience is rewarding and redeeming. They cite advanced technology, tidy incisions, and quick recoveries; they run in fundraiser marathons after surgery; they become "donor ambassadors." Amid this heroic assemblage of family members and friends, family and friends of friends, co-workers and co-workers' relatives, church and temple goers, former classmates (and even a kindergarten teacher who donated a kidney to a former student), how could you not donate to your own brother? Spare him the lonely, debilitating slog of dialysis? Improve – possibly, save – his life? Help the next person on the list and inspire others to do the same? You've never been a marathoner or a public speaker, but you could start now, couldn't you? Become a profoundly improved version of yourself?

To My Brother's Glass-Empty Sister

You, too, have combed: A donor's healthy kidney accidentally discarded; a donor's healthy kidney contaminated by a ceiling drip; a donor's healthy kidney placed in a misdiagnosed recipient; a donor's aorta sliced during surgery. You've read studies about risk and even watched a nephrectomy on video: the ligaments of the spleen divided with tiny scissors; the wet, squishy kidney "freed" within its webby white fasciae, the colon detached, veins cauterized, arteries clipped. If your body is your castle, you have sweat a knot of toads and dug yourself a treacherous moat.

To My Brother's Sacrificial Sister

Like Glass-Full and No-Nonsense, you are compelled to bestow a profound gift. But unlike these Sisters, you see your own life as something that was given to you. This donation to your brother has become your calling, a chance to repay a debt you've incurred just by breathing. You name your pre-ectomy kidney Agatha Left and start your farewells to her. Your body is no mere vessel of appetites, but rather a temple of communion and purification. Your body is no mere specimen of bilateral symmetry, but rather a life-giving vehicle with a part to spare. How then to go forth with two healthy kidneys when your brother has none? In the language of the King James Bible, your cup runneth over and the voice of your brother's blood crieth unto you. In the language of a widely quoted transplant surgeon, you were born with two kidneys, so you'd have one to donate.

To My Brother's Sheepish Sister

In the early stages, your brother rarely complained about the clusters of cysts that probably began forming on his kidneys when he was an adolescent, silently continued to accumulate fluid and, in his forties, began to rupture. Currently, his polycystic kidneys have swollen to the size of two footballs, raising his blood pressure to frightening levels and damaging other organs.

When you tell him you're worried about a nephrectomy's consequences to your personal plumbing, he replies that lots of women become incontinent after menopause, so what's the big deal? Your brother has a sense of humor; he also has a life-threatening condition. Maybe he's joking. Maybe he's not.

After the diagnosis, the immediate question around your father's breakfast table is not whether you had considered an elective nephrectomy, but how soon you can be tested for compatibility.

"You'd better start right away," says your father's caregiver.

"I wish I could give him one of mine," says your father, then eighty-nine. "My lamp is on its way out. Your brother, he's still young and sparkling."

One relative mentions another relative who donated a kidney to his brother; everything went well and both brothers are "just fine."

You: "Were he and his brother (like my brother and I) adopted from different birthparents?"

The relative: "No."

You: "When did you last speak to the donor?"

The relative: "A few years ago."

You: "Have you asked about any complications that showed up later?"

The relative: "No."

You: "Then how do you know the donor's 'just fine'?"

The relative: "Well, I assume I'd hear about it if he weren't."

To My Brother's Raised-Eyebrow Sister

Because your elderly father often helps people and because he talks tirelessly about his son's plight, several recipients of his generosity have offered a kidney. Two neighbors were in their seventies; one was on oxygen at night. One caregiver needed a car repair; another had met your father, then ninety-five, only twice and also needed a car repair. None of the above got tested for compatibility. Or even filled out the form. Some sought to reciprocate; some to extract. Each time someone offers, your father gushes with gratitude. Each time, he opens his heart and possibly his wallet. Each time, he has hope and passes it along to your brother.

To My Brother's Future Sister

In five years, you will be diagnosed with malignant melanoma; you'll have a second surgery before you've healed from the first. Nobody will know how long the cancer has lurked in your body or how long it will stay or whether it will ultimately be fatal. In any case, you will be ineligible to donate, even posthumously. Past transplant recipients – vulnerable from the immune-suppressing anti-rejection drugs – have already sickened or died from donated kidneys with stealth melanoma. Oddly now, it is by not donating a kidney to your brother that you will have improved his chances of survival.

To My Brother's Only Corporeal Sister

You and Sacrificial have long drifted. You and Future have not yet met. Unlike No-Nonsense, you have never healed quickly – not from injuries or bladder infections or even the flu. Unlike Glass-Full, you remain a mess of fear and shame and skepticism about the removal of a major organ. One day, when your brother gets that long-awaited call from a transplant coordinator, you will drop your life and go to him if you can, buy his groceries and fetch his meds. But ultimately, your multiple selves don't add up to the person you thought you were. And it is with this – its safety and its sorrow – that all of you must live.

Moulded

Phil Cummins

I put my thimble on the table
It tumbled down when it was able
I put it then upon the mat
Now thimble, tumble out of that
Down a sloping floor it dribbled
Into a hole a mouse'd nibble
Shopman, please, another thimble
One that isn't quite so nimble
– Anonymous –

"Daddy! Are you an' Mammy goin' to see de man gettin' graved up?" my five-year-old son asked me some years ago as I was readying myself for a local funeral. In my mid-30s at the time I smiled inwardly, secretly charmed by the grammatical alchemy contained in those words.

Graved Up.

Leave it to an inquisitive child untethered by political correctness to transform a dour noun into a candid verb.

Of course if I'd come out with a line like that as a young lad, my father would have berated me and given me a clip around the ear to go with it. Only grown-ups were permitted such flippancy. Where I perceived innocent charm, he'd have inferred impudent cheek. Such contrasts are the stuff of families.

My father was a brass moulder, an artisan trade that saw him spend most of his adult life working in old foundries in Dublin, his brawny hands teasing out the beauty hidden within lumps of base metals forged together in fire and sand. Mostly closed down now they were unspeakably filthy places, crumbling rat-infested dumps that would have made Dickens himself shudder with outrage. Health and safety had no place in his precarious working world. In one unfortunate incident his thumb was badly crushed while tinkering with some ancient mechanical contraption, his right hand thereafter brandishing a slightly mangled opposable digit; all the pain without the palliative of compensation. No union had his back. His was a hard, often thankless trade that he refused to countenance as a life for either my older brother or me.

He did allow me to work alongside him at the foundry in Church Street during the summer of 1987, but only because I was eager to earn a few quid before starting college. I was just shy of 19 years old. His ever-present cough, which had formed part of the soundtrack of my childhood, stemmed from the countless untipped cigarettes he'd hoovered down – the ones with the cheery little picture of the sailor on the front of the pack. The hellish air quality in his workplace also played its part, an acrid grimy atmosphere of dusty smoke and noxious solvents thick enough at times to hang your hat on. This latter I experienced first-hand. Piggy dirty from top to toe at the end of each working day that summer, I recall the great gobs of sooty black phlegm that came out of me. No wonder he didn't want that life for either of his sons.

One day during lunchbreak as we all sat around on overturned buckets and wooden crates reading the tabloids and drinking tea that could've easily passed muster as crude oil, he started coughing uncontrollably. Doubled over, red-faced and squinty eyed, his cough grew into a frightful gurgling thing that took forever to struggle out of him as if he was trying to drag it all the way up from his toenails.

"Are y'all righ', Christy? Are y'after swallyin' sumptin'?" the lads said jokingly, probably thinking as I did that a bit of his fig roll had gone down the wrong way. He took himself out to the toilet, bunched fist covering his mouth, where he hacked and spluttered out of him for an age. He finally emerged pale-faced and, gathering up his few bits and pieces into a plastic carrier bag, quietly announced that he was going home early, a rarity for him. From the drawn look on his face though, I knew something vital had wrenched loose inside of him that day and would never right itself again. It was as if all the sap had just drained out of him.

The foundryman's hands are worn smooth with sand. Sand is his blank canvas, the crucial fabric of his moulds. When mixed with a little clay and moisture, sand can be pressed into moulding brackets and made to take the exact shape of the desired template to be cast. Sand possesses the material strength to resist the searing heat and flowing pressure of liquid metal as it is poured into the mould in order to avoid warping and cracking of the final product. Such strength stems from the fact that sand was once rock. But its very existence also reminds us of the transience of solidity. That all things wear down. That time runs out.

"I know you are," she said. "It'll be all right. Sure I love you too."

I overheard Mam softly speaking into the hallway phone as I ate my breakfast on an early winter's morning of that same year, instantly discerning the words spoken from the other end of the line that drew such uncharacteristic talk out of her.

"I'm scared!" the nervous voice on the phone would've said. "I don't know what they're going to find. I love you."

I pictured Dad nervously clasping a palmful of coins for the public phone, a rumpled figure in his pyjamas and slippers looking out of place in the shiny new lobby of Beaumont Hospital. He had a short while to go before his biopsy and needed to feel the nearness of home. Of the two, Mam was made of tougher stuff, the more emotionally reserved one. It made hearing her talking this way all the more frightening, a rare glimpse of tenderness that drove home the gravity of the situation.

By mid-December the verdict was in, sentence handed down. It was as if a big celestial Use-By date had been stamped into him. "Six Months!" the doctors announced. "Come in number 48, your time is up!" Mam told me once that I whacked my head off the kitchen wall repeatedly when I heard the news, but I have no memory of that. He slipped out of the world by the end of the following spring, the life wrung out of him by lung cancer in his 49th year.

Dad's cancer took us all on a preordained ride from denial to acceptance. A cruel illness, it seemed to age him in two opposing directions, accelerating his previously tough body forward to crippling frailty and premature demise, whilst also triggering childlike fears to manifest themselves in his mind; fears of the dark, and of being left on his own, un-minded.

As he gradually succumbed to the cancer threading its way through his tissues like bindweed, honeycombing his poor lungs with tumours, an endless conveyor belt of pills and potions were summoned to ease his journey. There were drugs to fight infections, to ease constipation, to clear mucus from airways and to lessen the abysmal nausea that followed radium treatments; drugs to counter the side effects of other drugs; drugs to hold back the cyclical tide of pain. And towards the end, when illness had its pound of flesh well reaped, those drugs that evict you from your mind for a time so that you don't have to bear witness to your body's final pathological ransack. And through all this, he faced his illness with uncomplaining dignity, often entertaining us all with his funny little jokes and his poems about nimble thimbles and the curious contents of a little boy's pockets.

Sometimes he'd have a secret smoke, a sneaky suck of contraband that used to clear his chest and cheer him up no end. "Sure it makes no differ now," he'd say to me through a bittersweet smile. "The damage is done. Aughrim is lost!"

Our days were filled with awe-inspiring nurses and the charity of others, distant relatives offering condolences and former working acquaintances offering crocodile tears. My brother and I would crack jokes as we two made up our makeshift beds on the floor of the hospital waiting room, usually during one of his numerous visits home from a teaching job in New York to see Dad.

But most of all, I remember his hands.

Mumbling incoherently to himself in the hospital bed, opiates sluicing through his veins, his hands would gracefully dance over the bed covers, fingers fluttering over make-believe moulds as they skimmed away imaginary sand, moulds that would never be cast or give birth to their pretty brass treasure. He plied his trade to the end just as May's Festival of Bealtaine commenced, an ancient Celtic tradition ironically symbolized by fire, a vital element of his working life.

Dad was graved up in a local cemetery near Dublin Bay in May of '88, a 'boneyard' he would have called it when he was alive. In deference to his faith in his God we sent him off wearing the shroud of Mount Argos, the church of his youth. Afterwards we gratefully resumed the humdrum of our lives, purging our home of all the sad trappings of terminal illness.

In the years that followed, our entire family scattered like windblown seeds that eventually took root in Canada and America. Regrettably-long periods of time would pass by during which the graveside lay untended. As the gravestones in this particular cemetery are all laid out flat on the ground, the surrounding grassy border gradually crept over Dad's stone to partially conceal it, giving the impression of a wound scabbing over, as if the Earth itself was attempting to heal the passing of the grave's resident.

On a rare visit to the graveside just a few years ago, my brother and I, to our shame, struggled to find Dad's grave. We traipsed between the stones searching for anything that looked familiar, and after about a quarter of an hour finally stumbled across it and silently paid our respects. On the way out, we spotted a series of stone markers lining the exit pathway, each about the size of a dinner plate with a letter carved on it.

"Look!" said Dave, pointing to the marker on the end of Dad's row. "That's how we'll find him from now on. He's filed under F … for Fucked!"

He and I have now managed to overtake Dad's lifespan, a secret aspiration we only admitted to one another after I eventually followed my brother over that unspoken threshold of 48 years and 105 days. When we think about him now, we're looking back at a younger man; sadly, one who had become a complete stranger to me with the passage of time.

Until recently that is …

Brass is an alloy of two metals, namely zinc and copper, fused together at a temperature of nearly 2000°F. In an open furnace such as those used in older foundries, a large plume of smoke is released from the kiln when the two metals finally fuse together, an atomic birth announcement of sorts. Zinc imparts lightness and strength to the final alloy, whilst copper confers malleability and gives brass its pleasing golden burnish. It occurs to me that we are, each of us, an alloy of two different people, a mix of two different sets of traits defining the form and facade of the whole person, one set often striving for primacy over the other.

"You're just like your father!" my 80-year-old mother quite recently pronounced, some enigmatic word or gesture on my part sparking a remembrance of her now long-deceased husband. I said nothing at the time but her observation privately niggled at me, snapping to attention mental defences I wasn't fully aware of. How could I, now at 51 years of age, possibly be like someone who has been absent from my life for far longer than he was present?

Upon hearing Mam say this my mind lit up with some unflattering memory of Dad that I simply couldn't reconcile with myself. I instantly recalled, for example, the gruff working man demonstrating how TV could be watched through firmly closed eyelids whilst hogging the best armchair in the living room and snoring like a congested rhino, thick curls of cigarette smoke spiralling upwards from the overflowing ashtray beside him. The slightest move by any of us to change the channel away from the snooker would instantly awaken 'The Beast' and unleash a growled "I WAS WATCHIN' DAH!"

For the record, I neither smoke nor snore and I never watch snooker. To my mind in fact, he and I differed from one another on almost every conceivable level. Unlike me he was a man of strong Catholic faith, one who genuinely trusted in the power of prayer. His holy notions even extended to the belief that only Catholics had a valid ticket to get into Heaven. As far as he was concerned, all other faiths were at the mercy of scalpers.

He was also a man of deeply conservative mindset. Notwithstanding the irony of his own glaring recklessness when it came to matters of coin, the occasion of my mother audaciously opening her own bank account left him raising his eyebrows in stunned disapproval as he predicted our imminent financial ruin to his mates in the pub. I've occasionally wondered how he would have coped with Ireland's brave new stance in recent years on removing long-standing constitutional bans to abortion, divorce and same-sex marriage, overdue legal amendments to our constitution that I'm proud to have voted for. He would have cursed my secular heart as we took pot-shots at one another from opposite sides of the referendum divide.

"I am *nothing* like him!" I repeatedly told myself, mentally rattling off a long tally of dissimilarities in an attempt at self-justification.

The man had minimal formal education, never read a book, hadn't a worldly bone in his body despite presenting himself as a self-proclaimed expert on most matters, and never even held a valid driving license. This latter deficiency certainly didn't prevent him from getting behind the wheel of a car, usually a rusting pile of shit with dodgy brakes and tyres as smooth as a billiard ball. He also never harbored personal ambitions, never held a personal bank account, never held a passport nor travelled and was profoundly ignorant of health issues. And like many of his peers he was absolutely sports mad, openly mocking my teenage preference for books over Gaelic football.

But such contrasts are frivolous I soon reasoned, nothing more than a bubble-thin barrier flung up to keep out a simpler truth. To accept that he and I are alike would be to admit that I am steeped in ordinariness. That I am somehow shackled to his unsophisticated point of view. That I could be stolen out of the world in the same painfully wretched way as he. Such was the impact of his passing on my teenage self that I'm terrified to consider the possibility of these things, even now in middle age, so I kick back against any inference of similarity.

Like Simon Peter, I deny association and turn my face away.

Perhaps, I considered, my mother's words were referring to something more nebulous and tangled up in the roots of fatherhood. We associate a father with a male parent, the head of a family, a patriarch, a figure of authority and protection. "To lose your father is to lose the one whose guidance and help you seek, who supports you like a tree trunk supports its branches," proclaims Pi Patel, the protagonist of Yann Martel's *Life of Pi*.

The word itself derives from the Old English word 'Fæder' meaning 'He who begets a child'. Of course, begetting a child is the easy part; Dad begat *six* of us. Being a father to one is considerably trickier.

Societal expectations of fathers have radically altered over the last few decades. Fathers today attend to their partners during pregnancy and childbirth, video their baby's howling emergence into the world, cut the cord and help plant the placental tree. They proudly don baby slings, push strollers, change nappies, feed and wash their children, fuss over baby monitors, perform bedtime stories and help with homework. They view the notion of anyone smoking or swearing within 50 feet of their offspring as floggable offences. I've modelled my own fatherhood along such lines. In some selfishly twisted way, I even found an upside to my firstborn son developing asthma, figuring that at least it would keep him off the ciggies.

Such wholesome attitudes would never have graced Dad's paternal resumé. He never took that evolutionary leap from provider to caregiver. The poor man would have needed written instructions for a baby's rattle. Like most hard grafting men of that time, he viewed raising children as women's work. When we were youngsters, his version of childminding was to make sure my siblings and I each had a bottle of lemonade and a bag of crisps to tide us over sitting in the car whilst he downed a rake of pints in some pub or other. In the grip of tedium on one such occasion, my sister dared me to let out the handbrake of the car. I nearly shit myself as the car began to roll backwards, promptly bringing my father stomping out of the pub to push it back. He hopped off me for that one.

"YE LITTLE *BASTARD* YE!" he barked at me as I massaged the freshly clattered sting out of my reddening ear, hot tears flowing down my cheeks. And maybe I deserved that. He wasn't just angry with me. I'd given him a terrible fright.

When molten brass has been poured into moulds and allowed to cool, the resultant castings have spiky jagged edges, sharp enough to cause pain and to scratch and break the skin. The castings are placed into a barrel tumbler filled with tiny smooth stones of polished feldspar steeped in soapy water. The barrel is then set tumbling and eventually the brass figurines emerge with a smoother and more tolerable form, softened by the action of time and motion, made easier for one to hold. This could be a metaphor for how time and tide file away the rough edges off memories and allow us to look more kindly upon them.

It's too easy to remember a person's shortcomings after their gone, I realise now. To be fair to Dad, most of my memories of him are filtered through the arrogant lens of late adolescence, a time when sons see the world very differently to their fathers. He was a product of his time as I am of mine, the pair of us occupying different niches on the dadness spectrum. What was it the English poet, Matthew Prior, said? “Be to their virtues very kind; be to their faults a little blind.”

And so I’m also reminded of an oft-times caring, courteous and funny man, a talented tradesman, hard-working to a fault, and a perfectionist in his craft. I recall his teasing ways, his amazing ability to drive us kids bonkers with promises to bring us home spice burgers and chips after the pub closed. Or how, when we were all crammed like sardines into our tiny suburban living room to watch Starsky and Hutch, he would wrinkle his nose and make a big production out of blaming one of us for farting, his facial expression betraying his own guilt. And nobody could ever doubt that he loved his family beyond all else and encouraged each of us to reach beyond the working-class constraints that defined his own life. He understood the upward social mobility that education could bring, the education he was denied. And to my mind, this was the one thing that made him stand apart from so many of his fellow Dubliners of the day. I’ll give him that.

They say you can’t run from your roots, so if I’m being honest, more of him than I care to admit has percolated upwards through the gnarled trunk of his paternal tree to my particular branch. His bristly temperament and bullish obduracy certainly did, along with his formidable work ethic. “You didn’t lick it up off the stones, pet,” my wife likes to remind me.

And sometimes I even imagine I hear him whispering in my head. “Don’t be a feckin’ gobshite!” he says. “Don’t let what happened to me happen to you. Health is wealth. Live to see your grandchildren.”

He saw none of his.

And so I regularly submit myself as grist to the medical mill to be ground up and tuned up, to have lesions burnt from my scalp and latex-covered fingers crudely inserted into my body to probe for suspicious lumps; to urinate into jars and to have my wrist slapped for not trying harder to reduce my cholesterol.

So far, so good! My body appears to have a different agenda to his.

After a time, my curiosity piqued, I finally decided to ask Mam what she meant by her words, or were they just a casually reflexive thing that mothers say to sons. Her answer surprised me in its honest simplicity.

"You have a look of him," she said. "You and your brother. That's all!"

When she looks at me she sees a faint glimmer of him, a fleeting likeness of the man she once thought she'd grow old with. Amazing as it might seem I never even considered this, my genetic inheritance finally come to pass; a subtle reminder that even graved up his ghost still lingers and continues to mould me into his brassy form. No images of him hang upon my walls so he's remained out of my sight for many years now.

Staring into the bathroom mirror, I struggle at first to see any personal resemblance to the old photo of him I've dug out of the attic. But when I look really hard into the blue eyes of the middle-aged man in the mirror staring back at me, take in the shape of the jaw and the fleshy nose, the slightly prominent cheek bones and sticky-out ears, my eyes widen and I smile. For then I see.

Not just me.

Him.

Regeneration

Laura-Blaise McDowell

A modern myth in which I take great comfort is that of the seven year cell regeneration. According to this myth, the human body completely regrows itself every seven years, each cell replaced by a new one. In truth, while all cells have finite life spans, the length of life differs between the various types of cells. So while it is true that after, say, seven years one does not have the same cells as at the start of that time, the body has been constantly regrowing cells, and the seven year time frame is one picked at random – or perhaps not entirely at random. After all, human beings are, as a species, subconsciously obsessed with the number seven. We crave its magical relevance, its power. Magicians know that seven is the number people are most likely to pick between one and ten. Seven plays a role in every major world religion; Hinduism has seven higher worlds and seven underworlds; Christianity's The Book of Revelation contains seven churches, seven angels, seven seals, trumpets and stars. In the Old Testament, God rested on the seventh day, leading to our seven day week, while in the New Testament, the number seven represents the four corners of the Earth combining with the Holy Trinity. In the Quran, we are told of seven heavens, and during the annual pilgrimage to Mecca, Muslims circle the Kaaba seven times. In Buddhism, the new Buddha rises and takes seven steps. According to George Miller's 1956 Harvard University study, seven is the maximum total of numbers most people can recall short-term which is why the majority of phone numbers contain seven digits after the area code. Folklore upholds the seventh son of the seventh son or the seventh daughter of the seventh daughter, as the child destined for greatness. Seven is the jackpot on slot machines.

As such, it is of great comfort to me that I should learn what I have learned after such a significant amount of time has elapsed. I am ready to know now what I could not have known then. I am, after all, a new person.

The summer we were falling in love, we did so mostly from a distance. After a month of seeing each other as much as possible, a frenzy of first-time feelings, we both left Dublin on pre-arranged two-month-long trips. I went to Paris to work, he went to America to visit family. Often during that time, I would sit under a tree in Square René Viviani, leaves drifting every so often onto the pages of my notebook, remaining to this day pressed there. I would listen to Joni Mitchell on my iPod and look through the rose arch at Notre Dame. It looked like God had woven glass and stone between their fingers as a child would a string finger trap, and in their hands had begotten this darkly sparking, most intricate creation at which I was lucky enough to look, while in love. I thought endlessly about the pretty sorrow of loving someone far away, while I gazed at Notre Dame. I was nineteen. Whenever I listen to *Case of You*, I am swept right back there, to the cool beneath the tree, to the sounds of the city, the striking pink of the roses, the glimmering of life as I felt it beginning.

Seven years later, there is a message I don't know how to send until I send it. I write it and rewrite it. It is paragraphs long, but the gist is this: '*You probably know who I am. I've been checking up on you for years. I know what he's like. I know how it felt like the two of you were in on a secret that no one else could ever understand. I'm here if you need to talk.*'

The message is intended for the recent ex-girlfriend of the person I loved seven years ago. When they got together, it was about five years after we had broken up. I had had another relationship in the interim, a happy, healthy one. I didn't think about him anymore. But the photos on social media of them together bore captions written by his new girlfriend, slivers of text which could have been lifted directly from my journals from years before; paragraphs extolling all of his extraordinary, other worldly traits, just how deeply he had managed to sink his claws in somewhere else. I found myself periodically checking her social media accounts, seeing my past self in every post she made, waiting for the downfall, waiting for him to do the same to her, to break up with her out of the blue, break her heart. Hoping that he wouldn't.

And then one day, all of her photos of the two of them are gone. On her Twitter, she has posted that he 'did something awful.' I feel sick.

'Awful,' I say to friends. 'That's strange language to use, isn't it? That's something worse than a normal break up.'

They agree. I think about messaging her, but can't work out if my motives are ethical enough to justify doing so. Do I really think I can help, or am I simply nosy, curious, desperate to know what he has done? I write and rewrite the message, but I don't send it. I think maybe it is not my place.

Two months later, I am still thinking about her, wondering if she is alright, and how she feels now. Wondering if what he did is something someone could feel alright about after two months. I should add, he never did anything *awful* to me – he was a narcissist, definitely, and because of that, he could be manipulative; often, for want of a better word, a bit of an asshole, but never abusive, and even then it took me some time to move past our relationship – whatever it had been. Still. Something within me is so unsettled by *awful*. Something that knows, somehow, that he is capable of *awful*. So I message her. '*You probably know who I am. I've been checking up on you for years. I know what he's like. I know how it felt like the two of you were in on a secret that no one else could ever understand. I'm here if you need to talk.*' My palms sweat.

She replies straight away, thanking me for getting in touch, saying she knows who I am, he had talked about me. She tells me everything.

The person, whose very existence I once believed to be as miraculous as that of Notre Dame, this person who had convinced me that no one would ever understand me like he did, had done something awful.

A girl he had known for years, brave enough to get in touch with his now ex-girlfriend. A string of garbled messages detailing his actions.

He denied it at first, called the girl crazy, but then confessed. Cried and begged her not to leave him. She says she'll never forget his face when she believed the girl and not him. He was no longer looking at his own reflection in her eyes for she had finally seen him for what he was, and he couldn't stand to be seen as imperfect. And that is the crux of all this: his belief that he is perfect, and genuinely, without question, entitled to whatever he wants, whenever he wants. The moment the girl was brave enough to speak, he lost that. She says he still messages her sometimes.

In the wake of the break up, her friends divulged instances in which he had done strange and cruel things to them when she wasn't looking. They had been wary of him, too nervous to tell her. They said that recently, they had watched a popular new documentary about a serial killer, and at the point where it describes how charming and handsome, how appealing and intelligent, how completely convincing he was, and just how evil, they had looked at each other and said *his* name in unison.

We message constantly for a week, sending voice notes. She details the myriad chilling, insidious things he did to her, things she lived with, convinced herself weren't that big a deal, before the revelation. These stir memories of much less terrible, less frightening things he did and said seven years previously; things that appeared to be simply quirks at the time, silly comments, minor behaviours. But it seems that when we dated, he still had some grasp on reality. He was in college, forced to be social for hours a day, and so though some strange behaviours were definitely taking root – odd sleeping patterns and work hours, a belief that he and those he deigned to let close to him were truly superior to other people – they had not fully blossomed. I cannot emphasise how lucky he made me feel that he admired me, that he thought me good enough to be his. He was funny, and often kind and insightful. He made me feel like I was magic. Now his behaviours have become more extreme, she says. The bad far outweighs any good. His need for control usurps everything. His narcissism has reached unthinkable heights. She wasn't allowed to touch his face. He spoke often of the large golden statue of himself he intended to erect outside his mansion when he became rich. He would sleep all day, leaving her to her own devices. When he woke up, he would set his clock to 8AM, and begin his day then.

I was around when the seeds of these habits were beginning to germinate. I would sleep over at his house and he would sleep late, leaving me to wait for him. He was obsessive about what content I was and wasn't allowed to show him online – definitely nothing remotely related to a particular type of animal, as his fear of this creature was extreme and debilitating. Mysteriously, by the time he was in his new relationship, this aversion had vanished. She says he still 'shh's' – another way of ensuring that others know his thoughts are superior to theirs is by shh´ing them when they're talking, so he can have a momentary deep thought, then look back at them, thought complete, and say, 'go on.'

His charm, though, was intoxicating. He only let the facade drop once he knew he had us completely infatuated, completely sold on the idea that we were lucky, blessed to be chosen to be his companion, his sidekick. It was an honor for which we would put up with anything to hold on to. I didn't realise how much of this was still within me. After we had broken up, I was heartbroken, and then I moved on. I had another relationship, a great and happy one, and while in it, I thought of him little, embracing my new life of happy, easy love. Then I moved away alone and once gone, away from everything and everyone I had ever known, I began reflecting on my relationships, and the people I had been close to throughout my life. Only then did I realise that one was not like the others, that one had been very much worse.

Around the time we are talking about all this, Notre Dame goes up in flames. I watch its steeple tumble on the television, watch Parisians streaming by Square René Viviani, singing hymns to the burning icon of faith, of art, of stability, keeping watch as one might a dying relative, candles in hand. All over social media, people express their disbelief that such a thing could happen, that something so certain, so beloved and wonderful could blaze into the night and away from us, that so many memories, so many works of art would now feature the soul of something lost, rather than honor and pay tribute to an ancient, immortal place; the worship now retrospective.

After weeks of speaking, we finally meet. We spend the day together and have drinks with a mutual friend. It is one of the most cathartic things I have ever done. We go through a list of the seven signs of a clinical narcissist and he ticks every box. She tells me that the last thing she said to him – and I'm so pleased she got this in – was that he'd never be happy, and this is true. His narcissism will lead him to nothing but devouring his own life for the love of himself, unable to ever meet his own standards, unable ever to truly connect.

So I choose to believe the myth, I choose to think what I want to think. I can do that now, no one can tell me otherwise. The idea that the cells he touched are not mine anymore, I am not them, is endlessly appealing. It is helpful in coming to terms with the fact that for a year, even if it was only a year, I lived in the palm of a hand that never offered anything, a hand that reached out only to control, to manipulate, to wrap and twist and then to point back at its owner as if to say, *this guy, you gotta love him*. I gave so much to someone incapable of appreciation. I lived in the grip that at the time I thought was love. I thought the manic obsession he elicited, demanded, was the glory of love.

I have looked into the eyes of Narcissus and seen his love for himself reflected back and thought it my own. But that was seven years ago, and I am a different person now. I am someone who can be thankful that nothing actually happened to me, that he was just an asshole, just a bit of dick, nothing more. I am someone who can be there for someone else who was not so lucky, a person who deserves the world. We are seven hundred times the person he ever was or will ever be. And she and I will live lives seven thousand times more prosperous and fulfilled, golden and glowing than anything he ever promised us.

In seven years from now, who knows where we'll be – different again, I'm sure; better, maybe. The French government has pledged to reopen Notre Dame by 2024. We will have loved again. Paris will live again. Our bodies will have regenerated. And the people of the past will remain there, statues in the dawn mist, unable to see what is in front of them.

Leg Man

Alan McCormick

When I was twelve, I lived with my family in a housing estate bordered by an ancient vast Sussex wood. Along a path that snaked behind our houses towards the wood, my friends and I had to pass a large Tudor mansion owned by John Bonham, the drummer of Led Zeppelin, its high gates sealing off the outside world, the hysterical rumours of late night swimming pool parties, scanty debauchery, human sacrifice and alcohol. Don't loiter around there: move quickly on in case you're somehow ensnared and infected.

Deep in the wood, amidst needling carpets of twigs, gnarly fingers, small thin trees and tangled roots, an ugly squat tree with a thick trunk commanded attention. In its centre, scratched onto rough bark, a large red arrowed love heart defended its damp interior. On a carved-out shelf partially hidden behind a bow of intersecting branches, a series of smaller messages were drawn, declarations of love and lust, strange occult-like hieroglyphics from teenagehood, voices from an otherworld I had not yet experienced: unsettling, tingling, tantalisingly out of reach.

It was 1973, and I'd recently been thrown from a boy's prep school into co-ed schooling at the local grammar school, my daily journey down the corridor one of breathless embarrassment, girls in short skirts and knowing giggles my imagined huntresses and accusers.

Sex was arriving from everywhere into my confused hormonal orbit. Adam Burn, a badass devil, led me into an all-too-real, all-too-worldly brush with crime and sexual encounters with older girls.

Promenading Brighton's Palace Pier, Sweet's *Ballroom Blitz* pounding from the pier's speakers, Adam and I were cocksure and living it large, saturated in Brut, strolling in turquoise two-tone trousers and red platform shoes, flicking lighted matches into the cracks of the wooden slatted walkway, the sea circling, fermenting below. I lost sight of him for a moment, before glimpsing him clambering out of a kiosk in an amusement arcade. Then he came running towards me, a large shaven haired man chasing behind. Adam punched me on the shoulder as he passed and I started running too. We ran the length of the pier, notes and coins flying from Adam's grip. I ran straight into an old man in a grey windcheater, knocking him against the railings. I wanted to stop to see if he was okay but Adam pulled me away. The kiosk attendant, cursing all the time, chased us through Brighton into the hilly shopping streets of Kemp Town, and up an alleyway that ran behind the giant white American Express building. We got to the end of the path and I could hear the man slowing, his breathing getting more strained. There was no way he was going to catch us but Adam stopped, handed me the money, and ran screaming towards him. The man was twice Adam's size but he looked really scared. Adam jumped up, kicked and punched the man onto the floor, and then strolled back to me smiling, blood seeping out from the knuckle-duster on his right hand.

After that we couldn't go anywhere without a fight. Outside Crawley Leisure Centre, Adam was necking a girl of about fifteen whilst I stood staring at her silent, angry friend. It was dark and the car park was empty. Suddenly two boys came in from behind us. They said they were the girls' boyfriends. Adam turned without saying anything and head-butted the biggest boy. They ran off and the girls were impressed, and the previously disdainful one offered to snog me. 'No hickies or I'll bite off your tongue,' she said.

He decided that we were going to break into an empty sports pavilion in the park and rob their cash register. We got rid of the girls and drank miniature J and B's and shared a ten pack of filtered No 6's to get in the mood, but a sense of foreboding took over, and at the last moment I refused to join in.

'Come on, useless cunt,' he shouted, the phrase an unexploded grenade amongst my senses. I lay on a bench, watching through a lopsided drunken haze as he threw rocks at the pavilion window and climbed inside.

He celebrated the next night at a disco at the local secondary school, drunk and moving up close with an older girl. He told me to dance with her friend. As we shuffled aimlessly around she whispered, 'your friend's the best kisser in the world. So how come you're so pathetic?'

Adam's mother was in a wheelchair and unable to make it upstairs to inspect his den: its black walls, light bleeding from a naked red bulb on the ceiling, stinking overflowing ashtrays, stolen half-empty bottles of wine and whisky, posters of Newcastle centre-forward Malcolm MacDonald alongside Penthouse centrefolds, staple holes where I dared not look. He boasted about putting his hand in girls' pants and making them cry with pleasure. He talked about cunts, tits, pricks, johnnies, tonguing, and I didn't have a clue what he was on about. But I never asked him to explain, my silence suggesting I was complicit, in on everything.

Once my parents were watching Bernard Manning on Parkinson. I came in as he told a joke about thrush: 'Woman goes to the doctors. "Doc," she says, "I'm worried. My husband has been, well, sleeping around with some dirty cows. We don't have sex like, but I'm worried in case I might get something from the toilet seat after he's used it."

"Let me examine you!" says the Doc.

"Go on then, please yourself," the woman replies, lifting up her dress.

After a while up there the doctor says: "All okay downstairs, Madam, but you must have been eating the toilet seat because your mouth is full of thrush, you dirty cow!"'

My parents laughed, and then so did I. They looked at me, surprised, and I blushed: 'I'm shocked you understand the joke, Kevin,' Mum said. She was drunk, teasing me. 'Can you explain it to us?'

Dad looked uncomfortable – for me, I think. I was hoping the ceiling would fall down. I blushed more, held my breath and backed out of the room, hearing them laughing along with the audience after I closed the door.

Sex lessons at school also made little sense, especially as I missed the video of an actual naked man and naked woman holding each other, but my cheeks reddened at the grainy jerky antics of stick insects projected on the wall, and I avoided looking at the line drawings of limp penises and vaginas in the school's well-thumbed human biology textbooks. It was a step forward into near erotica from the obscure boring lessons I'd experienced before at prep school, with indecipherable words scribbled onto the blackboard by a sexually predatory teacher, the monotonous loop of images on a small black and white television of large flower heads opening and shutting in time with a Strauss waltz.

But in the double garage under my parents' bedroom, I had, despite my naivety, been indulging in a kind of instinctive sexual exploration, one disconnected from anything else in my life, including Adam Burn or school. The garage had been transformed into an adolescent speakeasy, a milk-bar brothel for the local kids to come and let go. Parents were barred but Mum innocently supplied us with crisps and peanuts, and I bought big bottles of pop from the Corona deliveryman and decanted them in plastic glasses for a small profit. Some parents complained to my parents about money changing hands and so that particular operation was stopped. If they'd known what was really going on they may have complained more and closed us down.

Strip poker with the door locked was our favourite game; the whoops and giggling as I got close to losing my pants were exciting and scary. I would cheat to keep my pants on but some kids loved getting naked, dancing around the room, shimmying their naked butts in our faces. In the face of full nakedness I was a young Chancy Gardiner, preferring to sit and watch. But on the green chasing, or in the garden playing football, we all took our chance to slide a hand into each other's pants, girl or boy, it made no difference, the tingle of abandon was overwhelming, the same.

This mad clumsy pubescent orgy occurred all through the summer of 1973, but I wasn't there the day of Nicola's striptease. In a friend's garage, Nicola, who was eleven, performed for a couple of boys a year or two older than her. Later, one boy claimed he had had sex with her (though we didn't believe him). The other described what had happened and kept yelling in a posh public school voice that 'she had a marvellous little cunt', the 'cunt' word laced once again with charged violence. Nicola asked him to stop saying it but he kept shouting the word until I told him to leave, my sensibilities disturbed, the Dionysian idyll of our early sexual adventures pulled out of focus, corrupted.

The same boy used to bring piles of his father's porn magazines into the garage. Whilst some boys leafed through them and exchanged mock bravado comments about the women's bodies, I was never interested.

The women seemed unreal, too posed, their overt flirtation and over-developed anatomies on display made me queasy rather than turned on.

Jocelyn was a regular at the garage youth speakeasy. She was older, maybe thirteen or fourteen, slightly stocky and already full-breasted. I loved her and I loved her breasts. Every time she appeared on the green in front of our house, a siren in her big frumpy dress, I was Roadrunner, out there like a shot, skidding to a halt by her side. She was such a sweet person and took me in hand, letting me kiss her when we walked into the woods. I felt like molten lava, my movements slow and liquid; my heart jumping in my chest until she undid her bra and rested her hand gently on mine to say I could touch her breasts, and when I looked into her big blue eyes everything was calm, everything was all right.

Dad was amused by my new energies and sometimes teased me. It was always a fond teasing but one day he said, 'you have lots of time ahead of you, stay young, enjoy yourself, but don't peak too soon.' He was warning me in a kind of cryptic adult code and I understood enough to blush. Dad's tone was light, only mildly concerned, merely wanting to protect me. But I'd been observed, and I began to feel self-conscious, worried that in some way I might be doing something wrong.

Dad was ill around the time of the 1974 FA Cup Final between Liverpool and Newcastle. Although he hated football as much as I loved it (I was a card-collecting, statistical obsessive), he made it down the stairs from bed to try and watch a little of the game, just as Steve Heighway scored the opening goal. He stayed at the doorway in his dressing gown looking grey and uncharacteristically unkempt and unshaven. Within a few minutes he went back to bed. Later, a series of tinkling sounds passed from the phone by his bed to the phone in the lounge, sounds made by his body contorting and writhing, the mattress shaking involuntarily against the receiver as he suffered a heart attack.

Dad nearly died but recovered after weeks in ICU. I lost my mojo during this period, the energies of puberty burrowing inward, my impulses dampened. I diverted my attention to humour, hiding away for years after in a giggling, geeky boys club in a classroom on the top floor of the school, as far away from girls as possible.

By 1977, my hibernation had taken its toll and I was dead boy walking at school, sublimating my own needs to become the sexless, comedic companion of several shyly eccentric, intense girls; girls with heavy knitted eyebrows and quiet, deep foreboding voices. One wrote a love sonnet in her own blood and posted it through our front door in an unmarked brown envelope on Valentine's Day. I practically had a heart attack, the threatening exotic twirl of her bloody pen filling me with dread, my own sexual desires locked up inside, the real hormonal world kept at bay.

I specialised in intense psychological relationships, incessant joking (on my part) blocking the chance of any physical release. A first date with Sammie, whom I liked, and who I knew fancied me, walked an uneasy line, to keep her close (I liked her attention) but not too close. We went to see Robert Altman's *The Wedding* at the Odeon on Tottenham Court Road, our unease distracted for a while by the black humour and dysfunctional adult relationships on screen. My heart was beating noisily against my chest, my palms sweating, I knew we were about to kiss and I was trying to work out if I really wanted to. When Sammie leaned over it didn't quite work, my lips were stiff and unresponsive so she gave up and became irritable, emptying our popcorn box onto my lap. In McDonald's afterwards, I bit into a hot apple pie and burnt the roof of my mouth and she laughed until tears ran down her cheeks.

Sometimes I could be momentarily liberated by a newfound taste for alcohol and dope. In Davey's mum's lounge, drunk and mildly stoned, I swayed up close to a series of off-duty bunny girls (Davey's mum was a seamstress at the Hilton Bunny Club), whilst she made mocking suggestive comments from the sofa. Barry White boomed out from the speakers and one of the bunny women jokingly clenched my arse. My cool façade momentarily faltered, my face reddening, as Davey's mum shouted: 'Go on, Kev, get stuck in!'

Back at school, a trendy Christian teacher, Mister Drinkwater, divided us into small groups for open and forthright discussions about attraction, sex and love. As a surprising number of other kids opened up, chuntering on about fancying people and needing to use protection, I grew hotter and hotter as if the radiators were on full blast against my back. I felt unable to breathe, let alone speak. But after a month of devoted monk-like silence, meditating on anything other than what was being talked about, Mr Drinkwater cajoled me into a response: 'Body parts, Kevin. What do you like most?'

I was in shock. What was I supposed to say? Someone had just said 'eyes'. Eyes were safe. Ears, 'ears' would be a ridiculous answer. After a prolonged silence I found myself blurting 'Legs. I like legs.'

'Legs? Oh, yes, of course, legs. You're a leg man, very good, I don't think anyone has ever said legs before. But legs are really nice, aren't they?'

The group murmured approval and Sally Raby, who'd always frightened me, patted me on the back and said, 'good on you, that was so brave of you!'

I kept quiet and stared down at her legs, and wondered.

What Are Young Men to Rocks and Mountains?

Maán Jalal

It's a truth – poorly concealed but still universally acknowledged – that an Arab boy from a good family does not cry. The People's Court will not accept it. And their acceptance is essential, if you're an immigrant.

As a teenager, I referred to this phenomenon as the Curse of the Arab Cock. And when I bought my first notebook towards the end of 1997, in Auckland, New Zealand, I dedicated pages to studying this curse.

The Curse of the Arab Cock:

Arab boys like soccer.
Arab boys like cars.
Arab boys like to fight.
Arab boys must be good.
Arab boys must be good at school.
Arab boys can't be sensitive.
Arab boys can't cry.

I'd never been told this explicitly, but these 'facts' were imposed on me from a young age. Despite being raised by parents who rejected many of these conventions, there was still an external pressure – an idea that to cry is wrong. To cry is shameful.

You may be wondering about the aforementioned People's Court. The People's Court consisted of a close-knit Arab community in Auckland, a city my family had migrated to from the Middle East.

The People's Court had no leader. It existed as a body of ancient binary ideas: good and bad, vice and virtue, masculine and feminine, virgin and whore, man and woman. There were no greys.

Their rules were enforced through a network of gossip and social ostracising. The fear of exile by any immigrant family from 'their people' was incredibly powerful.

A girl, a few years older than me, was chastised and her parents snubbed by the People's Court because she was seen walking after school, alone with a white boy from her class. She was wearing short shorts, apparently.

This system infuriated me and, at thirteen, I wanted to actively work against it. I just didn't know how. All I could do was retreat into fiction, my only solace, hoping it would cloak me with invisibility.

But then, two things happened that shifted my perspective on what it meant to be an Arab boy and what the People's Court actually was.

First, I stumbled upon one of the greatest novels of all time. Second, I got a job.

It was the middle of July and it was cold. I'd just finished reading *Roots* by Alex Hayley, the story of Kunta Kinte, an 18th-century African sold into slavery, and was finding it difficult to track down something as good to take its place. So, after school, as was customary, I walked to the Howick Public library.

After having no luck scouring the computer system for something similar to *Roots*, I walked aimlessly between the aisles. My hand grazed the spines of books until I felt one with a rough texture. It had a wide, olive green spine that looked out of place in the science section.

I pulled out the book and read its title: *Pride and Prejudice* by Jane Austen. The words were in faded gold lettering, the book was about to fall apart. I opened the pages carefully and read that famous first sentence. I was struck dumb – bewitched, besotted, intrigued.

I found an unoccupied chair and read the first few pages with laser-focused attention. I felt a connection to it, but I wasn't sure why.

By the end of the first chapter, which I'd reread a few times to grasp fully, I decided I had to take this book home.

The woman who was usually behind the desk wasn't there, instead there sat another librarian. The *Other* Librarian as he was referred to by some of the kids.

Tall with wavy strawberry blond hair, he often wore bright linen shirts paired with pink or red shawls. It was quite normal to see him in long skirts or overly baggy trousers, too.

That day, he was dressed in a ruby red shawl and a number of wooden beaded necklaces hung around his neck. Humming, he tapped his fingers on the table while he brought up my details on the computer screen.

What would the People's Court make of him? I thought.

'Pride and Prejudice?' he asked, looking down at the book. 'I thought we'd lost this one.'

His voice was completely ordinary, except he emphasised the end of each word. It reminded me of the dramatic way someone might tick a box on a form.

'Everyone loves Elizabeth,' he grinned. 'But I love Lydia. She's brilliant. No story without her.'

Reading *Pride and Prejudice* consumed my time completely. I'd fallen down a linguistic rabbit hole into a new facet of the English language. How I finished that book at thirteen, I have no idea.

I reread sentences and paragraphs until I understood them the best way I could. It took me a long time, but I was entranced and surprised every time I saw facets of my life in the story.

My elder sister had announced to my mother that she had a white, much older, boyfriend. My mother was upset.

It had been six months since my father left to work in Dubai, leaving my mother alone with five children. He called every Friday for updates and my mother wasn't sure how she was going to explain that his daughter was a fully-fledged teenager now.

It didn't help that my sister was purposely cruel. She was after all the Lydia Bennet of our family. It feels pertinent to mention that the boyfriend wasn't a catch. At least Lydia had taste. Wickham was apparently handsome and charming. My sister's boyfriend was toad like, wore clothes that were too small for him and smelt like cheese.

Rumours started to circulate about my sister in the People's Court and my mother was in a panic. She noticed a shift in how she was being treated by the Arab community.

Around this time, I got my first job – a kitchen-hand at an Italian restaurant. I had been obsessed with getting a job for some time. The People's Court, the Curse of the Cock, had hammered their mantras into my head.

Find a job.

Make money.

Don't be poor.

The restaurant was called Italiano and the owners were a husband and wife who were Bulgarian, not Italian.

Boris, the husband, was short, built like a square, and hardly spoke. His job was to bake bread and perform other tasks in the back office that were a mystery to me. I always assumed he was in there looking at porn magazines.

His wife, Maria, was the hostess and ran things like a strict headmistress. Maria was tall, with green eyes and dark hair. She told me once, nonchalantly while she folded napkins, that her hair was the reason Boris first noticed her.

In front of customers, Maria talked and moved in a measured, elegant way. But as soon as she was in the kitchen, she stumbled into things and hissed at us. Both of those Marias were uniquely condescending. She reminded me of Caroline Bingley. Her judgment of customers was based on how they dressed, the state of their teeth and what they ordered from the menu.

There was also the chef, Niko. Niko was Eastern European, swore a lot and didn't feel the cold. He wore the shortest shorts imaginable in the middle of winter and cycled to the restaurant every evening.

Sometimes when the restaurant was in complete chaos, he'd whistle to get my attention, throw a pan filled with sauce into the air and catch it with his other hand.

'I am a magician. See?'

The sink, my permanent office, was situated in one corner of the kitchen and behind me to the left was an open window that looked out onto the dining area. I was never allowed to look out of it when the restaurant was busy. I was expected to be invisible. This was something Maria was very particular about.

'No one sees the engine work, but it's the most important part of the machine.'

Maria and her rules were a People's Court all on their own.

Italiano was decorated to look like a cave. There were barrels with the words *wine, beer* and *honey* painted on them but inside they were filled with potatoes, onions and rags. The walls were painted with earth tones and the furniture was varnished to death.

There was a large painting on the wall that I realised years later in Art History class was influenced by *The Garden of Earthly Delights* by Hieronymus Bosch. It was a scene of a forest by a shore, the waves crashing while a group of naked figures were running around having an almost-orgy by a fire.

The restaurant was often busy. A few teachers from school came with their families, and one night I saw the Other Librarian with another man who had slicked black hair. When they came up to the counter to pay for their meal, the Other Librarian spotted me inside and smiled.

'You're everywhere aren't you?' he said. 'Didn't know you were running a sweat shop in here Maria.'

'You boys are so funny,' Maria said, followed by her hyena laugh.

She looked at me after the Other Librarian left, like it was my fault that he'd seen me.

One night, the restaurant was exceptionally busy, the sink was toppled over with plates and although I could hear Maria twirling and laughing from table to table, she'd come into the kitchen frazzled, and spitting out orders.

'Make sure those wine glasses are spotless, there is an important lady waiting for them!'

She sounded more on edge than usual. I dried the wine glasses quickly as she told Niko exactly how he should cook the next few meals. Before she took those meals out, Maria stared at the plates, examining how the food was arranged and made what she clearly thought were vital adjustments.

Niko slammed pans on the stove and cursed under his breath. When Maria left with the plates, I walked across and peeked out of the window to see who she was serving.

There was a couple with their back to me and in front of them at the same table was an older woman.

The first thing I noticed was how white this woman's hair was. Shockingly white. Perfectly white. It was pulled back in a bun. I couldn't stop staring at her. The woman, who was maybe in her late seventies, sat with a straight back and was wearing a blood red suit with oversized gold buttons.

I couldn't – though I desperately wanted to – study her more, as I heard plates being pushed in through a small window by the sink.

Then everything went pitch black and the music stopped playing. I couldn't see an inch in front of me. All I could hear was Niko cursing and people cheering.

Maria barged into the kitchen, moving around like the darkness wasn't an obstacle, lighting candles that she pulled out from one of the higher cabinets.

'Help me put them around the restaurant. Now!'

We later found out that someone had crashed their car into an electricity pole down the road, causing a blackout in the whole area. The customers, most of whom were somewhere between tipsy and drunk, didn't mind and were enjoying themselves. There was a new energy in the restaurant – everyone seemed livelier now that the lights were off.

Maria was flighty and nervous, seeing to customers with her hyena laugh. I stood at the edge of the restaurant, lighting candles by the wall, glad I didn't have to wash dishes for now.

Boris rushed out of the darkness and into the most candle-lit part of the restaurant. He was holding a violin that I'd seen before in the cabinet in his office and he started to play. The song was fast and people stood up to dance.

It made me think about the dances in *Pride and Prejudice*, and how the dance halls would have been lit by candles. I looked around to see if I could spot a modern version of Elizabeth and Mr. Darcy.

Then the music slowed down, and Boris closed his eyes as he focused on the movement of his arms and fingers. It looked like he was holding a baby instead of a violin. People swayed and a few were slow-dancing.

'You,' I heard someone whisper to me. 'I feel you're close. Who are you?'

The older woman in red was alone at her table, facing me, but her gaze was somewhere above. Her accent was peculiar. She wasn't from New Zealand.

'Do you need anything? Water?' I asked.

'No. Are you a waiter?'

'Kitchen-hand.'

Now that I was closer to her, I noticed she was even more beautiful than I'd initially thought. The woman's skin was wrinkled in a soft way, clear, like it glowed, her eyebrows – despite the whiteness of her hair – were long, thick and dark, her eyes a sea-blue, almond shaped.

For some reason, she wouldn't look at me directly, but over my shoulder.

'Are you OK?' I asked again.

'Sit next to me. My son is dancing with his wife,' she said, her hand on my arm pulling me down. 'I want you to tell me what's going on.'

I shouldn't have sat next to her, I knew Maria wouldn't approve. But my muscles and head hurt. I'd been standing for hours. I was tired, sweaty and smelled like grease.

'I'm blind.'

My immediate reaction was to apologise, but I was so stunned that I sat there and said nothing.

'Can you describe what's happening? I know there's a man playing the violin and people dancing. Tell me everything you see.'

I don't know if it was exhaustion or maybe the darkness made it easier, perhaps it was the music or the fact that she was beautiful, but as soon as I started talking, I didn't stop.

'Everyone is standing around Boris playing the violin,' I said, slowly. 'He's my boss. I didn't know he played the violin. There's a couple dancing, they look like this big photo my parents had in their bedroom when I was little. Next to them there's a woman, she's leaning on her chair and looks sad. Her husband just said something to her and she's smiling. Behind them it looks weird because there's a big painting of naked people, running around. Because the room is dark and there are candles it looks like the painting is another room in the restaurant, or we are all together in one big room …'

I kept talking about everything and everyone around us. She didn't say a word for what felt like a long time. Then she grasped my hand.

'You're a boy?'

'Yes,' I said, wondering what that meant.

'How old are you?'

'Thirteen.'

'You go to school?'

'Yes,' I said.

'Do you like it?'

I hesitated. 'No.'

She smiled. 'Did you know that you're a writer?'

I shook my head, then remembered that she was blind. 'What do you mean?'

'I know this type of person. You are one of them. Do you like to work here?'

'No,' I said, surprised by my honesty.

'You should quit,' she said, defiantly. 'You're too young to work like this. Go home and read and write. You like to read?'

'Yes.'

'What are reading now?'

I told her about *Pride and Prejudice.*

'I know this story, but I never read it. You are a sensitive boy.'

I winced. I loathed that description. It was one of those words the People's Court would not approve of. The Curse of the Arab Cock nudged me.

'Do you write?'

'No,' I lied.

I was too embarrassed to say that I did write now and then, little stories and descriptions of things on bits of paper that I often lost.

'You have to write,' she said, 'all the time. Write about yourself. Write about others. Write about me. You know, I wasn't always blind. I could see very well before.'

I can't remember what I said or how she responded but I'd written in a notebook later that week that, when the lights came on, it felt as though *someone had slapped me across the eyes.*

Maria was staring at me from across the restaurant. I got up and told the woman I had to go back to the kitchen.

I stayed in front of the sink, working away for the rest of the night. As the restaurant died down, I was hoping to get out of there before it got too quiet, but Maria called me from the window.

'A customer wants to talk to you.'

The old woman, her son and his wife were chatting as I approached them. Maria towered over us with a weird, crooked smile.

'Thank you for helping me tonight,' the old woman said as she shook my hand, passing something into mine.

If I were older and more experienced in the way of the world, I wouldn't have looked down and gasped when I saw $300 in my hand.

'This is 300 dollars!' I said, part of me thinking that maybe, since she was blind, she wasn't sure how much money she'd given me.

'I know. It's a tip. You helped me see tonight.'

This was more than my month's salary at the restaurant. Maria's crooked smile wavered. Somewhere behind me, Niko did a whistling sound.

'Thanks ... I'll split it with everyone.'

'You won't,' she said. 'If you don't take this money and keep it for yourself, I'll haunt you as a ghost when I die.'

Her son laughed and told me to believe her.

I pocketed the money, said thank you, and went back into the kitchen. A few minutes after the old woman left, Maria poked her head through the window behind me.

'Come into the office, please.'

I wasn't scared walking in there. I just didn't know what to expect.

'That woman gave you a lot of money,' Maria said, standing by the table while Boris sat in his chair, watching me.

I didn't say anything. I looked over at the violin that was back inside the glass cabinet.

'What did you do for that woman?' Maria asked.

'I talked to her when the lights went out.'

'What did you talk about?'

'I told her what was happening in the restaurant. She can't see.'

'You think I don't know that she's blind?' Maria asked, offended. 'What did you talk about? Tell me now. Don't lie.'

I suppose I should have told her everything, but I didn't want to. After my conversation with the old woman, I felt smart, which was something I didn't often feel as I was pretty much failing at school. It was something I wanted to keep to myself and not share with anyone – let alone Maria.

'No,' I said.

'You rude boy!'

I said nothing. My pruned hands were clasped behind my back, my fingers rubbing against each other. My throat felt lumpy. Don't cry.

'If you're dedicated to this job and want to stay here, you should tell me what happened tonight.'

I said nothing. Don't cry.

'We pay you good salary – cash. And this is how you repay us? If you don't tell us what happened, maybe you shouldn't come in tomorrow.'

As she kept talking, I turned around, walked out of the office and closed the door behind me.

In the kitchen, I called my mother to say I was ready to get picked up. Niko asked me what had happened, and Maria came charging from down the hallway, around the restaurant counter and poked her dragon head through the window.

'You're quitting?'

I didn't answer. I shoved my apron into the cabinet, took my bag and made my way out of the restaurant.

Don't cry.

'You can't quit because we fired you!' she hissed, following me. 'But I'll give you another chance. If you tell me what happened, then you're not fired. If you don't, I'll call your mother. She'll know you're keeping secrets. It's against your traditions. I know how the Arabs are!'

I didn't hear the rest. I was out of the restaurant and on the street where it was crisp and cold. I sat on the bench on the corner of the road by one of the streetlights and read about Elizabeth's first meeting with Lady Catherine de Bourgh until my mother picked me up.

Maria never called my mother. She was short a kitchen-hand, so she was probably very busy for the next week.

A few days after I quit (or maybe I was fired?) I was walking to the library from school. I saw the Other Librarian crossing the road, walking towards me. He had a big red bag and was wearing a swirl of yellows and whites.

'Faggot!' a group of kids yelled behind him. They laughed and yelled it out again. The Other Librarian spun round and stormed towards them.

'That's disgusting!' he yelled.

The kids, I think there were three of them, ran in opposite directions. Chasing after one of them, the Other Librarian tripped and fell.

I didn't know what to do. I ran over to see if he was OK. He'd scraped his shin and rolled into a small puddle.

'Are you OK?'

'Obviously not,' he said, collecting some of the things that had fallen out of his purse, 'Cruel, bloody kids.'

Standing up, he looked down at his clothes, half-drenched in muddy water.

The Other Librarian wasn't angry; he looked hurt, bewildered. He closed his eyes, tilted his head up to the sun and inhaled a few times. I didn't want him to cry.

The cut on his shin was bleeding. I didn't know how to help but I kept staring, staring at his red face, lips jutting out, eyes bulging. Don't cry.

'And what do you want?' he asked, looking down at me.

I didn't know what to say – how to register his emotions or my own.

'I'm sorry,' I said.

Neither of us were sure what I was sorry about. The Other Librarian swiped his purse from the ground.

'Do you have any other books by Jane Austen?' The words tumbled out of my mouth before I'd thought about them properly.

He looked at me curiously, and then walked away.

A few nights later, when I'd finished reading *Pride and Prejudice*, I cried for no reason. It wasn't a sad book. But I think I was crying for my mother.

The increased public spectacle of my sister's rebellion had enraged the People's Court. They completely exiled my mother. She was alone, in a foreign country with five children and practically no support.

My loathing for the People's Court was unparalleled at that point and I wasn't sure how to deal with it. They were present everywhere. Even as I cried.

It felt good to cry but I was also ashamed. There was that lingering thought that I was somehow less of a boy, less of an Arab because a book had made me cry.

Curse of the Arab Cock.

Curse of the Arab Cock.

Curse of the Arab Cock.

I had to find a way to break the Curse, to disestablish the People's Court, that I was starting to realise wasn't exclusive to me because I was Arab or a boy.

We all live in some version of Meryton. Me, Maria, the Other Librarian, controlled by a nasty word, the approval of others, the conforming to some invisible society.

But I remembered the old woman's advice – to write all the time. That's what I did, every single day from then on, using the tip she gave me on books and notebooks.

And every time I wrote, unknowingly, I was undoing the Curse of the Arab Cock and erasing the People's Court. I was also becoming more of what the beautiful, blind woman saw in me that I couldn't see in myself.

Poetry

Father

Coming in I often pass you in the hallway, in sepia,
your wedding day, June 1955. You couldn't believe your luck.
And sometimes I stop to catch a trace of something I missed.
Maybe it's the way the light catches the glass
I think I almost see you clearly
but mostly you give nothing away.
Clear-eyed, upright photo-stance,
a peep of handkerchief in your breast-pocket,
your first and last trip to the photographer's studio.
Right hand put away behind your back
your left-fingers folded in a fist,
elbow tentatively crooked for your new bride.

Going out, I sometimes glance at you again,
this time it's the other photo, a dozen years after the first.
Your farmer's grind cast briefly aside,
your brow furrowed, your slack half-smile.
And what do I really know? You were not for turning
from buckets and wells to pipes and plumbing,
from bicycle clips and tilly lamps to motor cars and electricity.
You knew land and fields and the cuckoo's call.
You said the best part of the potato lies under the skin.
These things hold steady when I pass through
angling to catch a glimpse of something new in the fading
greys and blurry edges of an overcast summer.

Peggy McCarthy

Some pleasures

Platinum, for how its hardness doesn't tarnish
or grow tired. Poodles that lie on their backs
on your lap, front paws folded down, cute.

The cold precision of scissors, pinking shears
for their name. A Steradent tablet dropped
into a glass of water, for the plop and the long

fizz of air leaving. Removing a man's tie,
the word *gravel.* Platinum was once tossed aside,
worthless, overshadowed by gold.

Chipping old tiles off a wall, but only
when they come away easily, as if agreeing enough
is enough. The Radiohead song that begins

a green plastic watering can. The sound barn owls make
when they mate. Pushing a thumb through the skin
of a satsuma in the run-up to Christmas. Bookmarks,

binoculars, cherry ice cream. Daydreaming
about next time round being a childless silversmith.
The word *couscous.* Lisbon existing over the sea

without me. Opening the window of a train
as it speeds through open countryside, taking off
my platinum wedding ring. Throwing it.

Vanessa Lampert

Wild and Alone

Our first winter together we rented Pilgrim's cottage
near Ballyconneely in the west of Galway, the wind-
tormented days spent desperately burning
turf; one night I found a mouse in the cutlery drawer
feasting on crumbs, and carried him out to the turf shed
where I released him. Our ancient neighbour, Val, who
had not yet learned to trust light bulbs, had a great strength
for the weakness, whiskey tasting of smoke, rain,
and the rogue Atlantic sea. I tried to pick a fight with Seán
when he stumbled in late under our old neighbour's influence,
so relieved he was alive I wanted to kill him. Does it get more
Irish than that? He wouldn't fight back, picked up his book
and pretended to read. I freed the frayed copy
of *Under the Volcano* from his hands and hurled it
on the guttering fire where it refused to burn, growing thickly
black. I didn't know, then, our love was doomed
to last. Watching as the mouse ran back up the path I'd so
recently taken, through the open cottage door into the sacred
heart of Mrs. Pilgrim's kitchen where he resumed his meal as if
to remind us interlopers *wild and alone is the way to live.*

Susan Musgrave

Shoegazers' Companions

"You miners are almost astrologers in reverse,"
said the hermit. —Novalis

Nowhere could be further from the truth
than here where jiveboats land, shove off.
Half-hearted jesters. Worst-case scenarists.
The palmist at the end of the line.

Divisive swill pouring in, us baling like mad.
Guys issuing RFID anklets,
setting on ready to privatize our parts.
"Let me hold that bike while you make a run for it."

In *The Largest Study of Its Kind*:

- the middle of the road hangs in balance
- sinking feeling from making the flat places plain
- shaky grip on iffy propositions

There are Certain parts of the country;
there are others less certain:
"If Bandera is the Cowboy Capital of the World,
you'd think we could get our cops to dress like it."

Nowhere could be farther from our mornings in bed,
alligator clouds bellying past open windows,
gliding behind walls we painted unclouded blue,
sun hat hanging on a wooden peg.

We ramble heurigen hills with the unaccompanied,
coalesce the loveless, tootle raclette railways
of centrifuging sound, particulating lights, highflying
as tides that sift calcined sky onto Pagination Street.

Allen Tullos

Dead Ant, Dead Ant!

Today I found an ant deep in the cleft of my library book.
So small, so black, for a second I thought
an "i" or an "l" had lost its footing on the page
and fallen into the margin.

I extracted the ant and examined it.
The Pink Panther tune popped into my head.

I got to thinking about the reader that trapped that ant.
Had they been a young mother at the park,
a camper on a shady river bank,
a hiker stopping to eat an apple and read a chapter on a lonely hill?

I thought about the ant itself.

Had its disappearance been noticed by the other ants,
or had they simply filled in the gap
and carried on marching in single file?

And had that ant been the type who, from birth,
was always one to take a different path,
wayward, curious, always dreaming of something beyond
its suburban nest?

Before it ended up flattened in a municipal library book,
had it been the type of ant who had always wanted to travel?

And there gazing at that ant, on a summery afternoon in my back yard,
I heard my mother's voice for the first time in many years, saying:
"Hitchhiking is always very dangerous".

Michelle North-Coombes

Edisto Island, May 2019

– to Rebecca

Between walks on the beach, or hearing the shush
of waves from our screened-in porch above the Sound,
we worked on the 1,000-piece puzzle, the image
one of gardening: white polka-dots on hot-pink gloves,
old-fashioned seed packets: antique scripts,

images of ladies in hats & lace collars.
Pale blue bird eggs, straw & twig nest, tulips,
violets, a butterfly in a cage, a spade.
So many pieces of black-brown shades,
& four-pronged leaves pointing the way,

Celtic crosses sprang from soil, if only for a season.
I thought we'd never have done, & was right. In three
days we finished dirt & leaves, but large gaps of dining
room table stared out like continents on a map of our lives.
If only we had one more day. Groups with like colors

& lettering puddled around the borders, immigrants
with no homes. But the saddest of all was packing
for departure. I boxed up loose pieces, separated
parts over which we'd labored, leaving
a few locked, in solidarity with future guests. Earlier

that evening, on the porch watching the sun melt
like butter into the surface, we two English professors
talked about "forming": the transience of words,
like nineteenth-century ephemera, or how stories
are not static but dynamic, shifting from moment

to moment, like building sandcastles soon
washed away, like boys finding treasures
they don't yet know their older siblings buried,
like Botany Bay, ever-changing as visitors hang shells
on protrusions of old driftwood trees; like sea turtles

who lumber across sand to lay eggs that crack open
to babies who fight to survive. Like how much we love
a country, or person, & how over time our heart expands
or shrinks according to how skilled we fit the pieces.

Celeste McMaster

The Taking of Caravaggio

A Meditation on "The Taking of Christ"
by Michelangelo Merisi da Caravaggio

I took a snap of the Caravaggio in the National Gallery.
I thought that hand upon Christ's breast
could lie unseen on my breast,
asking how it feels to be betrayed.

Judas is so strong, so self-assured:
there's little of his bleakness in the frame –
his eyes, his grip, his dirty hand,
the way he moves to plant his kiss.

Jesus yields to Judas' kiss,
downcast gaze, furrowed brow,
oblivious of the Roman soldier
whose metal-plated arm enfolds them both.

On the soldier's command, any moment now,
they'll go their separate ways,
Jesus to be tortured and to die, but rise again,
Saviour to the world,

Judas to be excoriated,
his body hanging from the tree
a warning not to emulate
the guy who brought about the Great One's fall.

But is it just as well, dear God,
that Judas played the part he did,
the ultimate sacrifice – eternal damnation –
meaning we could be redeemed?

Maybe that's why Judas looks so prepossessing,
and why Caravaggio, who knew a thing or two
about fervid down-and-dirty rows,
could paint him as an unrepentant dude.

Bill Richardson

My Glacial Erratic

In secret, he electrifies wood.
A shamrock, unexpected tree,
Bolts diverge, unfurls Lady fern,
Blooms by night. He blurs me.
Porous, bearded channels. I tried.
He sent me lines, mineralized.

I misinterpreted his spalted maple.

He fascinated me like glaciers
But I've never seen the Arctic.
Drenched in woods, I fell hard
Against rock, a glacial erratic.
The dog waited; consciousness
Came back, eyes deep in moss
Tickled my face, exfoliating.

Since that shock, I've grown
Obsessed; I've spent my nights
Delineating the dark-Romantic
Ecology of gothic heroines.
Let's call her "Emily," as she
Leapfrogs through stories,
From Radcliffe to Shelley
Across moors of the Brontës,
Seashores of du Maurier.

Bits of blue lichen, green pens
Fly off my papers; I botanize
Udolpho, Frankenstein, Brontë's
Poems, and *Mathilda*; I analyze
Incarnations of "Emily," both
Linnaean-botanist and poetess,
Wary of nightshade, briony, moss.

She's my eco-heroine, and
My glacial erratic: mysterious,
Preserved, as if stone, more wild
Plant, a natural history of flowers,
Ferns, marsh fairies; I chase
Her like Wollstonecraft's *Mary*
Pursues the will-o'-the-wisp.

Equally hidden, he clamps
Hot wires, making mischief
In his workshop, releases spores

And discards cartilage, reproduces
Intellectually – a high-voltage lore
Singed fingernails, his knuckle-hair.
Like Elizabeth, I fall for mad-genius
Victors, their spark-possessed elation
Of making and unmaking the world.

My mother watches the osprey
Swoop, mid-air, drop its catch,
Mussel shells, fish ricochet off
Her glacial erratic, whiplashed
By fishermen, centuries ago,
Who thrashed the granite,
Their lines, rope heavy from tar;
A needful lashing.

I wonder, by analogy, if that's what
He is doing, vices tightly gripped,
Veined, Celtic patterns he's turned,
Burning to understand his roots,
His dark ecology 'til the bitter end.

Leah C Stetson

On Reading Ecclesiastes 5 at St Patrick's Church of Ireland Cathedral

Life is useless, it reads,
and I read on, palms resting
on a lectern carved like an eagle about to take flight,

oaken feathers stained the colour of turf.
Here, the High King of Ireland lies buried.
Here, a 3,000-year-old statue,

Tandragee Man of the Silver Arm,
clutches his shoulder.
Here, I light a votive for your dead mother,

gone a year. I place it beside the other lonely flame,
drowning in a pool of its own paraffin.
Even a king depends on the harvest.

Oh, the silence, the weight of stone, the weight
of history, the stained glass
trying so hard in the weak sunshine to cast

shards of colour upon the Armagh granite,
a freestone, I'll learn later from a tour guide named Shirley
in her navy-blue cotton dress.

We leave this world just as we entered it – with nothing.
Your mother, gone.
How we disappointed her. Childless artists living abroad.

No interest in the marble-tiled villa,
the olive trees, the figs. The persimmons
hung with their fiery globes, shaped like hearts.

Kaki, you called them, prodding for ripeness.
And another Empire falls.
We labour, trying to catch the wind, and what do we get?

And I cry, not for the first time, but for real
this time. For your mother, for the way
she gripped the knife as she peeled the *kaki*,

flesh quartered and glistening.
Eat it with your hands she said, peeling
another, and another.

Angela Long

The Mothers and My Mother Tongue

(The parochial narrowing of the English vs the creative universality of English)

It's the English, *innit*?
Not the baronial, post-Colonial, old-Etonial phoney baloney of
frightful, entitled, unbridled billionaires.
Unfeeling wheeler-dealers, faking it, making it, raking it in,
riding pillion on the millions of taxpaying minions.
Thankless banking wankers, never paying their fair share,
moving their hoards abroad, offshoring. Yee-hawing their Tory story
to the still-unthinking, unflinching, un-sinking-in, giving-in-ones,
taken in and taken out by 'take back control',
that chronic, moronic, Tommy Robinson promise;
a baseless claim by the faceless,
embracing the fact-hating racists, racing for Brexit
in a lemming-like dash for the exit.
A nation sliding on a slime of jingo, now only dross.
A cross in a box, then a hot, cross bunfight.
A cross, bloodshed-red, on a white flag of surrender to the haters;
riven and driven to a sad, mad Mexican-wave goodbye.

No, it's the lexicon; the sexy phonic, melodic mother tongue we can flex it on.
Not wrung out, wrecked on the rack of the sad madness of '*Academisation*',
knackering the vernacular of a nation like the French,
who wrench each word back from the world, not yet formed
to conform to its normalisation, stationary on the stationery.
No, English bounces, flounces, announcing
hurtling herds of new words, stampeding;
some fleeting, some keeping their meaning.
With the biggest vocabulary, no constabulary can shackle thee
as you Scrabble free (taking the trouble to explore the double word score).
The tongue of Yeats, Waits and Shakespeare.
Of Eminem; eminently elementary my dear, what's on next?

The ringing, singing lingo of Ondaatje and Marley, Okri and Rushdie,
Sheridan, Gil Scott-Heron, Zephaniah; not some pariah
but a fire to inspire a choir of aspiring flyers.
A wealth of words in a wide world that welcomes wags
in the tongue that wagged,
English reigns supreme.

Shame about the English.

Geoff Burnes

Biographies

Winner of the Short Story Prize

Tracey Slaughter

is a poet and short story writer from Aotearoa, New Zealand. Her latest collection of short stories is *deleted scenes for lovers* (Victoria University Press, 2019). Awards include the international Bridport Prize (2014), second place in The Moth Short Story Prize (2018) and two Katherine Mansfield Awards. She lives in Hamilton, and teaches at Waikato University, where she edits the literary journals Mayhem and Poetry New Zealand.

Second in the Short Story Prize

John Mulkeen

is a writer and actor from Derry. He lived in Glasgow for fifteen years working as a chef. Although initially returning to Ireland on a temporary basis in2014, John rediscovered a connection with his homeplace and put down roots in Derry. In 2018 he completed an English degree at Ulster University. He's had work developed by BBC writersroom and is currently working on a collection of short stories, all inspired by the north west.

Third in the Short Story Prize

C S Mee

grew up in Birkenhead. After years studying literature and languages in the UK and elsewhere she now lives in Durham. She is a full-time mother to three small children and writes mostly between nappy changes and sorting collections of important pebbles. Parenthood is a constant source of inspiration. Her favourite stories view reality from an unusual angle and are often a little unhinged. She is currently working on a short story collection.

Runner-up in the Short Story Prize

Donna Brown

lives in Manchester. She is the mother of three wonderful children, the wife of one amazing husband and the owner of one crazy springer spaniel. When not writing, Donna loves hillwalking and gardening. She has also been known to bake the occasional cake, with toppings at a slightly rakish angle. Donna's work has been published in several places, and she was the winner of the Winchester Writers' Festival Short Story Prize in 2018.

Runner-up in the Short Story Prize

Stephen Flanagan

is a writer from Sligo, Ireland, who lives in Seattle, Washington. By day he works for Microsoft, and by night he often also works for Microsoft. But he writes when he can, and has been entering the Fish short story competition for fifteen years. He has self-published a YA sci-fi adventure novel called *M-World*, and a travel book called *0 to 66*. He used to occasionally have some spare time but now he and his much-adored wife, Katie, have a seven-month-old daughter. He's very happy with the trade-off.

Runner-up in the Short Story Prize

Rosie Cowan

was born in Derry, N Ireland. She is a former Guardian Ireland and crime correspondent, currently undertaking a PhD in criminal law at Queen's University, Belfast. Many of Rosie's short stories feature crime, mysteries or the supernatural. The heroine in her most recent novel is a crime reporter on a left-leaning London-based newspaper. She loves coincidences, all things strange and unexpected, and cheese.

Runner-up in the Short Story Prize

Sheila Armstrong

is a short story writer from the west of Ireland. She is currently working on her first collection of fiction.

Runner-up in the Short Story Prize

David Munro

lives and writes in the hot desert of Tucson, Arizona, USA. As a means to support his writing life, he earns a fair income as a carpenter, when he can.

Runner-up in the Short Story Prize

Róisín McPhilemy

started writing after a workshop on Rathlin Island. Her stories reflect the places she loves and the places she wants to be. She has an MA in Creative Writing and currently works in the Open University. Róisín is a member of the Belfast-based writing group Outside the Lines who meet regularly for coffee and commentary.

Runner-up in the Short Story Prize **Bruce Meyer**

lives in Barrie, Ontario and teaches at Georgian College and Victoria College in the U of Toronto. He writes to keep his sanity after grading papers. He is author or editor of 64 books.

Winner of the Flash Fiction Prize **Kim Catanzarite**

has been writing for nearly thirty years. When she's not writing, she's editing, and when she's not writing or editing, she's reading. Occasionally she watches movies. You can find her getting her steps every ten minutes to the hour. Kim lives in New Jersey with her husband and daughter.

Second in the Flash Fiction Prize **Mary McClarey**

uses her mixed heritage of West Cork and Northern Ireland to gain an insight – see the two sides of a story. She sidestepped the religious vocation her mother aimed in her direction and ran away to join the NHS. After a successful career as a nurse, she used *this* insight to inform another side of her life and turned to creative writing. She has two novels and a children's book under her belt.

Third in the Flash Fiction Prize **Anne Cullen**

holds an MFA in Creative Writing from Pacific University, Oregon. She lives in the San Francisco Bay Area and is currently working on a collection of linked short stories.

Runner-up in the Flash Fiction Prize **Claire Powell**

grew up in south-east London, where she still lives. She has an MA in Creative Writing from UEA, where she received the Malcolm Bradbury Memorial Bursary and the Malcolm Bradbury Continuation Prize. Her fiction has been broadcast on BBC Radio 4, and published in The Manchester Review, Harper's Bazaar, and other places. Her 300-word story *Valentine* was commended in the February 2020 Bath Flash Fiction Award. She works in advertising.

Runner-up in the Flash Fiction Prize

Jan Kaneen

started writing in 2015 as a sort of mindfulness therapy and now has an MA in Creative Writing from the Open University. Her flashes have won competitions at Flash 500, Molotov Cocktail and Retreat West. She's currently shortlisted for the Dinesh Allirajah Prize (Comma Press) and nominated for Best on the Net. Her debut memoir-in-flash, *The Naming of Bones* is forthcoming from Retreat West Books in April 2021. She blogs at https://jankaneen.com/ and tweets @jankaneen1.

Runner-up in the Fish Flash Fiction Prize

Stella Klein

graduated from Birkbeck's MA in Creative Writing programme in 2016. Her life-writing and short fiction have been included in several printed and online collections, including 101 Words, The Mechanics Institute Review, 100 Voices for 100 Years, Spread the Word's City of Stories and FlashBackfiction.com.

Runner-up in the Flash Fiction Prize

Jennifer O'Reilly

was brought up in a little village on the shores of Strangford Lough. It was an idyllic childhood in sharp contrast to her college days where her teacher training took her to the Falls Road, Belfast during some of the most violent years of the Troubles. After teaching English for a number of years she moved back to Belfast to work in a newspaper as an Education Officer writing curriculum material for schools.

Runner-up in the Flash Fiction Prize

James Wise

has been writing most of his life. His poems have featured in local Oxford anthologies – Hidden Treasures and Island City, alongside Helen Kidd, Paul Muldoon and Tom Paulin. Following an MA in creative writing from Birkbeck, James' short fiction has been published in MIROnline, Issue 14 of The Mechanics' Institute Review, The Cabinet of Heed and The Curlew. James tweets as @FreeQuayBuoy.

Runner-up in the Flash Fiction Prize

Rosie Garland

is a novelist, poet and singer with post-punk band The March Violets. She has a passion for language, nurtured by public libraries. Her work has appeared in Under the Radar, The North, Rialto, Mslexia and elsewhere. She is author of three novels, *The Palace of Curiosities*, *Vixen* and *The Night Brother*. The Times has described her writing as "a delight ... with shades of Angela Carter." In 2019, Val McDermid named her one of the UK's most compelling LGBTQ writers. http://www.rosiegarland.com/

Runner-up in the Flash Fiction Prize

Alan Passey

wrote a poem in his school Chemistry exam. He got an F for Fail. Undaunted he has been writing ever since, has shoeboxes full of the stuff (like everyone else). He had a brief dalliance with poetry publication in the '90s. Recent work has appeared in Domestic Cherry and been commended by The A3 Press. He recently published a travel book on Spain. He lives near Cirencester in the UK.

Winner of the Pocket Prose – Lockdown Prize

Paul McGranaghan

is from Northern Ireland, honestly doesn't mind the place, and frequents the wild places for peace and quiet in the company of the bonny wildfowl. When conspicuous by his absence it will be because he has gone to wander the earth, speaking in tongues and attempting to sleep in places that are not his. He fondly recalls nightmares incurred through such experiences. He is in reasonable health, carves wood, and enjoys receiving gifts.

Second & third in the Pocket Prose – Lockdown Prize

Shamini Sriskandarajah

is a therapist, bereavement counsellor, florist, writer, and editor. She writes poetry, fiction and life writing about the intricacies of loss, friendship, and family. Shamini also writes non-fiction about floristry and gardening, culture and society, and mental health and inequality.

Winner of the Haiku – Lockdown Prize **Lee Nash**

writes poetry, micro-poetry, flash fiction and non-fiction. An ex-pat still hoping to live the French dream (when she wakes up from the French nightmare), Lee was teaching privately when the lockdown put a stop to all but writing. In hindsight, this was not such a bad thing. She and her teenage daughter have survived by Lee's fly-by-the-seat-of-her-pants approach, home-cooking, and by the thought of exercise (stopping short of the actual exercise). https://leenashwriting.com/

Second in the Haiku – Lockdown Prize **Julia Travers**

is a writer and artist in Virginia, USA. She grew up near the Chesapeake Bay and now lives in the foothills of the Blue Ridge Mountains. She writes poetry, fiction, essays and news. Her creative works are published with Heron Tree Poetry Journal, Whurk Magazine, Ecological Citizen, On Being with APR, The Mindfulness Bell and others. juliatravers.journoportfolio.com, Twitter @traversjul.

Third in the Haiku – Lockdown Prize **James Allan Kennedy**

comes from Manchester in England. He has been writing for many years, mainly educational material but also fiction and poetry. His collection of poems *Silken Threads*, co-written with Mexican poet Ana Salazar and American/Israeli writer Barbara Kessel, was made available last year. These days, Allan splits his time between homes in England and Mexico, teaching, painting and writing. A life-long Manchester United supporter, he has neither a cat nor a dog.

Winner of the Breakout – Lockdown Prize **Emma Gallagher**

Emma Ní Suatman Gallagher is a recently retired homeschool-teacher; she is delighted that her children have celebrated her retirement so vigorously, so much so that she may return to the kitchen table school soon. She has been writing poetry of varying quality since her own childhood, brief though it was. Emma is currently working on her first collection of poetry, the work focuses on the inauthenticity of reality.

Second in the Breakout – Lockdown Prize **Jennie Ensor**

is a Londoner with Irish heritage. She is an author and former journalist. Her keen interest in social issues often creeps into her writing. Her poetry has appeared in Agenda Poetry, Ink Sweat and Tears etc. Her novels are *Blind Side* (Unbound); *The Girl in his Eyes* (Bloodhound Books, 2018) and *Not Having it All.* For her next novel, about teenagers who become trapped in a violent London gang, Jennie is immersed in urban slang dictionaries. www.jennieensor.com

Third in the Breakout – Lockdown Prize **Gráinne Murphy**

is a Cork-based writer, reader and coffee-drinker. She writes novels, short stories and poetry when big emotions need to be safely contained somehow. Her chief interest is family and identity in those moments where we have to stare life down and choose the person we want to be. Her debut novel *Where the Edge Is* will be published by Legend Press in September 2020.

Winner of the Poetry – Lockdown Prize **Rachel Parry**

has been making the pictures in her head visible for many years through her work as a visual artist (rachelparryartist.com) and more recently in words. She lives on the Beara Peninsula in Co Cork where the air is clean and she can grow her own vegetables. She is so happy that donations from the Lockdown Competition are going to Oxfam to help protect vulnerable people living without such luxuries.

Second in the Poetry – Lockdown Prize **Ash Adams**

is a photojournalist and documentary photographer based in Anchorage, Alaska, USA. She studied poetry and photojournalism at Ohio University, and continues to write poetry when not making images and tending to her two children. Her photography has featured in The New York Times, The Guardian, Mother Jones, The Wall Street Journal, The Washington Post, Rolling Stone, Stern, GEO, Smithsonian, and other national and international publications. Her poetry has featured in Narrative and the Fish Anthology 2018.

Third in the Poetry – Lockdown Prize **Rosaleen Lynch**

is an Irish community worker and writer in the East End of London, pursues stories whether conversational, literary or performed and believes words can make the world a better place.

Winner of the Short Memoir Prize **Noelle McCarthy**

lives in the Wairarapa, just north of Wellington, New Zealand, where she runs a podcast production company called Bird of Paradise with her husband. She grew up in Cork City.

Second in the Short Memoir Prize **Miki Lentin**

is a debut novelist, who completed his first novel Winter Sun while completing an MA in Creative Writing at Birkbeck, University of London. Originally from Dublin, he lives in London and took up writing while travelling the world with his family, and this year was a finalist in the 2020 Irish Writer's Centre Novel Fair. As well as writing his first book, he writes short stories and book reviews for MIR Online @mikilentin

Third in the Short Memoir Prize **John Martin Johnson**

was born in Leeds, UK and worked in design until success in a screenwriting competition occasioned a tyre-squealing change of direction. Since then, John has scripted many UK hit dramas including *Call the Midwife*, *Heartbeat*, *New Tricks*, *Monarch of the Glen* and *Where the Heart Is*. In 2013 he gained a Masters Degree in Scriptwriting from Goldsmiths College, London. John lives in Wensleydale, North Yorkshire with his wife and a red Ducati.

Runner-up in the Short Memoir Prize **Tom Finnigan**

is an Irish citizen with a Manchester accent. Married to Susie, he has three children and five grandchildren. Buying and selling cranes gives him a living. He came to Donegal in 2001 and joined Derry Playhouse Writers. He likes to evoke a sense of place in what he writes. BBC Radio Ulster and RTE Lyric FM have broadcast some of his stories; a few have featured in magazines.

Runner-up in the Short Memoir Prize

Julia Motyka

began writing with a combination of spoken word and narrative non-fiction work, which she performed at various benefits for World AIDS Day and Broadway Cares Equity Fights AIDS. She has received residencies at SPACE on Ryder Farm and at ARTErra, Portugal and is currently working on a memoir and an essay collection. She lives in NYC with her husband, daughter, and a menagerie of animals. Sometimes she posts things @juliamotyka_me and www.juliamotyka.com.

Runner-up in the Short Memoir Prize

Lisa K Buchanan

has had writing featured in Fourth Genre, Narrative, New Letters, The Offing, and Punctuate. She likes Brahms' short waltzes, spinach with mango, Downward-Facing Dog, and breaking the Rule of Three. She lives in San Francisco. www.lisakbuchanan.com

Runner-up in the Short Memoir Prize

Phil Cummins

is originally from Dublin, now lives in rural South Kildare with his family. As an academic and life scientist with DCU, he tries to figure out the mysteries of life. But when his day job is done and the dishes are washed, he retreats to his garret and tries to write about them. A keen diarist, essayist and short story writer, themes of interest include family, sense of place, 'otherness', and the absurdities of modern life.

Runner-up in the Short Memoir Prize

Laura-Blaise McDowell

holds an MA in Creative Writing from UCD. Her fiction and poetry have appeared in The Irish Times, HeadStuff, Sonder, Fly on the Wall Press and Still Worlds Turning, an anthology of new Irish writing from No Alibis Press. Her short story *Balloon Animals* was shortlisted for the 2019 Writing.ie, Short Story of the Year Award. She is delighted to appear in this year's Fish Anthology.

Runner-up in the Short Memoir Prize

Alan McCormick

lives with his family in Wicklow. His fiction has won prizes and been widely published, including in Best British Short Stories, Confingo, and online at Words for the Wild, 3:AM and Époque. His story collection, *Dogsbodies and Scumsters*, was long-listed for the 2012 Edge Hill Prize. His short memoir piece *Monty Modlyn* will be coming out in an anthology of recovery 'A Wild and Precious Life' later this year. www.alanmccormickwriting.wordpress.com

Runner-up in the Short Memoir Prize

Maán Jalal

is a writer of mixed Arab heritage who grew up in New Zealand and is based in Dubai. He is a manic bibliophile and lover of all things classic, from Italian tailoring and Renaissance masterpieces to Dad jokes and great pop culture debates and conspiracy theories. Apart from writing fiction and non-fiction about war, humor, the immigrant experience and keeping detailed notes of random people's conversations, he enjoys writing long Instagram captions.

Winner of the Poetry Prize

Peggy McCarthy

is currently doing the MA in Creative Writing in UCC and relishes the opportunity to spend time with other writers. She was a primary teacher for many years. She loves hiking in the glorious Comeragh Mountains or swimming in the sea! Born near Skibbereen in West Cork, Waterford City has been home since childhood.

Second in the Poetry Prize

Vanessa Lampert

recently completed an MA in writing poetry at Poetry School London. Since she works full time as an acupuncturist, something had to give so she gave up exercise and housework, saying these sacrifices were 'easy as hell'. She now needs a lie down and a massage after walking up a single flight of stairs. Since lockdown she has hoovered round resentfully and has no plan to repeat this in the foreseeable.

Third in the Poetry Prize **Susan Musgrave**

writes, "In June, my husband, a writer and retired bank raider, died; in July, my mother, and, in December, my handsome cat, Boo. I don't have a dog, but if I'd had one, I have no doubt he would have died, too." When asked for a bio-note that did not, "in the interest of originality", include details about her pets, she had this to say: "No comment." (Unique cat videos available upon request.)

Runner-up in the Poetry Prize **Allen Tullos**

is a professor of history and digital humanities at Emory University, is co-founder of the online journal Southern Spaces and author of two books of American Studies: *Habits of Industry: White Culture and the Transformation of the Carolina Piedmont* and *Alabama Getaway: The Political Imaginary and the Heart of Dixie*. "Shoegazers' Companions" comes from an in-progress poetry manuscript of memoir, history, and musical ekphrasis.

Runner-up in the Poetry Prize **Celeste McMaster**

is from Arkansas and now lives in Charleston, South Carolina. She is chair and a professor of the English Department at Charleston Southern University. Celeste writes poetry and fiction, enjoys yoga, traveling, and learning flamenco dancing. Lately, Celeste spends time being quarantined with her husband, Jason, and their three bulldogs. Instead of fretting about the pandemic, she meditates on beach time at Edisto and imagines a first trip to Ireland.

Runner-up in the Poetry Prize **Michelle North-Coombes**

has lived in South Africa and the UK and now lives on the beautiful Gold Coast in Australia with her husband David. Having never quite recovered from the thrill of seeing her first poem published (aged 8, school newsletter) she continues to write whenever her creative muse co-operates. Otherwise, she can be found shouting at pollies on the telly, beachcombing or working on her rather dissolute family tree. She has a BA (Hons) in Journalism from QUT.

Bill Richardson

Runner-up in the Poetry Prize

published some poems as a young man but wrote little during decades of teaching at second and third levels. A native of Dublin, he is now Emeritus Professor of Spanish at the National University of Ireland Galway and has re-engaged in recent years with his passion for creative writing. He enjoys swimming in the Atlantic, reading writers such as John Ashbery and Jorge Luis Borges, and practising tai chi to the music of Arvo Pärt.

Leah C Stetson

Runner-up in the Poetry Prize

is from Maine. She writes poetry beside a black-ash seep and a pond. Her writing has appeared in Off the Coast, Red Ochre Lit, and the Fish Anthology 2019. She holds a master's degree in human ecology, and is a graduate student in the Interdisciplinary PhD program at University of Maine in a tenacious pursuit of deep, Romantic ecology of wetlands. Last summer, Leah had an 'out-of-body' experience on the Beara Peninsula in search of the Hag of Beara.

Angela Long

Runner-up in the Poetry Prize

writes because she doesn't know what else to do, in any genre that will have her. Poetry remains her first love though and has helped her stay sane. Ever since the age of 14, when she wrote a sonnet for a stream, she has been hooked. She's originally from Canada but likes to wander. Right now she's living in Galicia, Spain.

Geoff Burnes

Runner-up in the Poetry Prize

is a writer, editor, musician, erstwhile business consultant, travel addict, environmentalist, opinionated political commentator and general smartarse. He lives with his delightful wife Elizabeth, who has tolerated him for many years, and has no children or pets, because they wouldn't. For most of his career, he wrote sales proposals and marketing documents, so he has a good grounding in fiction. He now writes mainly poems, short stories, long stories, song lyrics and polemic.

Writers' Retreats at Casa Ana

La Alpujarra, Andalucia

Casa Ana sponsors the Second Prize of the Fish Short Memoir Contest by providing a one-week place on a writers' retreat.

Casa Ana is a 400-year-old dwelling in the tiny Alpujarra village of Ferreirola. Once an important family home with a wine press, olive store, barns and stables, it lay abandoned for years. In 2004, London-based festival director Anne Hunt stumbled on the place, fell in love with it and spent nine years rebuilding, as well as creating a charming Moorish courtyard garden.

Today Casa Ana is a peaceful and beautiful place to stay, and provides an inspiring environment for writers and creative thinkers.

Writers' retreats take place four times a year, in March, June, August and November. Each retreat lasts for two weeks, with eight places available. A professional mentor is in residence for the duration and in 2020 the mentors include Mary Jane Holmes, writer and senior editor with Fish Publishing, and Nicholas McLachlan, published poet and Fish editor.

Days are spent writing in your room or on a secluded terrace; working one-to-one with the mentor if you wish or participating in facilitated group reading/feedback sessions; joining the other writers for meals at the house or drinks at the bar, or just watching moonrise from the terrace.

Anne Hunt: info@casa-ana.com
www.casa-ana.com

Anam Cara Artists and Writers Retreat

Beara Peninsula, Ireland

Sue Booth-Forbes donates one week's residency at Anam Cara for the second prize winners of the Fish Short Story Prize and the Fish Poetry Prize.

Anam Cara is set amid the rolling hills of west Cork's remote Beara Peninsula. The retreat, on five acres of gardens and riverbank, is surrounded by farmland that slopes down to Coulagh Bay.

Established in 1998 by Sue Booth-Forbes, an experienced writer and editor, Anam Cara accommodates five individual residents and up to twenty for workshops. Its main purpose is to provide a sanctuary from everyday life for writers and artists. As director and host, Sue is a supportive facilitator, who aims to provide what writers and artists need to 'slow down enough inside' to be productive. The north-facing bedrooms overlook Coulagh Bay, while the south-facing one faces Mishkish Mountain. One of the rooms can accommodate disabled guests.

In addition to private study-bedrooms, the house and the grounds offer many nooks and crannies for creative idylls – the bench swing in the conservatory, the sunken living room, the window seat in the gallery room, the 'island' near the waterfall, the low wall beside the stone fountain, the bench beside the duck pond.

Mealtimes provide an opportunity to share ideas and to socialize. For traditional music and perhaps set dancing, the local pubs are just a walk away.

Sue Booth Forbes: anamcararetreat@eircom.net
www.anamcararetreat.com

What is Fish Publishing?

The Fish Short Story Prize is an open door that's inviting writers to walk through it. It has to be encouraged, celebrated, congratulated.
Roddy Doyle

Fish is doing great work. It's an inspiration for all new writers.
Frank McCourt

I hail anyone who enters the Fish Prize ... It is difficult to create from dust, as all of us writers do. I know that the best stories are those that are still untold – so keep writing, keep creating, keep the faith.
Colum McCann

Fish is dedicated to fostering and publishing new and emerging writers. Since the first Fish Short Story Prize in 1994 we have published over 600 writers from around the globe. Over the years we have added the **Flash Fiction Prize**, **Poetry Prize** and **Short Memoir Prize.** Ten submissions from each competition, as selected by the judges, are published in the Fish Anthology. These prizes are annual, as is the publication of the Fish Anthology. The prize fund is over €8,000.

Critique Service: for short stories, poems, flash and short memoir – available year round online or by post.

Fish Editorial Service: provides in-depth professional assistance for anthologies of stories or poems, and for memoirs and novels.

Mentoring: for fiction, non-fiction and poetry.
Mentoring offers writers a long-term, tutor-writer relationship to work on a novel, memoir, collection of stories, poems, or work of non-fiction. Our team, led by award-winning writer and poet Mary-Jane Holmes, offers professional guidance to develop and strengthen your work. Duration 3 – 9 months.

Writing Courses Online: *Short Story, Flash Fiction, Memoir and Poetry.*
Courses provide useful and interesting ways to improve one's craft with one-to-one tuition. The courses are structured with set exercises, and feedback on each. Whilst designed to take about three months, the courses are completed in one's own time.

Details of all Fish activities are on our website

www.fishpublishing.com